To Jan,

Came away with me to Pier.

Love,
Nicki

Adamson's 1969

NICOLE BURTON

Nicole D. Burton

APC
Apippa Publishing Company
Riverdale Park, Maryland

First edition.
Visit NicoleJBurton.com for additional news and information.

Library of Congress Control Number: 2018900977

Burton, Nicole J.

Adamson's 1969/Nicole J. Burton. 1st ed.

ISBN: 978-0-9798992-8-7 (paperback)
ISBN: 978-0-9798992-9-4 (hardcover)
ISBN: 978-1-7321354-0-6 (ebook)

1. Fiction/Young Adult Fiction   2. 1960s   3. U.S. History

Manufactured in the United States of America.

To A. B. with love

NEW YEAR'S EVE
1968

"A pox on this party," Adamson thought as he trailed his mother Victoria through Stop and Shop, pushing a trolley of fizzy drinks and ludicrous food: Vienna sausages, cocktail peanuts, Cheez-Its, Ritz crackers, frozen shrimp, Cracker Barrel cheese, cans of pineapple chunks, boxes of eggs. What kind of party would this be? Where was the mac and cheese? The toffee apples? Chocolate cake? Bacon? Why did he have to stay home for New Year's Eve if he wasn't invited? Bollocks on his mother needing him "for heavy lifting." Was she planning to collapse and need hoisting to bed?

His younger sisters, Stewpot and Inkblot—Stella and Isabel—were invited to pass drinks and hors d'oeuvres. His father George had said he couldn't play drums in the basement or have friends over or go to Sal's or decimate the grub table but should "remain on hand in case." At home, Adamson carried crates of liquor from the boot of the car and set drinks to chill in the back yard. Americans loved their drinks icy cold even in winter. Passing through the kitchen, he spied chocolate cake mixes and two jars of jam filling and silently cheered that cake might be on the menu after all.

"Why can't I go over to Sal's?" he asked his mother again.

"We want you here to say hello. It's important for your father. All sorts of people are coming from the company plus neighbors. You can watch telly in our room. No," she corrected herself, "that's where we're putting coats. Hang this banner above the stereo, would you, darling?" She handed him a ridiculous purple and orange banner that read, "Groovy New Year—1969." His family had emigrated that summer from Swinging London. Now he was beached in the hinterland of Lexington, Massachusetts, while his parents invited strangers over to eat dollops of pigswill. "Happy New Year," indeed. From the kitchen, his father assessed Adamson's crooked hanging job. Before he could be assigned more tasks, he escaped to his bedroom, three stairs at a time.

In a last gesture of absurdity, his mother fed them hot dogs and baked beans for dinner while baking cakes then disappeared to "get beautiful." He could hear her chattering with his sisters as they tried on dresses, jewels, and makeup. Pathetic. Around eight-thirty, guests began arriving. He did door and coat duty, but after an hour or so the doorbell stopped ringing and the Grundig stereo was cranking out the soundtrack of *Hair* for the third time. The adults were beginning to totter about, which was what they called "dancing." He grabbed a couple of curried eggs and a fistful of nuts and headed upstairs to avoid witnessing more travesties.

He finished his December *Mad* magazine. Then he read a chunk of *The Hobbit*. He was lying on his bed in the dark, bored, listening to the bass thump of the stereo downstairs, when there was a knock at the door almost too soft to hear. Probably his sister.

"Go away!" he barked but the door opened and someone slipped in. Having lived his life mainly in school dorms, Adamson had decorated this, his first proper bedroom at home, by hanging satin sheets on curtain rods to create four distinct living spaces like a mini-apartment: the Entrance, where someone was now standing; the Study, containing his desk; the Lounge, with a small sofa, portable record player, and coffee table; and the Bedroom, with a twin bed and the lone window overlooking the yard. "Who's there?" he said. Whoever it was struggled with the curtains.

"What *is* this?" said a girl's voice. Hannah from across the street. What did *she* want? He raised the crimson cloth, then the navy one, and nudged her into the Study, stepping on her foot.

"Ow!"

"Sorry." She was tall and he could feel her breath on his neck. He turned on the lamp.

"Turn it off!" He did so. She draped her arms around his neck and swayed against him. Was she drunk? She pressed her lips against his and kissed him. He kissed back and only crunched her teeth once. He tried to apologize, but she kept kissing. Must not have hurt her too badly.

He was a virgin, eighteen years old, recently released from all-boys British boarding school. She pressed against him and undulated her hips. In the dark, his eyes bugged out and he became very aroused. He thrust and circled his hips, thinking of the Sussex Downs, those undulating green hills etched with giant chalk drawings of horses and Bronze Age men. She responded with a slow roll. He had studied James Bond's kissing technique in the movie *Dr. No,* and he'd kissed two real girls but hadn't had much practice in snogging, which Americans called "making out." Double-O-Seven always did something one-handed with a zipper. He felt around to see if Hannah's dress had a zipper, but she was wearing what felt like a lace tablecloth with something slippery underneath. He didn't recall any Bond scenes with a tablecloth.

"Music?" he mumbled and led her into the Lounge. He lit a candle and a stick of incense and put on his favorite song, Procol Harem's "A Whiter Shade of Pale." He patted the sofa next to him and she sat down.

. . . One of sixteen vestal virgins who were leaving for the coast . . .

They resumed. Oh, the Downs, those beautiful rolling hills. He wanted to make love to the whole landscape. She leaned back and he inched his hand up her chest till he felt her breast heave beneath his fingers. Heaven! As he moved his hand gently in a circle, she moaned lightly. What would his best mate, Alistair, say? "Make hay while the sun shines, mate," so Adamson traced her torso, lingering at her hip before gliding down to her delicious thigh.

As he moved his tongue into her mouth, she met his tongue with hers and he felt a surge of desire. Suddenly the partygoers erupted downstairs, singing and popping corks. His clock radio read 12:00. "Happy New Year," said Hannah and planted little kisses on both sides of his face and neck. He'd never been so blessed in his life. She shifted till he was almost lying on top of her and he rested his head on her shoulder.

"Groovy New Year 1969," he said, burying his fingers in her dark messy curls. The party was swinging again downstairs. He heard his mother's drunken voice and breathed in Hannah's woodsy scent.

"Is your first name Henry or Adamson?" she asked.

"At boarding school," he said, "they use last names. So I'm used to "Adamson" and I like it. I'm going to change it properly to be my first name."

"New country, new name," she said. She rubbed his nose with the tip of hers, then eased him aside and stood, straightening her dress. "You have a hair brush?" she asked. He found a comb and as she ran it through her hair, he reached up and stroked it. He barely knew her, a neighbor who drove him and Stewpot to school most days, but they'd never really talked, and they didn't have classes together.

"Don't tell. Maybe next time we can go all the way."

"Of course not," he said. Who could he tell? Who would believe him? She slipped under the curtain and out of his room. Life in America, he thought, is looking up.

1

JANUARY
1969

When Adamson came downstairs on New Years' Day, his father's face was grim.

"Franklin says your Christmas lights look un-American," George announced. Adamson had proudly strung a peace sign in colored lights on their garage roof. Apparently, the neighbor had made disparaging remarks at the party. George worked with Franklin at Dynamic Electric.

George was a radar engineer in C3—command, control, communications—and had recently retired from a similar though less lucrative position in the Royal Air Force. As a young lad in World War II, he'd installed mobile radar stations throughout India, Ceylon, and Burma, and claimed he'd never seen a shot fired during the whole war. "Had a whale of a time," he said.

Vietnam, George had told Adamson, was a few countries over from Burma. It had been Chinese, then French, now communist and fighting a civil war. Adamson's father said he didn't know why America was sending its sons to fight there as Vietnam had no oil or minerals to speak of but he was glad that *his* son was British and therefore ineligible for the draft. This was a relief to Adamson as well.

George cooked himself two poached eggs every morning and was polishing off the last bit of egg with his toast. Victoria was washing the saucepan George had used to poach the eggs and talking about returning some chairs to the store. George cleared his throat and began to speak but instead wiped a spot of yolk off the table with his napkin.

"Morning, darling," said Victoria, brightly.

"Morning, Mother," he said, sitting at the pine kitchen table.

"What's on today?" She laid a coaster down and placed her coffee mug on it.

"Sal's," Adamson said, bracing his arms and stretching.

"Why not take Stella? She likes Sal."

Adamson dropped his chin to his hands in despair. "I know."

"Don't be like that, darling. Tell him not to be like that, George."

"What, dear?" George was biting his fingernails, studying his cuticles. He found a hangnail and bit it firmly.

"Being mean to his sister. You never used to be like that. She's feeling down."

Adamson rose to his feet. "All right. If she wants to." Snogging Hannah had left him feeling magnanimous.

"Lovely! Corn Flakes or toast?" Victoria opened the cupboard over the dishwasher and pulled out cereal boxes and Pop-Tarts.

"I'll eat at Sal's," Adamson said, but he sat back down and watched his mother move around the kitchen.

George found another hangnail but when he bit it, it bled. "Damnation."

"What are you up to today, dear?" asked Victoria.

"I don't know!" snapped George and went upstairs for a Band-Aid. Victoria sat down and sipped her coffee. Isabel skidded into the kitchen like a puppy and flopped down next to her mother. She stroked the little girl's hair off her forehead and kissed her ash blonde waves.

"Hello, love. Nice sleep in? What a good girl you were at the party."

"Stella won't let me in her room," said Isabel. "I hate her. She's fat."

Victoria sighed. Adamson's sisters didn't get along. He used to be chummy with Stella but lately she'd become annoying and moody. He hated that they went to the same school, which had never happened in England. She *was* getting fatter. Every day after school, she ate baked cinnamon buns that came in a tube. Drinking Tab, gorging on sugar buns, and watching *Lost in Space* on their parents' giant bed was her after-school ritual. His mother cooked her special steaks and salads according to *The Doctor's Quick Weight Loss Diet* everyone was on, but Stella gobbled sweets and made the effort useless. Victoria was always "slimming," which meant she ate hard-boiled eggs, Ry-Krisp crackers, and black coffee instead of real food "to keep her figure."

"Can I, Mummy?" Isabel was asking.

"What, darling?"

"Have ice cream?" Isabel snuggled her mother's arm, loving her into submission.

"Not for breakfast. Have cereal or a poached egg." Victoria stroked Isabel's pale skin.

"A nice poached egg for Inkblot?" Adamson crooned in a sing-song voice. Isabel tried to kick him under the table but he deftly deflected her attempt and squeezed her chubby foot, causing her to squeal. She hated his nickname for her but annoying his sisters was one of Adamson's great pleasures.

"No one lets me do anything!"

"We'll go shopping," said Victoria. Isabel often accompanied Victoria because the others didn't want her around.

"Can Barbie have a new outfit?" Isabel sneaked a cookie from the beehive jar and nibbled it.

"If we see one you like. Run and get dressed. Darling," she said to Adamson, "would you mind coming with us? I have to return those velvet chairs, they're too big. I'll drop you at Sal's on the way home. Please?" He raised his hands spreading his fingers like Struwwelpeter, the fairytale character with long, menacing fingernails. "Thank you, darling. Pop them in the back of the wagon, would you?" she said, topping up her coffee.

He loathed and loved her at the same time. There was something helpless about her that demanded rescuing, the girl about to fall into trouble, but she was also stubborn as he was, refusing to accept suggestions, insisting on doing things her way. He watched her walk down into the den, gazing at the trees in the back yard. She opened the sliding door and stood in the tracks, sniffing the frigid air. A bird chirped in a tree. She stepped out into the yard and touched the blue shingle of their house. He knew she loved this house, the only one she'd ever owned, but really, it was just a house.

It was a stupid day to return furniture. With difficulty, they carried the rejected chairs through a throng of New Years' Day shoppers to the second floor of the department store. Victoria produced the receipt and flirted with the salesman. Adamson studied his feet as she laughingly inquired about the balding man's New Year's Eve and told him about her party. Why does she do that? On the way up, she'd pawed some plastic containers in Kitchenwares but didn't buy anything. Her endless shopping jag seemed sated. In the past six months, his parents had bought mattresses, sheets and towels, beds, a sofa with matching wrought iron lamps, chairs, rugs, silverware, casseroles, everyday dishes, pots and pans, coffee percolator, kitchen clock, two televisions, tray tables, a used Pontiac, and a new Oldsmobile.

While she was giving rocking loungers and mirrors the once-over, he lay on a big bed. Inkblot bounced on it next to him. "Daddy says I can have a big bed when I'm fourteen." She was trying to annoy him. His parents wouldn't allow him a full-size bed even though he was six feet tall and eighteen. "Can I have an ice cream cone, Mummy?" she asked, winding her arm through Victoria's and looking up with a grin. Victoria smiled back.

"What shall we do for dinner tonight?"

"Bangers and mash!" said Isabel.

"Americans don't have 'bangers.' I can't even find chipolata sausages. What about macaroni and cheese, Adamson?" He didn't answer, cracking his knuckles, which he knew she didn't care for. He was going to Sal's.

"We forgot to look at Barbies!" shrieked Isabel as they approached the exit.

"Can we wait till next time?" said Victoria. "I don't think I have it in me." She put her arm around Isabel's shoulder and they walked that way to the blue Pontiac. On the way home, Isabel sat in the front watching the cars going by, and Adamson drummed on her seat back.

As they waited at the light, Isabel said, "I don't want to move again, Mummy."

"Who said anything about moving?" said Victoria.

"Daddy was talking on the telephone about Italy. I thought we weren't moving again?"

"We'd better not be," said Adamson, though he wouldn't mind returning to England.

"He was probably talking about someone else," said Victoria, "at the company."

"I don't think so," was all Isabel said. Victoria pulled up next to Sal's house and Adamson hopped out without saying goodbye. She waited as he knocked. There was no answer. Where in the blazes was Sal? Adamson shuffled back to the car. Bleeding rotten New Years, he thought, till he remembered Hannah.

At dinner, Adamson plowed through a top-rate mac and cheese while Isabel, who'd sneaked cookies all afternoon, moved hers around the plate. She and Stella were excused to watch telly. George marched through his dinner as usual while Adamson had seconds.

"More, darling?" Victoria asked George.

"No, no," he said.

"Darling," said Victoria, beginning to clear plates. "Isabel said the silliest thing today." George was biting his nails again. "We aren't moving, are we?" George didn't answer and the doorbell rang. Sal, arriving for band practice.

* * *

Their band desperately needed a name. "How about 'Hieronymus Bosch?'" offered Sal. Adamson drummed to Eric Clapton's guitar solo, playing on his portable stereo in the basement.

"Can't spell it," yelled Adamson. 'The Troggs' was taken. What about 'The Grunts?' Or 'Gravy Train?' His friend Alistair might have a good idea. Alistair, his almost half-brother, his better half, said he might come visit soon. He could play percussion. Adamson whacked the drums and shook his tousled blond hair as Sal thumbed the bass line. All they needed was a lead guitarist, a singer, and a name. Adamson could sing, but drumming took most of his concentration. Victoria came down the stairs, smiling and wiping her hands on her apron.

"Sounds good, lads. Can I have a go?" Adamson wiped the sweat from his forehead with the back of his hand. Say what you will, she defended his drumming to his father, who said it was pure noise.

"Sure," he said and passed the drumsticks to her. She sat on the stool.

"What do you do?" she asked.

"Give her a bass line," he said to Sal, who thwacked the E and A strings. "Pick up the beat with the bass." He reached in with his foot and slapped the pedal. "Boom boom-boom boom boom boom-boom… "Then tickle the cymbals." He took hold of her hand and lightly rang the cymbals until they buzzed. "You do the bass," he directed, and she thumped the pedal to the beat as he rang the cymbal. "Now we'll add some syncopation," he said, and moved the sticks over the other drums in rolls and crashes. She kept good time with the bass and was putting her heart into it when George's legs appeared on the stairs.

"I thought we were… Gracious, what on earth…?" George ogled the aluminum foil wallpaper that Adamson and Sal had recently hung on the basement walls.

"Far out, Mr. Adamson," said Sal.

"Indeed," said George. "I thought we were going to Boston to look at the lights?"

Adamson gripped Victoria's hands and let forth a crazed punctuation before releasing her. Sal closed with a strumming frenzy.

"Far out, Mrs. Adamson," said Sal as the last note died.

"Thank you, darlings," said Victoria. "Would you like to join us, Sal? We're going to Boylston Street to look at the Christmas lights."

"I'm not sure…" began George.

"If we take the station wagon, the girls can sit in the way-back. It'll be fun." Victoria disappeared upstairs.

Sal shrugged. "I'll check with my dad." Adamson bounded after Sal, leaving George alone in the basement.

As they backed the car out of the driveway, Victoria pulled on George's sleeve. "Stop darling, there's Hannah. Maybe she'd like to come too." George scowled but she didn't notice. "Wind down your window. Hannah, darling? We're going to town to see the lights. Sal's coming. Would you like to come?" Hannah yanked the black-and-white spaniel she was walking and leaned in the car window. "Have you seen the lights this year?" asked Victoria. Adamson cringed in the back seat.

"Americans don't 'do' the lights, Mother."

"Why not?" Victoria said.

Hannah smiled, taking in the family outing. "Thanks so much, Mrs. Adamson, but I have to walk Snaps, then we're going to Dad's boss's house for drinks. Have a great time. I want to hear all about it, guys," she added.

"Such a nice girl," said Victoria as George drove on. "She'd be perfect for you, Sal."

"Maybe I should ask her out," said Sal.

"Lovely manners," said Victoria.

Adamson's stomach lurched as if he'd biked over a hump. He felt sick and his skin went clammy. He never wanted to see Hannah again and also prayed to 'go all the way' with her. His sisters argued in the way-back and he was grateful for the distraction. Suicide? Maybe it wouldn't come to that. He didn't even know if he liked Hannah. If only she'd keep quiet. As the dark trees sped by, he remembered his hand on her thigh and touched himself through his jeans.

The window displays of the Jordan Marsh and Filene's department stores were Christmas predictable: reindeer, Santas, elves, and fluffy white snow, unlike the dirty ice mounds lining the curbs of Boston. One set was different. Two mannequins, dressed in dark robes, stood with spotlights trained on their gazes. White and black snowflakes hung from the ceiling. In the first window, the woman stared passionately at the man, who gazed back. Had they gone all the way? In the second window, the couple had turned away from each other. The woman's eyes were lowered (in shame?) and the man stared at a distant horizon (had he been drafted?). What was the store trying to sell? Love? Loneliness?

Cheerful Christmas lights spanned the boulevard. People milled about in the night air. His family drove to the North End for Italian cocoa. In the cafe, the customers yammered incomprehensibly. Christmas decorations festooned the windows, counters, and tables. Everyone exuded an irritating holiday glow.

"What's wrong?" asked Sal, who'd been flirting with Stella. "She's just a kid."

"Nothing," said Adamson, his heart heavy. "Mother, can we call Alistair tonight?"

"It's too late, I'm afraid, with the time difference."

He missed Alistair terribly. Alistair's parents lived in Hong Kong, and their son had spent Christmas and sometimes Easter holidays with Adamson's family for years. When they were together, Adamson wasn't afraid. He felt brave. Alistair pulled his shoes on without untying them, driving down the backs of every pair, driving his schoolmasters mad. He once hid leftover fish in his pocket and forgot it till it began to stink. He'd fling his greasy hair and grin and refuse to give a damn. Adamson hated this country with its overenthusiastic people and inscrutable customs and no one to talk to, even Sal. He downed his cocoa and moped after the others to the car.

On the way home, Sal went in the way-back with Stella, Isabel sat up front with her Daddy, and Victoria sat next to Adamson. Isabel tuned the radio to a station playing Christmas rock 'n' roll.

"Penny for them," Victoria whispered. He was staring out of the window, miserable. She put her hand on her big son's arm and briefly touched her head to his shoulder. She squeezed his arm in the dark. Her compassion made him fight back tears.

"What's wrong with Henry?" asked Isabel, swiveling around, her radar for someone else getting attention activated.

"Turn around and find another station," said Victoria. She whispered to him, "We all get sad sometimes." Her grasp of the situation made him feel worse and he bit his lip to keep from crying and tasted blood. Every Christmas, Alistair had been with them. He sniffed, and Victoria passed him a tissue. George cleared his throat, a signal he was about to talk.

"Have you decided which universities to apply to?"

"No, I haven't," Adamson said, bitterly.

"If you don't go to U. Mass, you could go to Blackburn Junior College. It's easy to get in," said Sal.

"We must know soon," said George.

"Are we moving, Daddy?" asked Isabel.

George cleared his throat again. "Might be."

Adamson stared at his mother. It was her turn to bite her lip and avoid his eyes. Adrenaline shot through Adamson's system. "What's going on?"

"Might have to go back to Europe," said George.

"When?" Adamson asked. "Why didn't you tell me?"

"I knew," chirped Isabel. George slapped her leg before either of them knew what was happening. Isabel burst into tears.

"George! Uncalled for!" Victoria reached over and comforted the howl-ing Isabel.

"You're going to bloody strand me in this godforsaken country, aren't you?"

George remembered too late that Sal was in the car. "Talk about it at home," he said through gritted teeth.

"If it makes you feel better, I didn't know anything either," said Stella. "Where to this time? Back to England? We were supposed to stay in Amer-ica," she said to Sal. They rode along in stunned silence.

George put his hand on Isabel's leg. "Sorry, darling. Not your fault." Isabel snuggled up to him, pals again, and picked a new station playing the Monkees. Sal and Stella whispered in the way-back. Adamson stared accusingly at Victoria, who looked out of the window.

"You'll settle in at college," Victoria said in a low voice. He told himself college would be just like boarding school, but in his heart, he felt doomed without Alistair or the familiar tastes and smells and sounds of England. He bit his knuckles to suppress a roar. It didn't even hurt. Couldn't his mother do something? She refused to return his gaze, and he wanted to hit her, hurt her. His granny and cousins and uncle and aunt were an ocean away. He could go back to England but he'd have to repeat a whole year of school. He was pretty sure American classes wouldn't count. Sacrificed again on the altar of his father's bloody career! Victoria touched his arm, but he yanked it away. How could she? He watched her stare into the dark, lips pursed, entering her own private storm. Even his mangy sisters would be gone.

2

FEBRUARY

Of the three girls they auditioned for the band, Hannah was the only one with lungs. "I'm in love," said Sal, licking his lips as the three band members huddled to make a decision.

"You're in heat," said Adamson, tipping a carton of chocolate milk over his head to catch the last drops in his mouth.

"Same thing."

"What now?" asked Ron, the guitarist who'd joined the week before. Ron wore thick glasses and had acne but when he wasn't hanging out with weirdos in the Computer Club, he was busy practicing being Jeff Beck. He wasn't half bad.

"Want to do the honors?" Sal asked Adamson.

"No, go ahead."

"But then it looks planned if I ask her out," said Sal. "It's your basement, your band, really."

Adamson sighed and approached the sofa. The girls sat up. He clasped his hands behind his back and they burst out laughing. He didn't inspire seriousness.

"Thank you, ladies. You were all very good, but we think Hannah has the sound we're looking for. But you were all tops." The two unchosen pantomimed disappointment but Hannah's smile was like sunshine. "Welcome to The Grunts," he said and shook her hand, which seemed silly. Sal swooped in, disconnecting them, and twirled Hannah to her feet in a surprise pirouette.

"We can't call ourselves The Grunts with a pretty singer like this."

"How about 'Torpid Gerry'?" said Adamson.

Sal looked at him as if he'd lost his marbles. "Stick to drumming, man. What about Paisley Something?"

"Paisley Alarm Clock?" said Hannah.

"There's already 'Strawberry Alarm Clock.' What *shouldn't* go with 'paisley?' Peanuts, palm trees, parade..."

"Paisley Straitjacket," said Hannah. "Paisley's psychedelic, and Straitjacket because... well, we're all a bit crazy." Adamson thought she winked, but it might have been the strobe light. They chewed on this.

"What kind of music are we going to play?" Sal asked.

"Blues," said Adamson.

"I can sing blues," said Hannah and began wailing like Janis Joplin.

Sal was still mulling. "Paisley Parade, Paisley Patrol..."

"Paisley Peacock!" Hannah piped up, looking from face to face. She didn't know males could not use a word like "Peacock."

"Paisley Scarab," said Adamson.

"What's a scarab?" asked Hannah.

"An Egyptian good luck charm," he said.

"I thought it was a dung beetle," said Ron.

"It is a dung beetle," said Adamson, "but it's also an ancient symbol of luck, and you have to admit, the name, The Beatles, was very lucky for some. Paisley Scarab... it's mysterious and memorable. I could paint a scarab on my bass drum." They nodded silently. Sal walked over to Adamson and extended his arm, then Adamson placed his hand on top of Sal's, and they all stacked hands and roared in agreement.

"Paisley Scarab is born!" Sal proclaimed.

"Can we play now?" asked Ron. "I have to clean out our garage at three." They ran through some blues standards, and Hannah knew most of the words. When she sang "I Love You More Than You'll Ever Know," she clutched the microphone with such heart, Adamson wanted to stop playing and stare.

If I ever leave you, you can say I told you so
If I ever hurt you, you know I hurt myself as well ...

Her version was even better than Blood, Sweat, and Tears', and Sal destroyed the guitar solos. We're bloody geniuses, thought Adamson. They ended with Sly and the Family Stone's "Dance to the Music." Great song for drumming! Sweat was flying off him left and right by the time they finished.

"Far out," said Sal, wiping his brow with a sleeve. "Rehearse again tomorrow? We'll make up a playlist and then we can talk gigs."

Adamson watched through the gauze curtains in the living room as Sal walked Hannah home. They chatted a few minutes on her front steps, then Sal went to his car and drove away. Adamson flopped down on the Yeti, a huge rocking lounger upholstered in gray fake fur that dominated one end of the living room. His mother turned on the Grundig stereo and soon Tom Jones was pleading with Delilah,

My, my, my, Delilah
Why, why, why, Delilah . . . .

Did he dream the incident with Hannah? That would account for her lack of embarrassment. No, it definitely happened and she definitely said next time they might go all the way. Sal was smooth. Adamson had watched him at school, smiling at this girl, touching that one's shoulder, slipping his arm around the waist of the head cheerleader. He wasn't even good-looking. Half the time he had spots on his face, but God, was he smooth.

Alistair was smooth too but different. Adamson closed his eyes and thought of the time they went to the Golden Egg Restaurant on Oxford Street. Alistair had found a hair in his eggs and they ended up with the whole meal free. Alistair's strength was his fearlessness, it made him irresistible to women. Sal was confident but Adamson knew Sal really cared what people thought, he just pretended he didn't. Sal played the field more than Alistair. Of course, there was more field to play in America. Adamson and Alistair had gone to an all-boys school and their only chance to meet girls was by accident on the weekend at the movies or on the street. Sal's entire education involved meeting girls. Lucky mug.

Sunday lunch was roast chicken, and his mother was already drinking. "Care for a drop?" Victoria tilted the Mateus Rosé bottle in his direction.

"I prefer moo juice," said Adamson.

"I'll have some," said Stella, pushing her glass forward.

"You were always cosmopolitan, darling," said Victoria.

"There's a magazine called *Cosmopolitan*," said Adamson.

"Is it good?" asked Victoria.

"It's stupid," he said, drumming his index fingers on the table. He knew Stella had secretly bought a copy at the supermarket.

"Not as stupid as *The Hulk* and *Captain America*," replied Stella. "Isabel, don't you think our brother looks like The Thing?"

"Tell me about *Cosmopolitan*. Why is it stupid? And what do you think, Stella?" Victoria always got over-sincere when she drank.

"It's about having orgasms and how to paint your toenails so men notice you," Adamson said, breaking off a crust of bread and chewing it fiercely.

"I prefer *Seventeen*," said Stella.

"More like *Twelve*," said Adamson. Left herself open for that one, he thought.

"Henry," growled his father, "don't antagonize."

"What's an orgasm?" asked Isabel, and the table went silent. Stella and Isabel looked at George, though Stella's expression was a touch mocking. Let's see him worm his way out of this one, Adamson thought.

"More chicken, darling?" asked Victoria.

"Daddy…" began Isabel.

"I don't know and it's not suitable for the table," said George. "Finish your plate, little thing, you're holding us up. Henry, have you decided on a university? The deadlines are coming up."

"Sal's going to U. Mass but he says it's huge, thousands of students. I don't want that."

"If you beat around the bush much longer, you won't go anywhere."

"You'll have to come to Italy with us," said Stella in a singsong voice. With one swipe, he could obliterate her from the face of the earth. He saw her head fly off, smashed into pieces against the wall. He didn't want to go to Italy. To do what? He couldn't go to university there. He didn't want to repeat the year in a lower form than all his friends in England. He didn't know what to do.

"Can't you talk to someone?" Victoria was saying. "Surely they must have an advisory master?" She sipped rosé and fluttered her eyes. Adamson tutted rudely and looked at the ceiling. She was right, though.

"They do have a guidance counselor," he said, remembering a sign under the stairs and someone saying something about college guidance at the start of term.

"I suggest you ask for an appointment," said Victoria, pleased with herself. "I'm sure he'd be delighted to talk. Anyone for Friendly's?" It was snowing when they piled into the car but that didn't stop them. Adamson had a fudge ripple cone, Stella and George had maple walnut, Isabel had rainbow sherbet, and Victoria had a cup of black coffee and a taste of each cone. The road looked as if it were covered in coconut as they drove home. They'd had snowstorms in England but no more than a few inches and not every year. The radio weather forecast predicted six to eight inches before tapering off to flurries. At home, Adamson pulled on his windbreaker to shovel the driveway. "You can't shovel in that!" said Victoria and gave him her camel duffle coat. "Put this on, it's got a good hood."

"Mother!"

"No one's going to see you, it's thick as pea soup out there." He took the coat, leaving it unbuttoned as a concession to his pride but once he got into the driveway, he pulled the hood over his head, took the gloves from the pocket, and did up every hook and button he could find. The sky was filled with snow. It floated down and stuck wetly to his face. He put his tongue out and caught some flakes. Snowflakes crept down his neck. He wiped them off and shoveled.

Which songs should they rehearse? A few Jeff Becks. Ron was inclined toward Jefferson Airplane. What did Hannah like? He looked up as her front door opened. Her father came out and opened the garage. Perhaps they were going to church. Americans were always going to church, bloody religious fanatics. He remembered Hannah was Jewish. Did Jews go to church?

Mr. Wardheimer shoveled his driveway without acknowledging Adamson. There were already eight inches on the ground. Bet we'll have a foot by tonight, Adamson thought. Wardheimer put his back into it and soon had the Wardheimer Edsel warming up in the driveway. He drove off alone, perhaps going to the office, not church. He went to the office a lot on weekends.

Adamson indulged himself by chugging like a steam engine as he pushed the snow shovel down the driveway. He glanced around to check no one was watching but the street appeared asleep. He was red-faced when he came in, stamping his feet in the foyer, leaving wads of snow and his boots by the front door. In the kitchen, he boiled the kettle for a cup of cocoa. Isabel and Stella were watching telly in the den.

"Bet we won't have school tomorrow," said Stella.

"Could be," said Adamson. He sat on the carpeted steps leading down to the den and drank his cocoa. Could he call Alistair? He wasn't sure what to dial. He'd have to wait. His parents had gone to their bedroom for a siesta with the newspaper and cups of tea.

"Can I have some cocoa?" asked Isabel, presenting herself before him.

"Help yourself," he said. Her lip went out and she folded her arms.

"I'm not allowed to touch the kettle."

"Why not?" He gazed up at her then made a grotesque face that set her laughing. She was easily amused. He made her a cup and began to ask Stella if she wanted one but checked himself. God, I was almost nice to her, mustn't let that happen again, he thought. Still, might throw her off guard...

"Like some cocoa, Stee?" he asked.

"Why?" she demanded, suspiciously.

"Made one for Inkblot."

"Don't call me Inkblot," said Isabel.

"It would probably be contaminated," said Stella.

Probably, he thought. He'd once made her "a cup of coffee" out of mud, milk, and warm water. She'd taken one sip as he ran out of reach so she couldn't throw it on him, all that field and track practice paying off. As fast as she ran, he always ran faster.

Adamson acquiesced when Stella pulled out their old Monopoly set. He loved a good game of Monopoly, and you couldn't play alone. Stella played cautiously, trying to amass as many £200 payments as possible, missing opportunities to invest. He bought as much property as he could, especially utilities and railway stations. Isabel played on and off, drifting in and out of the game to tend her dollies or sneak cookies. Even so, she managed to beat them both through a combination of disinterest and luck. As the game broke up, Victoria came into the kitchen.

"Can't seem to stay awake today," she said, turning on the kettle. She peered out of the kitchen window into the back yard. "Have you ever seen anything like this? Imagine those poor people on the Mayflower. What does the news say?"

"Someone's going to have to shovel the driveway again but it won't be me," said Adamson.

"I don't mind," said Stella.

"That's what she says," he added.

"We had snow at Woodside Park but nothing like this." Victoria stood with her hands around her tea mug, meditating on the white scene. He went to the basement to practice. He brought his record player down and played along to the whole of *Sergeant Pepper's,* Pink Floyd's *The Piper at the Gates of Dawn,* and Jeff Beck's *Truth.* Musically, he liked British blues and regency pop but Sal was tutoring him in American rock 'n' roll. He liked playing his records really loud.

"Daddy says to turn it down or you'll have to come upstairs," spoke Stella's knees from the top basement stair.

"All right!" He switched the volume from 9 to 6, then to 5 as a precaution. Anything was better than watching *Seven Brides for Seven Brothers* with his sisters. He gently blew dust off the needle. He and Alistair used to play rec... Damn, Alistair! Bounding upstairs, he found Victoria emptying the dishwasher and singing along to the telly.

"We've got to call Alistair!"

"It's too late, darling."

"It's always too bloody late!"

"I told you, there's a four-hour difference. You can remember as well as I can," said Victoria. He was trembling. He'd tried calling all week. Longer, weeks, months. He couldn't remember how long.

"Actually, since it's four-thirty here, it's only eight-thirty in the evening there. What would you be doing at school at eight-thirty Sunday night?" Adamson had momentarily forgotten Alistair would be at school, boarding school, where they brainwashed you into wanting a boring job, a whiny wife, and a set of sticky children. As feeble as America was, it had released him from the harassment and compulsory sports of British boarding school. "Get his number, lad. The worst that'll happen is Matron will bark." When Adamson returned with his address book, Victoria lifted the phone receiver from the kitchen wall. "Operator, I'd like to make a transatlantic call." Adamson danced around, drumming on the appliances. "She'll call us back when she has a line."

"How long?"

"Five or ten minutes." The operator called back at six forty-five, and even Adamson had to concede that almost eleven at night was too late. Victoria gave him a quick hug. "Next Saturday," she said, and wrote on the wall calendar, "Call Alistair, two o'clock, six U.K. time."

"We'd better make it nine their time," said Adamson. "Sometimes they let us go to the pictures but only the early show." She changed the time to five o'clock. "We'll be practicing downstairs."

"You have to remember but I'll help." She reached into the cupboard above the refrigerator and produced a large bar of Cadbury's Milk Chocolate. Adamson's eyes widened. "Your father's secret stash."

"Thank you very much," he said, sounding like John Lennon, "thank you very much indeed." He poured a glass of milk and went to rock on the Yeti, munching on the chocolate. Victoria walked through the living room, down to the foyer, and opened the front door. She flicked on the light. Lots more snow had fallen since he'd shoveled. Across the street, Hannah's house was dark.

✳   ✳   ✳

"Henry," whispered his father, "you must come see this. It's extraordinary." Adamson's clock radio read 6:05. "I was letting Bella out ... come, see for yourself." His father sounded excited. Since George was seldom excited at six in the morning, Adamson rolled out of bed and followed him downstairs. "Look!" said George, speaking from the darkened den. Adamson stepped into the den and joined George and the dog at the back door. It was perplexing. Someone had built a white wall behind their house. George flicked the light on. The sliding glass doors that led to the back yard were covered from top to bottom in snow. Their house was buried.

"What do we do?" asked Adamson.

"Dig a tunnel for Bella, for starters," said George.

It became known as the Big Snow of 1969. Over four feet fell on Sunday night, drifting to ten feet in places. Adamson helped his father dig a latrine for the dog and went to wake his mother. When he returned, George was in front of the house shoveling the steps.

"What ho, Father!" he shouted. The street sparkled in the sunshine. No school today!

George leaned on his shovel and smiled. "Not a bit like Brighton."

Stella brushed past Adamson and plunged down into the snow. "I can hardly move, it's up to my chin!"

"I could use a hand," said George. "Where are you?'

"Over here!" she announced. She was clambering through the snow toward the road. "Hey, Hannah!" Hannah was out shoveling.

Feeling brave, Adamson called over, "Ahoy, matey." He lurched like a giant down his driveway. She put down her shovel and joined him in the road.

"Dad's car went into a ditch at work last night when he was leaving. He's snowed in there," she said. Truly, no car could drive down this street. "Why don't you come over for cocoa when you're finished?" She gestured toward his driveway. "My mom and sister are in New York. I'm home alone," she said, impishly.

Shoveling his driveway in record time, Adamson was already tearing off Hannah's clothes in his mind. He went inside to change into a fresh shirt, downed an OJ, and tucked "protection" into his pocket. Throwing a casual "Tally-ho" over his shoulder to no one in particular, he sauntered across the street and made it to Hannah's without being seen.

A woman of her word, she had two mugs of cocoa waiting in the sitting room. He'd never been this far into her house. He'd stuck to the threshold on days that he'd waited for a ride to school or when he had to fetch a cup of sugar for his mother. The sitting room was over-furnished in gold brocade and decorated with photographs of ancient relatives. No fake fur rockers or Spanish murals here. The carved wooden furniture and heavy curtains reminded him of a European castle.

They gazed at each other across the cocoa. "Know what today is?" she asked. He hoped it was the day he went all the way. He put his cocoa down and moved close enough to kiss her. She relaxed in his arms, just like in the films, and after fifteen minutes of delicious snogging and stroking her breasts, he was panting like a dog.

"Can we go… to your bedroom?" he asked. Her room was the one that was Stella's in his house. Fancy having it on in your sister's room. She slipped off her clothes and he hastily undressed, but he couldn't get the sheath package open. Hannah tore it with her teeth and handed it to him, but he dropped it on the floor and fell off the bed trying to reach it. She was laughing so hard, he snapped, "I'd appreciate a hand if you don't mind." She was rolling naked in hysterics as Adamson tried in vain to put the sheath on himself. Blasted penis didn't fit.

"We don't even need that," she said, getting control of herself. She inched her bottom closer and slowly enclosed him around the waist with her legs.

"I'm on the Pill," she said. He kissed her.

"How does it work?" he asked. Of course, he'd heard of the Pill.

"I got a prescription from a doctor," she said. Being so close with nothing on was amazing, yet he didn't want to make a mistake. Her father could come home and catch them naked. She could get pregnant; teenage girls seemed to get pregnant in a snap. He wanted to have sex, of course, but in films, girls ended up preggers all the time. His erection began to deflate. From her bedside table, Hannah produced a round plastic container filled with small tablets marked for each day of the week. "Monday" and all the indentations preceding it were empty.

"How do you know it works?" he asked.

"Because I'm not pregnant."

"Who else have you done it with?"

She snorted. "None of your business. Do you want to get it on or not?" He wanted to be sure he wasn't stepping into quicksand.

"Tell me where, how, and when you got the Pill." She wrapped her legs around his torso.

"Last year, New York City. My mother's cousin's doctor. She's married but she's young. He gave me a prescription. I filled it at a drugstore on 14th Street." Adamson knew the Pill was revolutionary. Girls could have sex and not get pregnant and men didn't have to wear sheaths, like swimming naked.

"Don't you have to be married to get the Pill?" he asked. He wondered if his mother took the Pill. What an awful thought.

"I told him I was 19 and engaged." He'd never been this close to a girl before. He was about to enter the tunnel of love and change his life. He looked into her eyes and watched her nostrils flare as she adjusted herself even closer. They kissed, and he took the plunge. What a pleasure palace! He couldn't help coming almost immediately, but she said she'd give him a second chance, and she did. They made love three times that afternoon, interrupted on the third blissful time by her father phoning. She told her dad she was okay being home alone. "I'll get together with the neighbors if I get bored," she said, and stuck out her tongue at Adamson. What a tease. He loved her.

School was closed for three days. He sneaked over to Hannah's two more times, built several snow monsters, buried Stella and Hannah with their consent, drank at least thirty cups of cocoa, split open his lip sledding downhill while standing up, tunneled to Ron's to play music, beat Isabel at Monopoly, and forgot to do his history homework. All in all, time well spent.

Back at school, he was knocking on the door marked "guidance counselor," wondering what to say, when Hannah appeared in the hallway.

"Need some help?" she asked, balancing her books on her lovely hip.

"Getting college advice."

"Aren't you going to U. Mass with the rest of us?"

"Not sure. Maybe Brown Junior…" Hannah confused him. After their delicious "snow dates," she'd gone to see a film with Sal, and it was hard to ignore Sal's salacious comments at rehearsals. The door opened and the counselor, Mr. Wallace, smiled thinly as if to say, "Not another bleeding complainer."

"See you later," said Hannah, who swung on her heels, flipping her tartan skirt as she clip-clopped down the hall past a bank of lockers.

"Can I help you?" Mr. Wallace was saying.

"I'd like an appointment."

"How about now?"

"That would be fine, thank you." Adamson bent down to enter Wallace's office. Once inside, it was spacious for a cubbyhole under the stairs. On the wall behind his desk was a poster of a glorious tropical sunset at the beach.

"Makes up for no window," said Wallace as Adamson stared.

"Ingenious," said Adamson.

"I don't think I know you. Sit down." Adamson introduced himself and explained his predicament. He needed to pick a college. His family was leaving the country and they wanted him settled. Wallace listened, forearms resting on a calendar blotter. When he finished, Wallace removed his tortoiseshell glasses and polished them. "You've missed the deadline for many of the schools."

"Have I?" said Adamson. Idiots dishing out the obvious, like at boarding school.

"Do you have any other family in the States?"

"No, sir."

"And does your family have money for college tuition?"

"I think so. What does it cost?"

Wallace sighed. "Why don't you go to U. Mass? They take almost every-one. You have to be in school because of the draft. What are your grades like?"

"Last semester I got three Cs and two Bs."

"What's your GPA?"

"Pardon?" Wallace waited. "Did they give them out at the beginning of term, sir?" asked Adamson. What the hell is a DBA, he thought, member-ship in the Dung Beetles Association? Wallace opened a file cabinet drawer and handed Adamson an application.

"I recommend U. Mass," he said.

"I can't go to U. Mass, sir," said Adamson, surprising himself with his own resolve. "Personal reasons." He set his lips in an implacable dash. The possibility of seeing Sal slobbering over Hannah every day was too much, plus Sal said U. Mass was ten times bigger than high school, which was enormous.

Mr. Wallace shifted direction. "Look through this book then, and pick a college that fits your preference and checkbook. I'll see if I've got the forms on file."

Adamson took the proffered three-ring binder and turned a few pages. There were too many bloody choices. He flipped a few more pages, then started from the back of the book. University of Bridgeport. Sounds nice. A bridge, a port. Students: 3,000. Not too large. Tuition: $1,600 per semester. Sounds reasonable. Art, literature, French, photography, biology, chemistry, history, physics.

"This one seems good."

Wallace had returned to a mountain of paperwork and swiveled back to Adamson. "What's that?"

"The University of Bridgeport, Bridgeport, Connecticut. It's convenient, right?" Wallace looked at him as if he were mad. Adamson wondered if he'd got his states muddled up, maybe Connecticut was on the other side of the country, but Wallace read the description, stuck out his lower lip in reluc-tant approval, and nodded his head.

"Not bad. Couple of hours from the folks…" Realizing his error, Wallace recovered like a pro, "… and friends and familiar surroundings. Good value, not too big, and you have till… March 15 to apply." Wallace swiveled to the file cabinet and swiveled back, placing a Bridgeport application on the desk.

"It's customary to apply to more than one, in case..." The firm dash on Adamson's face returned. Wallace refiled the U. Mass application. "Let me look it over before you submit." He stood up, signaling the end of the session but Adamson wanted to ask him something.

"Sir, my father says I don't have to worry about the draft because I'm English." Adamson had been seeing terrible things on the television. The new President, Richard Nixon, said he was going to end the war, but all the politicians said that. Adamson couldn't imagine himself in uniform killing people ten thousand miles away and he wanted to make sure that his father hadn't missed something about the draft in the fine print. "Is he right?"

"I can check. How old are you?"

"Eighteen, nineteen in October."

"Do you have a green card?"

Adamson nodded. Wallace came around his desk and patted Adamson's shoulder. "Fill out the application and bring it back next week. I'll get you an answer... uh, son." Adamson could tell Wallace had forgotten his name and couldn't get back to the blotter where he'd scribbled it.

That evening, he was reading a comic while his mother watched the news. Isabel was using crayons in a Barbie coloring book, her pink tongue flipping side to side in concentration. Yelling came from the telly.

"Students protesting at the University of Massachusetts," said Victoria. The picture was jerky as police arrested a clutch of young men and pushed the cameraman.

"Thirty-three arrested... " announced the broadcaster. His father was finishing the Yorkshire pudding left over from the weekend.

"Henry, you have got to get organized with your college business!"

"I have," he said. Heads turned his way. "I'll show you." He skidded upstairs and returned with the application.

"What? The University of Bridgeport? What about that community college?"

"I thought you were going to see the guidance master," said Victoria, looking over George's shoulder at the application.

"I did. This is what we decided." His parents looked at him blankly. He elaborated. "I talked with the counselor, and we decided this would be a suitable school. It's reasonably priced, good value, and not far from friends and familiar places." Adamson thought he sounded a bit like an advertisement for Butlin's holiday camps. "Mr. Wallace says he'll look over the application after we've filled it in."

George scowled. "What about some others, like the University of Massachusetts?"

"I don't think we want him going there, dear. That's where those students were arrested today." She gave Adamson's shoulder a rub. "Well done. I'm sure he could use your help filling in the details, George." When she wasn't drinking or in a dream world, Victoria possessed the knack of making people feel comfortable. George pursed his lips.

"I suppose we'd better get cracking," he said. "Good job."

George went to his bureau and brought back three sharp pencils, blank sheets of paper, and his checkbook. At the kitchen table, Adamson filled in the blanks and George made computations. Victoria shushed the girls and ushered them upstairs. When he got to the financials, Adamson passed the application to his father and sat back. In the glow of the light above the table, he felt quite adult. He didn't relish his family leaving. In fact, it made him feel sick and lightheaded, but the adventure stretching before him was magnificent to behold: A bridge. A port. And he was the Captain who set the whole thing in motion.

3

MARCH

Driving to Cambridge was Victoria's idea. It wasn't quite spring, but everyone was dying to get out of the house and *do something*. "I'll pick you up from school and we'll go to Harvard Square. We could have a snack at Zum Zum and go to the Coop for records, and perhaps the Fogg Museum."

"I'll skip the Fogg, thanks," said Adamson, relishing the thought of poring over the record section at the Coop.

"Perhaps it's too much for one afternoon. Still … " He knew his mother would love traipsing through rooms of Titians and stone-faced Puritans.

"All right but only *after* we look at records," he said. It was always hard to park in Harvard Square. Victoria dropped them at Zum Zum and it was half an hour before she got back to the restaurant. They were finishing their hot dogs and antsy to go. She ordered a coffee and a small sausage for herself and cookies for Isabel. Students plodded by the plate glass windows. Isabel twirled around and around on the counter stool and told her mother about her friend's doll collection. Victoria peeled off two tens, giving one each to Adamson and Stella, and arranged to meet them at the Coop.

By the time Victoria got there, Stella had browsed the clothes and bought some colored pencils. Adamson was torn between the new Lennon/Ono record and Cream's *Disraeli Gears*. "We're going to dash across the Yard to the Fogg, darling," she said to Adamson. "Meet us there." Adamson actually wanted to go to the Fogg, not so much for the poxy pictures but to be with his mother in a gallery again. They used to go when he was young and showed talent in painting. Galleries gave you freedom to think unusual thoughts, even say unusual things. Soon he wouldn't be able to spend any time with her at all. He thought of them leaving. Their departure shadowed his waking moments and even his dreams. He replaced the Lennon/Ono and hurriedly bought the Cream for $3.69.

He caught up with them as they entered Harvard Yard. The Yard was full of students, not the ordinary stream crisscrossing between classes but a big crowd milling around, as if a show were about to begin. Victoria craned to see over the lanky lads in front of her. "Oh my, police," she said. "You don't suppose there's going to be trouble?"

Adamson, who topped six feet, stood on tiptoe and turned periscope-style. "There's a platform." Above the din of students and cars honking on Massachusetts Avenue, a speaker was barking an incomprehensible point again and again. The crowd quieted and began to listen.

"WHAT DO WE WANT? TO END THE WAR.
WHEN DO WE WANT TO? NOW!"

The crowd picked up the chant and surged forward. Victoria held Isabel's hand tightly. The speaker continued yelling encouragement through a megaphone. The chant changed. "HARVARD LIES AND SOLDIERS DIE!" was what it sounded like. What had Harvard lied about? Isabel grabbed his leg. The crowd moved forward like floodwater around them while they stood marooned.

"We'd better forget the Fogg today," said Victoria, as a chair crashed through a window of the Administration Building. Students swarmed the stone stairs and tried to open the locked doors. A thrown object broke another window. Adamson saw the police moving in from the heart of the campus carrying sticks and transparent shields.

"Time to go," he said, reaching protectively for his sisters, but Stella pushed him away.

"I'm staying."

"Stupid! They might start shooting!" he barked. Victoria and Isabel were struggling to go back in the direction they had come but Stella stood firm. Just as Adamson yanked her arm, a man with a portable tape recorder asked her a question.

"I support the student struggle!" Stella yelled as Adamson yanked her. Another young man pushed his way in with a cine-camera. Cripes.

"Stee! Come *on!*" He couldn't budge her and didn't want to be filmed assaulting his sister.

"Stella! This instant!" Victoria screamed, having swum back through the chaos with Isabel. She must retrieve her children from the madness. As Victoria reached Stella, the cameraman addressed her straight on.

"What is your position on the war, ma'am?"

"I think we should all go home right now!" she snapped and pulled Stella's arm, marching both girls like a general back to the Avenue. Adamson glided in their wake. On the edge of the crowd, Victoria let go of them and fluffed the crown of her hair.

"Goodness gracious!"

"Mummy, I'm thirsty."

"What excitement. Let's get to the car first, darlings." She was too upset to make a proper dinner so they had grilled cheese sandwiches and crisps on tray tables in front of the telly. Isabel wanted to watch *Gilligan's Island* but George insisted on the news.

"That's where we were, Daddy!" said Stella.

"Bystanders expressed their opposition to the war as students smashed the windows of Harvard University's Administration Building today," announced the news anchor. A clip panned the packed Yard and they could hear breaking glass in the background.

The television showed a close-up of the reporter with the tape recorder, who intoned, "One housewife expressed her frustration with the Nixon Administration…" Then an angry Victoria appeared saying, *"I think we should all go home right now!"*

"There's Mummy!" cried Isabel, pointing at the telly. The news moved on to other stories: John and Yoko were planning to marry and North Sea oil had been discovered off the coast of Britain. In the Adamson den, George tried to formulate a question. Victoria was explaining. Stella was shrieking, "We walked into it, Daddy! I didn't want to leave. Then the camera came. I'm going to more demos!"

Adamson looked at his father and saw the wide-open eyes of a man falling over the edge of respectability into the abyss of counterculture chaos. His teenage daughter wanted to attend demonstrations. His wife was on the evening news. His son played drums at an excruciating volume in the basement. His youngest, merely a child, papered her bedroom wall with boy posters from teen magazines.

As Adamson poked in the kitchen cabinets, looking for chocolate biscuits, his father slotted his plate in the dishwasher. George went into the living room and put his favorite record on the Grundig. Soon, the soothing sounds of "Moon River" and "I Left My Heart in San Francisco" rose over new demonstrators arguing on the telly. Victoria went into the living room. Adamson couldn't help overhearing them.

"You oughtn't to have talked to the cameras," his father said. "I'm liable to hear about it at work. I have top secret clearances."

"I'm sorry, I was angry with Stella, she was being very naughty," said Victoria, "but I meant it. They thought I was talking about leaving the Yard and I was, but I don't like this Vietnam War one bit." She faced George. "I've felt this way for some time."

＊　＊　＊

Adamson had a free period after lunch and wandered into Lit. Mag. to avoid the corridor police. The room buzzed with activity as he hovered at the edge.

"Hello." He turned to see Paulette, a brainy girl from Algebra. "Can you copy-edit? I've got to lay out these pages and I'm late. Just look for typos and punctuation errors. Ignore the poems." Adamson took the pages and the proffered red pencil. "You can sit here," she said. She made space at the end of a row of desks where she was working. Adamson read through three short stories and ignored the drippy poems as instructed. Mostly about love. He liked Paulette's story about a black family in Boston. Nothing really happened, the main character, a grandmother, didn't die or anything. Her Jamaican dialect and the descriptions pulsed with life. He wasn't a strong speller but he found a couple of errors, marked them, and gave the papers back. Almost time for Math.

They walked down the hall together and up the stairs. He stood a head taller, but she bounced along with good posture. A few people greeted them as they passed the lockers. Others stared.

"You just ruined your reputation," said Paulette, as they took their seats. "What do you mean?"

"Don't you notice something about me?" He looked her over. Nicely dressed in a black-and-white sweater, black skirt, a bit long but all right.

America was a fashion-backward place in 1969. They hadn't discovered miniskirts, at least not where he lived. Paulette's hair was brown and curly and it looked soft. Her eyes were brown; her face was light brown. He couldn't tell if she was wore make-up, but nothing seemed out of place. "I'm black," she whispered.

"You mean . . ." He rubbed the back of his hand. She nodded.

"Shouldn't we walk together?" She smiled and he noticed what lovely teeth she had. Against her brown skin, they were especially white and looked straight and strong, not like your typical English teeth.

"It doesn't matter," she whispered, as Abrams instructed them to open their books and began marking on the blackboard, "what other people think." He didn't have a chance to respond because Abrams called him to the board and made an ass out of him for the rest of the lesson. Enjoyed himself too. "Would you like to study tomorrow?" she asked. "That test is going to be a doozy." He didn't know what a doozy was but the brown of her eyes was delineated from the white, like sand from the sea or the black-and-white diamonds on her sweater so they arranged to meet.

The Edsel, his ride home, was already started by the time he sprinted through the parking lot. "Sorry," he panted to Hannah, who drove her younger sister, Adamson, and Stella to school most days.

"What were you doing?" said Stella.

"Your brother's got a girlfriend from Roxbury." Hannah swiveled and backed the car out of the parking lot.

"Adamson only likes reptiles," said Stella.

"Hmm," said Hannah, "that's not what I heard." She rolled her eyes at him. He felt it best not to step into this pudding of American race politics. He still loved and slightly feared Hannah. What accounted for her cavalier approach to boys and sex? How had she learned everything she knew? He wished she'd teach him more.

When he walked into his house, Sal and Ron were sitting at the kitchen table drinking chocolate milk and eating Pillsbury iced cinnamon buns. Hannah had gone home to change clothes. Their first paying gig was coming up, a birthday party for one of Sal's friends. Victoria was chatting with the lads and doing ballet stretches at the sink. He hated when she did that but his friends didn't seem to notice.

Stella took her milk and buns upstairs to watch *Gilligan's Island*, *Lost in Space*, and *I Spy* till dinner. She was blimping out. The lads went down to the basement and when Hannah arrived, she gave Sal a kiss, and unwound her microphone. "What'll it be? 'Just Like a Woman?' 'In-A-Gadda-Da-Vida?'"

"You can't sing 'Just like a Woman,' it's a man's song," said Ron. She tossed her hair. God, she was beautiful. But was she more beautiful than Paulette? He mulled this as they debated songs for the party playlist. Paulette was shorter, more compact, with those lovely brown eyes. Hannah's eyes mocked. With Paulette he felt comfortable. He didn't have to duck her putdowns. Hannah's hair was madness in his hands, but wouldn't Paulette's feel nice running through his fingers?

"Adamson!"

"What?"

"'House of the Rising Sun!'"

"Right!"

Stella came down to listen. She was nursing her crush on Sal. Adamson watched Sal play to Stella and Hannah at the same time, encouraging attraction without jealousy. What a player. Hannah's mum called her for dinner and rehearsal broke up.

George was quiet at his end of the table while Victoria was chatty. The bottle of rosé was half-empty.

"I thought we'd go to Marshall's tonight for supplies," she said to Adamson.

"What for?"

"University."

"Tonight?"

"Why not? Good a time as any," she said.

"Perhaps wait till the weekend," said George.

"You'll be gone by then," Victoria snapped.

"Gone?" asked Stella and Adamson together. George's expression was full of discomfort. Why was his wife setting off land mines?

"Your father's leaving on Saturday for his new job, didn't you know? We'll be packing up alone in the house we were going to spend the rest of our lives in, and he will be jetting off to Italy. Cheers!" She drank her wine and poured another glass.

Three long, young faces stared at George. He wasn't the perfect father, but they'd liked having him around for a change. They were just getting used to living together, and now, he was off again. Isabel cried and nestled her face in her father's arms. Stella looked uncomfortable. Adamson felt sick to his stomach. He'd been denying the approaching void. Saturday would bring the first departure.

"When *were* you going to tell them?" asked Victoria.

"There, there," said George. "Look…" He closed his eyes as if to gain strength and steady himself. "I shall be back. I'm just going over for a few weeks to hire some chaps and get things started. Then I'll be back to pack." His eyes shot to Victoria but ricocheted away, a sore point indeed. "You'll come at Christmas, lad. It'll be like Alistair and Hong Kong."

"We forgot to call again," said Adamson.

"Get the number." Victoria went to the phone.

"We can't call now! It's eleven at night there." His parents were Mrs. Fruitcake and Mr. Bloody Idiot. Victoria wrote on a sheet of paper, "Call Alistair" in big letters and taped it to the kitchen cabinet. "First thing tomorrow! Before school." She cleared the table noisily. Stella left to do homework.

"Shall we go anyway?" He turned to find his father behind him.

"Where?"

"Marshall's. I'll take you."

"I want to go," said Isabel.

"Not this time, little thing. It's your brother's turn." Adamson couldn't remember the last time the two of them had done anything together. Must have been years ago, when George sometimes drove him back to boarding school instead of dropping him at the station to catch the train.

"What do I need?" he asked.

"Nothing. We'll be back, darling. Any requests?" George kissed a surprised Victoria on the lips and was at the door before she could respond.

"Make sure he gets underwear and socks," she said.

As George backed the car out of the driveway, he asked, "Is there someplace you'd rather go? I'm not very fond of Marshall's. I can't ever find anything, but it's up to you."

"Dunno."

"Let's go to Burlington Mall. They've got Jordan Marsh and some other places. We might even be able to stop for an ice cream," he said, with a twinkle. Adamson realized this was a rite of passage: the final shop for socks, underwear, and whatever else he could get away with, records, comics, jerseys. This was it. The last time he'd shop with his parents. He didn't hear his father's nervous patter. He didn't see the houses or the mounds of remaining snow. He didn't smell the scent of thaw. His fingers, moist, nervous, itchy, tightened on the seat like those of a child rising in the car of a big dipper. He braced himself, mentally. Any minute, he'd be flying downward, careening toward adulthood.

George parked as close as he could to the Jordan Marsh entrance. "Right," he said, turning to look at Adamson sitting next to him, face frozen in a grotesque masculine mask. His father put a hand on Adamson's shoulder and tried to pull him close, but Adamson resisted. "There, there, old chap, sorry about tonight. Your mother means well…" He stopped, realizing that Victoria's behavior was beside the point. He continued to rub Adamson's shoulder and Adamson felt himself relax a little. Being with his father made him feel like a little boy.

"Where will I go?" he whispered.

"You'll be at university, in the dorm," said George.

"But where will I live when everyone leaves next month? University doesn't start till September."

"Quite," said George. "We'll go see Sal's father tomorrow. Come to an arrangement. If not, perhaps the Wardheimers?"

"No, I can't… no, not the Wardheimers," he said. He could barely go into their house without getting vertigo from guilt and lust. The idea of living there… no.

"We'll settle soon, I promise. And we'll call you often and send you money for whatever you need. You won't be stranded, old boy, I'll see to that." George opened the car door. Meeting over, on to the next agenda item. Adamson had to admit his father was efficient.

They stopped just inside Jordan Marsh to get their bearings. Menswear was upstairs so they rode the escalator, leaving perfume and ladies' scarves behind.

"Where shall we start?" said George, heading for underwear. Adamson dutifully selected two packages of Fruit of the Loom jockey briefs, size 32. George moved to socks.

"I could use a few of these myself."

Adamson stood before the dress socks. He hated socks, preferred to go barefoot even in winter. He picked out a bag of cheap gym socks to be a good sport.

"What about a dressing gown?" asked George. "That would be handy staying at someone's house and in the dorm. How about this one?" His father held up a bright green flannel number with an angler theme. He was enjoying this. Adamson could not repress a smile.

"A bit fishy, Father," he said. The next one George picked out had post-cards all over it. Adamson raised his eyebrows and George put it back.

"Here you go, just the ticket." Plain royal blue with white piping around the pockets.

"That one's all right," said Adamson.

"Not too David Niven?" His father liked shopping, unlike most blokes. When he went away on business trips, he always brought back dresses for Victoria and the girls that actually looked nice. He had the knack. He couldn't remember his father ever bringing *him* back any clothing. He usu-ally got a book on reptiles or Viewmaster slides.

"Let's look at trousers and shirts. Do you have anything decent?"

"Like a suit?"

"No. Sports coat, slacks, that sort of thing."

"Sports coat?"

"For going out."

"Where?"

"I don't know, boy. Don't be dense. Going *out.*"

"Oh, *out.*"

"Say you were taking out a young lady. What would you wear?" George looked over the display of madras shirts. "These are very American."

"What I'm wearing now."

"But if you wanted to impress her parents. Say, you were picking her up from her house, wouldn't you want to wear something a bit more..." George gestured at Adamson's blue jeans and gray T-shirt.

"I wouldn't buy it here," he said.

Music blared from the front of the Rag Shack and a strobe light assaulted them as they walked in. Adamson nodded to the beat, this was better. He moved to the rack of tie-dyed caftan shirts and picked out one that was blue with silver thread. Too posh. He moved to another rack of loose Indian shirts and picked out a blue one with white embroidery around the neck and cuffs.

"This one's good," he said to George, who was standing ten feet away, deafened by the music. Adamson picked out two tie-dyed T-shirts and some pairs of cotton drawstring pants and put them on the counter.

"All done," he said, smiling at his father.

"Well done," said George, and extracted his wallet. After they stepped into the quiet of the mall, George asked, "What about shoes?" In Thom McAn, George wanted to buy Adamson a pair of brown lace-ups but Adamson balked, and they emerged with a pair of black-and-white high-top sneakers. "I'm bushed," said George. "How about a Friendly's ice cream?" George ordered a double dip of coffee and Adamson had chocolate. They ate their cones contentedly, surrounded by shopping bags. "I'm done in. What if I give you money for school supplies? You don't know what you'll need exactly, do you?" Adamson nodded. As they walked toward the exit, they passed a camera store. "Mind if I pop in for a moment?" asked George. "I want to look at a new model."

Adamson followed him and wandered from case to case. He owned an Instamatic camera but had recently taken a few shots with the Nikon belonging to a boy on the Lit. Mag. The boy tried to tutor him in photography basics. Adamson felt himself to be thick as a brick about anything technical but since the boy had a harelip and Adamson felt sorry for him, he let him show off the camera's features and explain the F-stop stuff. The pictures came out well enough. Perhaps he wasn't so thick after all. He looked along the Nikon case to see if the camera was there.

"Nice pieces," said George, standing next to him.

"I used that one at school last week."

"Did you?" George stared as if he had announced that he'd climbed Mount Everest. Eventually the clerk came over and offered to show them the model they were interested in. "Let me see that fellow on the left, the 1000, is it?"

"Excellent camera," enthused the clerk, lifting it out of the display case. "Semi-automatic features with manual overrides, the best of both worlds. I'll give you a good price because they're coming out with a new one next month, but between you and me," the clerk leaned in, "this is the better model." George held the camera, sighted it, weighed it in his hands, and handed it to Adamson.

"It's lighter than mine, nice feel. What do you think?"

"It's the same one. It takes good shots. This boy at school is trying to teach me so that he doesn't have to take all the yearbook pictures." George bit a cuticle and chewed his lip.

"Let's wrap her up and take her home, shall we?" He winked at Adamson and turned to the clerk. "Take a check, I trust?" It was Adamson's turn to stare at his father.

"Is that for me?"

George glowed. He put his hand over Adamson's and gave it a squeeze. "Take good care of it."

When they got home, everyone was in bed but Stella, who was stretched out on the daybed in the den. "What *are* you watching?" asked George.

"*The Day of the Triffids.* I tried to sleep but I couldn't."

"Didn't you watch it last night?" asked Adamson.

"And the night before. I'm going for the world's record, five nights in a row."

"I'm off to bed," said George. "Don't stay up too late. Tomorrow's a school day."

"G'night, Daddy," said Stella. George stepped down into the den and across the room. He leaned over and gave his daughter a light kiss.

"Good night, love." He patted Adamson's arm, "Good night, old chap. Jolly good show this evening."

After he heard his parent's bedroom door shut, Adamson got sucked into watching the evil rhododendrons try to take over Planet Earth. "Are you looking forward to Italy?" he asked.

"I'm happy to miss exams. And we're going to stop in London first."

The whole thing was bizarre. They'd traveled thousands of miles, immigrated to a foreign country, with foreign food, difficult dialects, peculiar customs, for all practical purposes a different everything. Left behind boarding school, Royal Air Force, cousins, pets, to "put down roots" that less than a year later, they were tearing up. Off we go, back to Europe. Sorry, old chap, you go to university, have a nice life, ta-ta!

"Are you scared?" she asked, eyes glued to the Triffids, "being left here by yourself?" Was it so obvious that his cretinous sister could see? He shrugged. He didn't know how he felt. He'd miss his mother, maybe his father, and possibly... no, he wouldn't miss his sisters. "At least you won't have Inkblot to put up with."

"All she wants is everyone's attention all the time and fistfuls of choccy biccies, a simple lass."

Stella eyeballed him. "Not like us."

"No," he sighed, "not like us." He got up and stretched. "Let me know how it turns out." Stella rose and turned off the telly.

"I think watching two-thirds counts as the whole thing, don't you?"

❊ ❊ ❊

Adamson kept staring at Paulette in Yearbook. Something was different. Finally, she turned to him. "Yes?" She had a red pencil tucked behind her ear, which was terracotta-colored and curved like a Mexican pot he'd seen in a museum.

"Sorry." He was proofing photo pages. If American football were discontinued tomorrow, he thought, his life would be unchanged. "Did you do something… to your hair?" He blinked, which he realized from her blush, she took as a wink. He looked down, squinting at the photos, then back at her. He was probably blushing too.

"I tried Sun-In. What do you think?" She was blushing for sure now. She was ever so pretty. He didn't know black girls blushed. He wanted to reach out and touch the little pink roses in her cheeks.

"Different. But nice. Want to go for a frappe when we're finished?"

"Sure. I'll be done in fifteen minutes." He swiveled around so she wouldn't see his mouth flap open and shut like a guppy's. He'd asked her out! On a date! She'd said yes! He didn't even plan. It just floated out of his mouth like a gift from God. Hallelujah!

"You okay, Adamson?" asked Ron, who was alphabetizing yearbook order forms.

"Toothache," Adamson said, covering.

It was a good hike down to Friendly's from school but the wind had lessened and the late winter sun shone pale through the trees. Tufts of green grass were sprouting by the roadside. He carried her book bag and listened as she chattered about Lit. Mag. and Yearbook.

"You should be a newspaperwoman."

"Or television," she said. "Think I'm photogenic enough?" She flashed a saucy smile.

"Of course."

"They'd have to start hiring black women first. The thing is," she said, "if I could break a really good story… hey, we could do it together. You could take the pictures, and I'd do the interviews and write the story." They walked into the ice cream store.

"Frappe?" he asked, after they were seated.

"Did you see the way the hostess looked at us? Why can't white people get over themselves?"

"What?" He looked toward the door, as if he might have missed a fire-spitting dragon.

"I like you, Adamson, because it all goes over your head." He bobbed his head agreeably.

"The ignorance-is-bliss type." She squeezed his hand then pulled it back as the waitress approached to take their order. He wasn't even sure she'd done it.

"Chocolate frappe, please," she said.

"Make that two."

"Two chocolate frappes?" asked the waitress, whose hair was coiled in a vertical whirl. It reminded him of neatly coiled rope on the deck of their boat in England. His father, the captain, liked a nicely coiled rope on deck.

"That all?"

"Yes, thank you," said Paulette, giving the waitress her phony smile. The waitress left. "What are you doing a week from Saturday?" asked Paulette. "It's the first anniversary of Martin Luther King's assassination. There's a demo in Boston. We could cover it. For the yearbook."

"Did they ask you?" he asked. She flashed an impish smile. "They didn't, did they?"

"Better to beg for forgiveness than ask for permission," she said. The waitress with the ropy hair placed the frappes in front of them. They gazed at each other as they sucked through the straws. "So, are you in? It's in Roxbury."

"Where's that?" he asked.

"You'll see."

APRIL

The street bustled as he looked up Bluehill Avenue. He'd arrived in Roxbury on the MTA. One glance confirmed he was the only white person in sight and he wished he could camouflage himself. This must be how the black students at school feel, he thought. He nodded at several people, and they nodded in return. The American custom of greeting strangers had been entirely new to him. In England, if you didn't know someone on the street, you ignored him. Why wouldn't you? But in the States, to ignore random passersby was tantamount to rudeness. It was best to be polite.

This was his maiden voyage as a photojournalist. Adamson touched the Nikon hanging from his neck and adjusted the shoulder strap of the camera bag in which he had packed provisions: two extra rolls of film (one color, one black and white), lens cleaner and cloth, and a cheese sandwich. He headed down Lawrence Avenue toward Martin Luther King Middle School, the designated kick-off point for the rally. Dozens, perhaps hundreds of people milled about. He couldn't make eye contact with everyone so he focused on giving every tenth person a quick nod and a pursed-lip smile.

He scanned the crowd for Paulette. He hadn't realized there would be so many people. He saw a few other white journalists with notebooks or cameras. He waved his hand but none responded. They were the proper journalists: CBS, ABC, NBC, all the professional alphabet guys. He was only representing the Lexington High School Yearbook, but many of them had probably started out in high school.

"I'll meet you at the middle school at eleven," Paulette had said. It was only ten forty-five but she said she'd be early too. Three little girls had drawn a grid on the sidewalk with chalk and were playing hopscotch. He raised his camera and found them in frame.

"No taking pictures of my babies!" He looked up to see an angry woman planted in front of him with her palm toward the camera.

"Sorry, they looked happy," he mumbled.

"We don't want pictures of "happy pickaninnies" today. This is a serious day of remembrance. It's about time you white people woke up!" She grabbed her children's hands and hauled them down the sidewalk. Great, he thought, no pictures. People around him averted their eyes in embarrassment or looked through him. Is this what Paulette has to deal with at school, being "odd man out?" A march organizer announced something over the microphone and he managed to hear, "... starting in a few minutes." Another man at the mic began praying, and all around him bowed their heads. She was missing it. He bowed his head and looked at people's shoes.

Adamson was never sure what to do during moments of prayer. He himself never prayed. Prayer was for foreigners and the elderly, and for especially emotional occasions like christenings and weddings and funerals. Prayer was not for 18-year-old British schoolboys. At school assemblies and mandatory church services, "Let us pray" had been the signal to shoot spitballs at the chair in front. Alistair had once dropped a young toad down Adamson's shirt during a moment of standing meditation. He mustn't forget to call Alistair. The toad became his pet, which he kept in a wire mesh cage fashioned from a borrowed portion of the kitchen garden fence. Walter B. Toad grew large, and Adamson fancied at times he caught the toad smiling. Walter eventually escaped near the end of term but Adamson imagined a dynasty of great kitchen garden toads that he'd played a role in founding. You might say that during prayer, Adamson thought of toads.

A speaker was announced from the Southern Christian Leadership Conference. He exhorted the crowd and a banner of the Reverend King was unfurled above the stage. Adamson listened to the pleas to "follow the dream." Which dream were they talking about? He'd missed American History as it was taught during 11th grade. I'll ask Paulette, he thought. Where is she?

He had to find a way to photograph without causing dissension. After the speeches, the crowd sang "We Shall Overcome" and another song before starting to march. He followed, craning for a glimpse of Paulette. While standing and waiting for the walking to begin, he'd rediscovered the top viewfinder on his camera. By flicking it open, he could look down, train the lens on an object, line it up, and click the shutter, all without bringing the camera to his face, the telltale and objectionable action. Though most of what he saw holding the camera at waist level were coats and arms, if he moved to the edge of the crowd and leaned back, he could catch some faces too.

Crowds lined the avenue and children waved. The marchers passed through Roxbury, picking up people as they went. He worked on his walking-leaning-viewing-shutter-clicking technique till they halted before the Black Panther Party storefront. Here a man made a speech about Martin Luther King and others who'd been killed that Adamson had not heard of. At Humboldt and Townsend, another man spoke and at the end of his speech, people in the crowd punched their fists in the air, yelling "Malcolm! Malcolm!" He clicked his camera nonchalantly.

He thought he heard his name and scanned the crowd but almost everyone had rounded Afro hairdos like Paulette's and he didn't see her. Leaning against a storefront, he took a few more pictures and ran out of film. The sun was too bright to reload on the avenue, so he ducked into an alley. On an old table behind a store, he removed the spent film and wrestled with the winding mechanism to reload. Some men strolled by. He nodded to them as the film slipped again from the sprockets. Dammit. He snapped the camera closed as a blinding crash took him to his knees. Clutching his camera to his body, he felt a sharp kick that knocked him flat on the ground. His chin scraped on wet concrete. His side throbbed and he flung his arm over his head to ward off blows. I hope I don't die, he thought.

"Get up!" yelled a voice and someone yanked him. "Get up, Adamson, you drunk bastard!" He squinted. Paulette stood above him, scowling, hands on her hips. "Get up, or I'll beat your butt!" she yelled. Then she actually kicked him.

"Ow!" he said and got to his knees. She wrapped his arm around her shoulders and yanked him to his feet. He glanced at the hooligans glowering from the alley wall.

"What you looking at?" Paulette spat. The men shrank back visibly. "You never been drunk in the wrong place? Go beat up some other honky. This one's going home." Squaring her shoulders, she walked him down the alley away from the march. After they turned onto the next street, she glanced behind her and dropped him onto a stoop. "You are one sorry-looking honky," she said, and pulled out a tissue. "Spit," she commanded. He spat in the tissue, and she scoured his face and neck and examined his head. "Just a scratch," she pronounced and sat down next to him.

"Thank you," he said, not sure if he was thanking her for dragging him away from a beating or dismissing his clubbed head. The sunlight was too bright and he didn't know where he was. "Where were you?" he asked.

"My brothers were supposed to go to tutor... never mind. Your camera's beat up." The Nikon was scratched from hitting the ground. He lifted it to his eye, focused on her grim face, and clicked the shutter. It resounded appropriately.

"Seems to still work," he said. He checked the back. "Seems tight. I don't think I'm cut out for photojournalism."

"Pfft!" was all she said. She started walking down the sidewalk. "Come on."

"Where?"

"We can rest at my house till the brothers get drunk and go home." She sounded dejected. Adamson hobbled beside her down two blocks and over three. When he wasn't sure he could go on, she climbed a set of brick steps and unlocked the door of a row house. Inside, he was struck by a woodsy smell spiced with curry. Music played somewhere. A bare bulb lit some hooks where she hung her jacket. He put his jacket over hers and followed her back to the music in the kitchen. The house was toasty warm and he involuntarily rubbed his hands together like Scrooge. In the kitchen, a woman was playing singles on a little record player and drinking beer. "Hello, darlin'," she crooned at Paulette, who bent down to be kissed. "Bam-bam," went the song rhythmically, "Bam-bam," then the singer went falsetto.

"Mom, this is Adamson, my friend from school. This is my mom."

"This a pleasure," she said, getting up and moving toward him, her nose and eyes wrinkled in delight. "What brings you to town, Adam's Son?" She took his hand to shake it and he saw alarm cross her face. "Boy, you as white as a sheet. Paulie, give the boy a chair. What you do to 'im?"

"Some brothers smacked him in the alley," said Paulette, rinsing out a cloth in the sink and bringing it to where Adamson was sitting, doing his best not to pass out.

"In broad daylight? What this world coming to?" He watched as the room went black-for-white. The women's voices sounded as if they were talking in a tin can. "Need the hospital?" he heard Paulette's mother ask. He wanted to lie down.

"In Lexington, he'd go to the hospital," said Paulette. "In Roxbury, we'll give him tea and see what happens." Her tone was harsh.

"Water, please," he said. She handed him a glass.

"Maybe this is what he needs," said Paulette's mother, lighting a hand-made cigarette. "Worst thing, he take a nap. Look like he need one." She offered him the cigarette. "Take a little puff."

"I don't smoke," he said. Paulette shook her head. She took the cigarette from her mother and inhaled deeply, holding the smoke in her lungs. When she exhaled, he smelled the sweet scent from the hallway.

"You may as well keep us company," she said. He took the cigarette, now a little wet at the tip, and inhaled a small puff and blew it out. Not unpleasant.

"Is this marijuana?" he said before he could stop himself. I'm an idiot, he thought. "I mean, it is, isn't it?"

"He's a cute one!" said Paulette's mother, puffing on the cigarette, passing it to Paulette, and around it went. The ladies puffed, inhaled a little air, inhaled some more, and let it out. He'd sworn he'd never smoke, having put up with Victoria's vile habit his whole life. The room shifted but instead of fighting it, he slipped like Alice down the rabbit hole. Paulette helped him to a sofa. When he awoke, the telly was on. His mouth was dry and his head throbbed. He lifted his head but the throbbing got worse. He slept again.

"Tea?" He opened his eyes. Paulette was sitting next to him, a cup in her hand.

"No, thanks."

"What do you drink except water?" She went to refill his glass. He pulled himself up on an elbow.

"What's time is it?"

"About four. You've been asleep."

"I should go home," he said, but he reclined on the sofa. She sat beside him, cradling the tea in her hands. The cozy living room was bathed in the warm light of an old standing lamp. Paulette had never said where she lived. He knew she was one of "the Roxbury kids," bused to an all-white school in the suburbs every day, but he'd never thought of her as actually "poor."

"You could have been killed this afternoon," she said.

"It was stupid to go in the alley."

She slipped her hand in his. "You're a stupid boy, all right," she said. She smiled at him. On the telly, the newscaster announced that there were half a million American soldiers in Vietnam.

"Why is America fighting in Vietnam?" he asked. She shook her head.

"White people got to be in charge of everything," she said, "even Cracker Jack countries a million miles away." He touched her forearm with his index finger and traced a line back and forth between two moles. Her brown skin was soft and warm. He felt a sinew rise beneath his finger. She watched him with deep interested eyes. Back and forth his finger traced as they sat in silence.

At seven that evening, he walked into his kitchen at home, spent from his injury and the long ride on the subway and bus back to Lexington. Isabel was lying on her tummy on the floor of the den in front of the telly, reading a pop star magazine. Stella was curled up on the daybed with her mouth twisted in a squiggle. His father, newly returned from Italy, was sitting in a large wicker chair watching the telly, arms folded in front of him. The air was thick with accusation. Victoria was doing leg exercises in the kitchen using the counter as a barre.

"Evening all," said Adamson. He'd called from Paulette's to let them know he'd be late, and his mother had sounded cheery, asked if he'd had a good day. He found a plate with roast chicken, leftover mac and cheese, and green beans. He poured an OJ and ate. His head still ached. Victoria did pliés at the kitchen sink.

"Bloody fools," sputtered George. He snapped off the telly and poured a glass of chocolate milk. "I don't want to see you demonstrating." He scowled at Stella, then Adamson. "Where have you been all day?"

"I told you, darling," said Victoria, sweeping her arm over her head and watching her hand open gracefully. "He went to Boston to see his friend from school. Did you have a good time?"

"Quite good," he said. His day would be difficult to explain to his parents. George handed him a letter. Adamson looked at the return address: University of Bridgeport.

"Oh, God." He looked up in horror.

"I'm sure it's an acceptance," said Victoria. "You did quite well on the entrance exam. We've been waiting for you to get home." He stood, paralyzed. His mother gently took the envelope and opened it, handing him the letter. He scanned the text.

"I'm in!" He looked joyfully at his parents. "I'm going to university! To Bridgeport!"

Victoria kissed her son's cheek. Stella bounded up to investigate and Isabel followed. The victorious tale was retold. "It's astonishing. Your brother has been accepted to university," said George. It wasn't till he heard his father explaining that he realized he hadn't expected Adamson to get in.

"What is university?" asked Isabel.

"A school for big boys and girls. Where they study and prepare for what they'll do with the rest of their lives. He'll have to work hard, won't you?" Adamson nodded. That made his head throb, but he was going to the University of Bridgeport. He was going to be a university man, like his father. George re-read the letter. Probably looking for a mistake. Victoria hugged him again. George chewed on his cuticle.

"No more bloody demonstrations though," said George. Victoria shot a look at her husband. "You have to keep your wits about you over here. It's a different country."

"Will do," said Adamson. As he brushed his teeth before bed, he grinned in the mirror. University Man. Why didn't his father think he'd make it? He climbed into bed with a Thor comic but fell asleep immediately.

Sal woke him around noon. "Someone stole my car last night in Cambridge." He sat on Adamson's sofa, totally dejected. "I'll never get her back."

"Stolen?" He'd been dreaming of walking on a beach with Paulette amid palm trees and sunset.

"She's probably in pieces in some Back Bay chop shop." Sal's eyes were bright with tears. His rebuilt 1962 blue Mustang meant the world to him.

"Have you called the police?" asked Adamson, wanting to help.

"What are they gonna do?"

"Catch the thieves?"

Sal shook his head, holding back from crying. "Man, I loved that car." Adamson shrugged into a sweater and a pair of jeans.

In the kitchen, his mother called to him, "Darling, shall we try Alistair? Five o'clock on a Sunday afternoon would be a good time to catch him, wouldn't it? Coffee, Sal?" Adamson had lost faith he'd ever talk to his friend, but Victoria placed a request with the operator. Over coffee and orange juice, she coaxed out the sad tale of the missing Mustang.

"What about insurance?" Victoria asked.

"I don't know," said Sal. "I haven't told Dad yet."

"If your father has insurance, you can at least get the money to buy something else, not that it could replace Mona." She respectfully used Sal's name for his car.

"He'll be pissed off. He helped me fix her up. I let him borrow her when... when he needs it." Adamson looked at Sal in alarm as Victoria rose to answer the phone. Sal rolled his eyes. He had been about to say, "... when Dad has a hot date." He and Sal had agreed not to share Sal's dad's proclivities with Adamson's parents. Victoria unwound herself from the phone cord and passed the receiver to him.

"It's ringing."

A smooth English voice answered, "Richmond College." After a halting start, Adamson asked to speak with Morris, Alistair. He forgot to mention he was calling from America and had to wait five long minutes before the lady returned. "The boys are coming in from Evensong. Morris will be with you in a minute."

"Any luck?" asked Victoria. She was biting her thumbnail, trying not to calculate the escalating cost of the call. At that moment, a panting voice came on the line.

"Back, back, Base Troll!"

Adamson responded on cue: "Back to the Stygian depths from whence thou emergest at the dawn of time!"

"So much for calling as soon as you landed, matey," said Alistair. Adamson hugged himself. His best mate, Alistair-the-Bear!

"It's bloody tricky here. The clocks don't be'ave. Night is day, day is night."

"Same when I talk to my parents only worse 'cause it's fifteen hours earlier in 'ong Kong, he said. "I don't bother anymore. Just send money, I say. So what's it like to go to school with girls? Tell all, lad."

"As different as…" he ducked around the corner to the dining room to avoid Victoria and Sal's eyes and ears. "…going to school with aliens. Girls everywhere!"

"Everywhere?"

"Very good but mighty confusing. I mean, can't talk about it right now," he said, lowering his voice.

"You're not going to Vietnam, are you?" asked Alistair. "I heard every boy in America gets drafted at nineteen. Don't let 'em take you, matey. Fight to the death!" Alistair grunted and Adamson could tell he was stabbing the air on his end of the line.

"Adamson," Victoria poked her head around the archway, "just a few more minutes."

"Will you come over soon?" The sound of Adamson's own voice touched him.

"Write this down…" Adamson scrambled for paper and pencil. "July 12th, my Pater will be in San Francisco on business," said Alistair, "and so will I and so will you."

"Me?"

"No, you bombastic boob, the Duchess of Windsor. Of course, you!" Alistair's voice dropped till Adamson could barely hear him. "I'm aiming for early release from this rat-trap, family hardship, miss me Mum and Dad, boo-hoo. Can't go into details, but get thee to San Francisco second week in July and your services will be amply rewarded." Alistair resumed his regular tone. "Details by post, it's good as done."

"Count me in," said Adamson, "but make sure you send the details 'cause it's a bloody battle getting you on the phone."

"Adamson, give Alistair our love. Tell him to come see us in Italy."

"Me Mum says 'Oogle-oogle, snog-whiz-bam potato, m' lad.' I think she likes you." Victoria parked herself in front of Adamson, her presence insisting he terminate the call. "Gongs and whistles to yer, matey," he said.

"Gongs and whistles, and to your Mater and Pater," replied Alistair.

"Ali," said Adamson, turning to face the china cabinet, "can't wait to see you. Write to me."

"Summer she blows, matey. Good as posted." Adamson heard the receiver click. He wished they could talk on and on into the night as they used to. God, Alistair's socks smelled!

✳ ✳ ✳

Monday, Adamson delivered the University of Bridgeport acceptance letter to Wallace's converted broom closet. He sat watching Wallace read, eyes darting from line to line till the counselor nodded his head in approval. Adamson got up to leave, but Wallace raised his hand. "About the draft…" he said. Wallace was rubbing the stubble on his chin, seeming to take a measure of something. There was nothing to look at but Wallace and the sunset poster. "As an immigrant with a green card, it turns out you can still be drafted."

"What?" Horror spread across Adamson's chest. "But my father…."

"I was surprised too," Wallace continued. "What does your dad do for a living?" Adamson tried to form words, then bit his lip. "An accountant? Engineer? Teacher?"

"Engineer," Adamson managed.

"Aeronautical? Mechanical?" Wallace was peering at him.

"Radar."

"And what did he tell you about the draft?"

"He said I couldn't be drafted because I'm English. I have a British passport."

"You arrived last July and now the rest of your family is leaving for Europe?"

"I don't even know where Vietnam is."

"Southeast Asia, it was a French colony and after the French left, the Americans sent advisors to help the South Vietnamese defeat the Northerners, which they couldn't do. Now we have thousands of troops there. It's a quagmire. The South Vietnamese are our allies and the communist North Vietnamese are China's and Russia's allies."

Why didn't they teach us global politics in England? Adamson thought. All he'd learned was ancient stuff—Beowulf, Glastonbury Village, Battle of Hastings, Magna Carta, Henry the Eighth's six wives, chop, chop, chop off their heads.

As Wallace explained the Cold War, Adamson realized that his father had been fighting in the Cold War. Whenever he told his friends that his father was in the Royal Air Force, they assumed he was a pilot, but he wasn't. "I once asked my father what he did," Adamson told Wallace, "and he said he listened to things, under the sea, on the ground, and in the air, using radar."

"Sounds like a Cold Warrior to me," agreed Wallace. "With China and Russia arming North Vietnam and America arming the South, their civil war has become part of the Cold War. When you turn nineteen, you'll get a draft notice telling you to report, like everyone else. You'll show up, they'll test you, but even if you qualify, you can get an educational deferment, meaning you can put off going into the service till you finish college, which is what you'll do. I assume you don't want to go to war?" Was this a trick question? Adamson thought.

"No, I'm not Army material, sir."

"Many young men feel the same way but some feel obliged to serve, so I ask. You've been accepted to college, that's the first step." Adamson recalled the joy he felt when he received his letter, his invitation to join the adult world. Now it seemed like a life-preserver as well. "You must stay in school and keep your grades up, Cs or better. If you fail classes, they can place you on probation and your deferment will be in jeopardy. Do you follow me?"

Adamson's eyes had started to glaze over. Deep down, he still felt panicked. He was still trying to place Vietnam on the map and sweep the corners of his conscience for any sense of duty. "What about when I finish university?"

"Don't worry about that." Wallace grinned a crooked smile. "The war will be over in four years. Of course, we were supposed to defeat the North Vietnamese last year, and the year before that. Ever hear of the Hundred Years' War? Just joking, it won't last a hundred years. We'll blow the Chinese to kingdom come before that. After you finish, you can go on to grad school and extend your deferment. Or marry and have a baby." Adamson registered astonishment. "The point is, you're set for now as long as you stay in school. Enjoy yourself. Your college years can be the best of your life." Wallace shook Adamson's sweaty palm.

"Thank you, sir," quavered Adamson. "Thank you very much."

"Anytime. Come back even after graduation. I like to see how my students get on. What will you major in at Bridgeport?"

Adamson didn't know what majoring meant so he feinted. "Hard to say, sir."

"Choose something you like, something you're good at. Don't let your parents choose for you. That's sure to backfire. Good luck." Wallace shook his hand again. Backing into the hallway, he collided with Hannah. Was she following him? He dropped his math book and struggled to pick it up without staring up her skirt.

"We need to talk." Her voice was distressed. She must have been waiting the whole time. She hugged her books protectively and twirled a corkscrew of hair. He waited. He longed to touch her shoulder or her cheek, not to be sexy but because he cared. He knew that would be misconstrued. Girls were a mystery. "I have to quit the band," she said.

"We have a gig coming up!" he exclaimed. "This weekend. Lisa's sister's whachamacallit, Bat Whiskers Party."

"I can't. Because of Sal," said Hannah.

"Is he bothering you?" He felt protective plus Paisley Scarab was the best thing going in his life. Dear God, change her mind, I'll do anything, I'll stop tormenting Stella, I'll take out the rubbish, no complaining…

"I dig him but he's started seeing someone else," she said, tearfully.

"Can't you…" Adamson saw the futility of his arguments as Hannah cried. She buried her face in his shoulder. She'd never been tearful over him that he knew of. He awkwardly held her elbows while she sobbed, then gingerly put his arms across her back and left them there. She'd never said she dug him. He didn't have a tissue but she pulled out a whole packet from her pocket. Well prepared, our Hannah.

"You're so sweet. I'm sorry. My shrink says I'm impulsive." She closed her eyes and took a deep breath. "I've got to go to lab," but she didn't move away. She looked up and smiled a wee smile. "I have to go." He still had her in his arms. He briskly dropped them and clasped his hands behind his back. She laughed.

"You always do that. It's so funny." She caressed his cheek, the very gesture he had wanted to make to her. "Sorry about the band. Hope you can find someone else."

"Hannah?" he called after her but she was already a speck in the distance. He liked her but she was an enigma. He hoped she'd invite him back to bed one day. In the meantime, all-instrumental set? Maybe one of the other girls could step in? Or Sal? Maybe he could learn the vocals by Saturday?

Adamson opened his locker. His new band was on the rocks before they'd started, but he was going to the University of Bridgeport. He wouldn't have to go to Asia to kill people he didn't know if he made Cs in his courses. And a young woman with whom he'd recently had sex had sought comfort and cried on his shoulder. And soon he would be alone in this strange new American world.

5

MAY

The Cadillac Coupe de Ville in Hannah's driveway was the biggest car Adamson had ever seen. Hannah's dad had just bought it. Gold with a cream leather interior, it had two colossal doors that closed with a satisfying "thunk." He'd heard it from across the street and waited till Wardheimer went indoors to sidle over to Golden Boy. You couldn't hide an automobile this impressive. Adamson traced the long, sleek fin all the way to the tip of the crimson rear light. Ouch! Not quite sharp enough to cut yourself on, but ouch anyway.

He'd never loved a car before he saw Golden Boy. His father's English Rovers and Fords were nice and serviceable, full of old world charm with walnut dashboards, leather upholstery, and middle arms you could lower to keep your poxy sisters at bay. He'd sat in a Jag once, even a Rolls Royce. They were luxe and grand, but none made his breath go shallow or his hand tremble as he caressed the fender. Golden Boy was excessive, that was the thing. For all its yardage, the Wardheimers could barely fit their family of four into it. It was intended for you and your lady and perhaps her luggage. It had a boat-sized boot. Adamson fingered the Cadillac seal, walked to the driver's side, and peered in. "Trunk latch" read the handle. Trunk, not boot, he had to remember that.

"No sticky fingers." Wardheimer startled him from his reverie.

"Nothing sticky, sir, " he said, holding up his hands as if for the sheriff.

"Want to ride to the grocery store?" Wardheimer unlocked the door.

"Don't mind if I do," said Adamson. He dashed to the passenger side and heard the "thwock" of the automatic lock, half-rolling his eyes in pleasure. Opening the door, he brushed his pants off before getting in. Wardheimer looked alarmed.

"You are not dirty from the yard?"

"No, not at all," he said, lowering himself into the spacious front seat. Wardheimer eased the shift into reverse, turned around, and with one hand flat against the steering wheel, backed Golden Boy into the street. Then he swung around, pushed the handle into Drive, and they were rolling. "He's a beauty," said Adamson, taking in the interior and the ride.

"The performance is surprising," said Wardheimer.

"How so?" asked Adamson, ready to learn something new. Wardheimer did not expect a follow-up because he mumbled something like "for a car this large." Adamson stretched his long legs out. Never enough room for a good stretch in the Bonneville. If this were his car, he'd move the front seat back six or eight inches but Wardheimer was small and needed to be close to the pedals.

"I hear you're moving," said Wardheimer as he steered past the pond and down the hill into town. The woods were vibrant with the green leaves of springtime. Adamson nodded. He'd already begun detaching though he felt a stab when he saw the boxes come in and when he watched his mother linger over each candlestick and lampshade. What did they mean to her that her eyes glinted with tears? For the most part, he was looking ahead.

"I'm moving in with Sal," he said as they turned into the Grand Union parking lot.

"I'll just be a moment," Wardheimer said and walked into the store. Adamson waited until he was inside before trying the radio but Wardheimer had taken the keys. He pulled down the visor and saw his reflection in the mirror. His hair was tousled. He hadn't brushed it before leaving the house. He hadn't even brushed his teeth. He'd gone outside to look for a special pen that he'd lost while playing badminton. Embossed with the Dynamic Electric logo, the pen telescoped and could be extended into a three-foot-long pointer. His father had given it to him. Adamson had been poking in the grass when he fell under Golden Boy's spell.

The car was warm in the sun. He wished he could open the window but he couldn't do that either without keys. In the back seat was a vinyl briefcase, the kind that opened when you pulled apart the top edges. A magazine poked out. Adamson looked at the store entrance; no sign of Wardheimer. Extending an arm behind him, he extracted the magazine far enough to see it was *Playboy*. He pushed it back, but when Wardheimer hadn't appeared, he casually pulled it out again and glanced over his shoulder at the pretty blonde on the cover. She looked a bit daffy, dressed in a tight red-and-white checked apron outfit, as if she were a hillbilly lass whose clothes had shrunk. Her breasts loomed like mountains. He imagined shaking his head between them, getting good and clobbered. He read the article titles: "Miranda's Adventure in Spain," "Playboy Interview: Marshall McLuhan," "San Francisco's Smashing Girls." That article might come in handy when he met up with Alistair. He jumped several inches when Wardheimer opened the trunk. With the lid as cover, he tipped the magazine back into the briefcase and they drove home in silence. He fingered the leather and played with the ashtray in the door handle. How to get his hands on a *Playboy*? He'd ask Sal. Sal's father probably subscribed.

"What do you know about Salvatore?" asked Wardheimer, holding the steering wheel tightly as they sat at the stoplight near the skating rink. Adamson hesitated. If he said, "Nice chap," that might not be good since Sal had apparently initiated the break-up with Hannah. If he said, "Bit flighty," he'd feel guilty. Perhaps Sal broke it off because the Wardheimers didn't like him, and they were thinking of giving him another chance. He decided to be honest.

"He's my friend," Adamson said, "and an excellent bass player." Nice and simple, take it or leave it.

"Why didn't you ask her out?" asked Wardheimer. "Is it because she's Jewish?"

"I... uh..." Blimey, that's a sticky wicket.

"You don't have to apologize," said Wardheimer. "I know the English." He glanced at Adamson.

"I happen to like Hannah very much, but it wasn't reciprocated. I mean, she fell hook, line, and sinker for my best mate. What could I do?" He hoped he wasn't wandering into treacherous territory. He didn't exactly want a relationship with Hannah. She was very attractive, but her moods shifted with the weather. Hannah required warning signs: Dangerous curves. Caution. Speed trap ahead. In contrast to Paulette, with her soft sweaters and brown curls and delicious brown eyes set in white-whites. Paulette was like clean, fresh sheets. Straightforward, friendly, even when cross. He understood Paulette without thinking. Hannah gave him a headache.

Parked in front of Wardheimer's garage, as Adamson daydreamed about Paulette, Wardheimer said, "One more sing…" With his German accent, he said "sing" for "thing." His hands still gripped the steering wheel, as if listening for instructions from an invisible Kommandant. Adamson wasn't keen on Germans. Victoria had taught him what they did during the World War II, including killing her fiancé in Czechoslovakia, and, of course, killing the Jews, but Wardheimer himself was Jewish so that was confusing. "We will be happy to help you when your family is gone," said Wardheimer. "We know what it's like to lose family and live in a strange country."

He would have dismissed the offer out of hand if Wardheimer hadn't added the bit about a strange country, and if his voice hadn't betrayed a crack of emotion. For a moment, Wardheimer peered into Adamson's soul and they were frightened boys gazing at one another. Then suddenly, the rat was back, and Wardheimer's boy fled into the labyrinth of his unconscious. The exchange only took a second but Adamson's palm was damp when he touched the door handle. The door was locked. He looked for the button but there was no bauble on the top of the lock to pull, no way out. "I have to get home," he said.

"Remember, we will be here." The door lock popped and Adamson sprang from Golden Boy. He walked straight to his house, up to his room, and played "A Whiter Shade of Pale" as he lay on the sofa with his eyes closed. Wardheimer gave him the creeps. He knew about men who preyed on boys, but that didn't seem to be the problem. Was Wardheimer trying to get Adamson involved with Hannah? That didn't make sense. He let the song seep into him. His cousin had given him the record when Adamson played it over and over at his aunt and uncle's house. "You can have it," the cousin said, "if you promise never to play it here again." After re-playing it twice, Adamson felt fortified. Perhaps he'd imagined Wardheimer's strangeness or he was feeling guilty about the *Playboy*. He went over the conversation in his mind and saw there was nothing menacing.

Cardboard boxes had sprouted around the house, a familiar scene to what the Americans called "Army brats," the children of servicemen. He'd lived in and out of boxes, trunks, and barrels his whole life. New quarters, new neighborhood, new friends, then move, and start all over. At the center of their family was his father George, handsome in his officer's uniform with a rainbow of mysterious insignia on the left breast. He wore medals on special occasions for "Meritorious Conduct" or "Honorable Acts of Valor." Nothing like the Iron Cross, mind you, but he cut an impressive figure. Now boxes blocked the entrance to Adamson's room. "Daddy says you need to get cracking," said Victoria.

"You're not leaving for two weeks."

"We're going to a hotel first," she said.

"What?" Just once, he would like to know what was going on before it happened.

"We're renting the house. I need your help." Adamson sat on his sofa, head in hands. "Darling, he's left us again. It's up to you and me. The movers will do most of the heavy stuff but you'll have to do your room and help me with the china. I don't want strangers packing it. I would never have bought this house and all these things if I thought we'd be packing up again."

"Don't bring that thing in here, please," said Adamson, smelling her cigarette. He heard the hiss as she tossed it in the loo and flushed. She sat down next to him.

"It's nice the way you did this room up," she said. "You could go into interior design. I once thought of that but didn't get a chance. Made nice homes, though, didn't I? Remember Woodside Park? That was a lovely house, French doors opening onto the back garden. Better than quarters. Ruislip wasn't bad. Marham was drafty. Which was your favorite house?"

He couldn't remember much about the houses they'd lived in. He came home from boarding school six weeks in the summer and was mainly out on his bike or on the boat. A month at Christmas, a few weeks at Easter. He remembered his childhood more by their pets: Hercules and Draco, early lizards; Tavish, his first box turtle. He couldn't remember the names of the other turtles. There was Sugarpuss, a proud black-and-white cat; King Crimson, his king snake; and Zippity-Doo-Dah, a corn snake that disappeared before they left England. Like a pair of bookends, Adamson and Victoria sat in his dim room reflecting, he on aquariums, pet shops, and turtle cages, she on sitting rooms and French doors. They'd had to leave Sugarpuss last year. Only Bella, the younger of their two dogs, was allowed to come with them to the States.

"I might get a lizard when I move to Sal's," he said. She didn't answer, lost in thought, fingers opening and closing as they did when she couldn't light a cigarette. Sometimes he wanted to shake her awake her to the joys and horrors of real life. Perhaps that's how it is with mothers, they're always thinking of something else, planning dinners, making a mental note to darn a sock.

She turned to him. "Don't forget to feed him, your new lizard." She *had* been listening. She'd fed his reptilian and amphibian menagerie when he went away to school; she didn't like giving live mice to King Crimson but she'd done it. "We're going to the hotel Saturday. Let's ring Sal, make sure they're ready for you. It's good of them to take you in." She rose and drew herself to her full height. "You will come over at Christmas?" As if he had somewhere else to go. Italy was one of those drippy places advertised on American Express commercials with worm-eaten art, fountains, gondolas, and endless bowls of spaghetti. It wasn't a place he'd choose to go but he might be ready for Victoria's homemade mac and cheese. "Stella will miss you."

Now she's off her rocker, he thought, but he flashed on the hours of bike riding he and his sister had done together, how she'd patiently watched his reptile demonstrations, and he'd fed her curiosity about his record collection. Poor kid, she'd have no one to guide her tastes. "I'll write to her," he said, knowing he wouldn't. Victoria looked around his room till her gaze fell on her big son on the sofa, all knees and drumming hands. "You rang?" he asked, feeling awkward.

"Haven't done such a bad job, have I?" She was fishing for compliments.

"Not bad," he said, "for a Nottingham girl."

"Prettiest girls in England," she said, and left the room smiling.

Adamson disassembled his curtains and folded the silk sheets. The band had decided to go on hiatus since they would now lack a rehearsal space *and* a singer. Adamson would be taking over Sal's basement, which already had a bed and a sofa, so they couldn't rehearse there. Sal's dad used the basement bathroom as a darkroom but Adamson could shift the equipment to operate the sink and loo. He packed his stuffed turtle, his Asimov novels and comic books, and unplugged the study lamp on his desk. As Adamson was a senior, his classes had been basically over since mid-terms. He still worked on the yearbook and Lit. Mag., and he struggled in Math, but the teachers didn't care if he came to class. He was a graduating senior. He'd made Bs and Cs and their work was done. After morning classes, he usually went to Yearbook where he could count on seeing Paulette. She typed up her short stories on the yearbook typewriter between classes but seldom let him read them.

The Yearbook and the last issue of the Lit. Mag. had turned out well. He thought he might work for a newspaper or a magazine when he finished college. He liked working to deadline, helping out, learning whatever skill was required. He liked the matey atmosphere, followed by publication and attention. He liked being part of a team that did something but wasn't sport or rifle drill. He liked getting compliments, being pointed out by strangers, being part of an in-crowd without having to don cleats. That's a good name for a band, he thought, Don Cleats, maybe a solo singer, kind of an anti-sport, anti-cocktail lounge crooner. But no one in Lexington, Massachusetts in 1969 would get it, he thought, as he moved linens from the hall closet to a box. Towels, tablecloths, embroidered napkins, where did they come from? Who used them? At Christmas, they'd had a formal dinner in the cramped dining room. Victoria had made a real English Christmas cake and decorated the snowy frosting with traditional green brush-like trees and a little red house, but a fight ensued when Adamson added tiny plastic lizards that Alistair had sent from Hong Kong. The person most offended was his sister Inkblot.

"It's supposed to be nice, Mummy," she wailed. Stella and Victoria were amused, George couldn't see any reason for the fuss, but his sister cried so hard that Adamson picked the scaly fellows off the cake and refused to eat it. Poxy concoction anyway. He hated the rummy taste of fruitcake and couldn't stand marzipan, and the icing was as hard as concrete. Best part about it was the lizards.

Adamson hauled the box of linens marked "Italy" downstairs to the living room. Stuff for storage was near the record player. That was going into storage, too. You couldn't take a Grundig to Italy; the current was wrong. He ran his hands over the polished wood and opened and closed the sliding top lid. No matter where it was manufactured, this was an American music machine.

He stood before the corner cabinet in the dining room. "Shall I pack the plates?" he shouted to Victoria. She was by his side in a minute, must have run up from the basement.

"They're breakable, darling. I'll do it." She selected a large bowl with a fitted lid that matched the rest of the china, blue and white with a delicate black pattern. Looked like it belonged in a museum or at the headmaster's table, definitely not here in Lexington. She placed the bowl reverently on the table and lifted the lid. A tiny spider had built a web across the top. "It's a soup tureen," she said. She took several sheets of newspaper and wrapped the lid, then the bowl, and placed them in the box atop the last of the linens. "You get them out. I'll wrap, and you pack, how's that?" Plates, bowls, candlesticks, and his favorite, a white ceramic platter with two dozen oval indentations: the family deviled egg platter.

"Is this a hat?" he asked, balancing it on his head. It slipped.

"Don't!" She grabbed the platter and hugged it to her chest.

"It's only a dish," he said, sulkily. He placed the remaining pieces on the table.

In his room, he opened his closet and stuffed a box with coats, corduroy trousers, and sweaters. He carried the box downstairs and marked it "Sal's/Winter Stuff." On the closet shelf he found a boarding school photo album. In one picture, Adamson was frowning at Alistair, who had pinched him the second before the shutter clicked. Adamson gazed at the starched white face of what's-his-name, the twit who had been his last prefect. In the photo, Twit stood next to his squad of uniformed underlings. Looking down at his bare feet and the tie-dyed shirt he'd made with Paulette, Adamson realized how much his life had changed in less than a year. Good-bye, afternoon tea. Goodbye, fagging.

He'd been shocked to learn that in America the word "fag" meant buggery. He explained that in England, "fagging" meant dorm chores performed by a younger boy for a designated senior student, for example, polishing shoes, fetching mail, washing dishes. "Fag!" went the cry, and the boys listened to determine whose sixth-former was calling. "Yours, Adamson," and off he'd tear. There were some who wanted more than chores. One senior had wanted a friend of Adamson's as his fag so intensely the matter went to a fistfight. The Head Boy had reprimanded the sixth-former, who found a more compliant lad. He threw the album in the bottom of a box, along with books, posters, and leather shoes, glad to put boarding school behind him. He marked it "Storage."

The movers came mid-week. He'd expected tough guys with tattoos but four college boys not much older than he showed up, one in charge with a clipboard. Numero Uno sat at the kitchen table with Victoria reviewing the list. This to storage, that to the container to Italy, don't touch the boxes marked "Sal's," which Adamson would move himself. He watched the skill with which the boys worked, hoisting tables and cabinets as if they were made of balsa wood, barking "go high," or "let me have it." One mover told Adamson they made "big money," but when Big Money gashed his hand on Victoria's bureau and had to go to Lexington General for stitches, Adamson decided big money might not be worth it. Was there ever big money in photography, which involved blows to the head but was more rewarding than shifting crates?

He loaded his boxes, record player, and records into the Bonneville station wagon. Victoria forced another box on him containing sheets, towels, and oven mitts. "Why do I need poxy oven mitts?"

"When you go to the dorm, there's bound to be a stove," she explained. "You might want to make tomato soup one night." She was bright-eyed. Wine again.

"Oven mitts?"

"You wait. None of the boys in the dorm will have them and you'll save the day." This was too much. His plan centered on traveling light. He fished in the box and pulled out tea towels, a frying pan, and a set of piggy salt-and-pepper shakers.

"Save the day, will I?" he said, waving a little pig in each hand. "Don't panic, chaps, I've got the cruet!" Victoria laughed and Stella joined in. He performed an elaborate dance, sprinkling them with salt and pepper, while they sang, "I've got a lovely piggy pepper pot" to the tune of "I've Got a Lovely Bunch of Coconuts." He laughed till it was too much, like emerging from the woods to find oneself at a highway coursing with traffic. Where was he? Where were these cars going? Don't get hit! Victoria slipped her arms around him for the last mad totem dance of the Henry family. Boy-Child was going forth, home no longer. Actually, his family was going forth, leaving him stranded.

They drove to Sal's house, an older home on a hilly side street with big oak trees. Sal's dad, Lou, helped them carry in the boxes and offered a cup of coffee. Another smooth mover. Victoria explained they would put money in Adamson's new bank account. She offered to contribute to food and utilities, but Lou wouldn't hear of it.

"Glad to have the boy," he said, smoothing the tablecloth with his left hand. "Keep Sal out of mischief." The grown-ups laughed.

"Where is Mrs. Salvatore?" asked Victoria, looking about as if she expected her to pop out of a cabinet.

"Ah," said Lou.

"My parents are separated at the moment, Mrs. A.," said Sal.

"Oh," said Victoria, her mouth remaining in the O shape after the sound disappeared. She made eye contact with all three of them and appeared to be waiting. Lou jumped into the breach.

"My wife and I are taking time to explore the changing nature of our relationship," he said. "She's a dorm counselor at the community college but she stops by all the time. Adamson will be well-cared for, I assure you." As he said this, Lou pressed Victoria's hand, and Adamson felt creepy.

Victoria insisted on helping him set up his room. He tacked up posters as she unpacked socks and T-shirts and hung up his trousers, shirts, and jacket in the closet. On his chest of drawers, she placed a framed photo of Adamson, Stella, and Isabel sitting on a fallen tree by the edge of the River Thames. "To remember us by," she said, wafting a candlewick bedspread over his bed and tucking it in around the pillows so it looked like a hotel room. The bedspread was lilac. Maybe Paulette would help him tie-dye it. Victoria sat on the bed and watched him put his books into a bookcase at the foot of the stairs. "I hope you'll write to us," she said, handing him a folder. In it were stamps, writing paper, and envelopes. He picked up the sheet of stamps that showed the Earth rising beyond the moon, with the caption, "Spaceship Earth."

"Crazy wallpaper," he said, holding them up.

"I'd better go. Want a ride home or are you coming later?"

"What's for dinner?" Dinner at Sal's was usually a box from the freezer. Victoria might have something more appealing.

"I have no idea," she said. He followed her upstairs, remembering to stoop to avoid the pipes that had caught the crown of his head twice.

"Everything shipshape?" asked Lou. His eyes raked Victoria up and down so quickly you'd miss it if you weren't watching. Adamson had seen Lou in action at school functions where any double-X chromosome got the flit-flit treatment, as if he were cataloging the Known Female World. If he found the object attractive, he'd stop, smile, and make small talk. If not, he moved on like a honeybee collecting nectar, flit-flit, flit-flit, flit-flit. Probably doesn't even know he does it, thought Adamson. His father was known to give young ladies the eye, especially if they were wearing mini-skirts, but then, who wouldn't? But George didn't make it a hobby like Lou. Funny how people are different. Lou couldn't care less about food while George loved his meals, grocery shopping, even washing-up. Adamson was more in Lou's camp. Food was fuel; he enjoyed it with a cheesy savor or a cinnamon aroma but life was full of things more interesting than eating. Like sex. Drumming. Doodling. Reading comic books. Bashing Stella in badminton.

After waving Victoria goodbye, he returned to his basement. He plugged in the transistor radio and tuned it to WBCN. Stowed the two issues of *Playboy* borrowed from Sal under the comic books in the bedside table. Rearranged the two small carpets. He had a good sense of composition, liked things pointing in the right direction. A lot of good that'll do me in life, he thought, but it made for a comfortable room. He switched on the bathroom light, which glowed red. Another switch lit a high-intensity lamp on the counter. Negatives hung on a line over the bathtub. He unclipped a six-inch strip and held it up to the light. Who was that woman? He closed the bathroom door. How did Lou get her to pose like that? No wonder he does his own film development! Kodak had rules about what they would print when you took your rolls in for development. George had told him they'd call the police if they found anything "lewd." They would definitely find Lou's pictures lewd. He wanted to look at all of them but a voice in his head with Wallace's tone said, "How would you like Lou to ogle pictures of Paulette?" "Bugger off," he replied to his conscience. Lou had left them hanging for any teenage boy to see. He pulled down two more strips but they were boring studies of shadows on a wall.

He went home for dinner, but it wasn't worth it. Victoria tossed a few TV dinners in the oven. Couldn't feed a flea on that. She made herself some cottage cheese with sliced tomatoes and poured more wine. When he complained he was hungry, she suggested he make a sandwich. Adding to the inconvenience, all his clothes were at Sal's, so he trekked back in the dark and spent his first night in the basement. He only awoke once. The electric clock hummed softly and read 3:10. The refrigerator upstairs gurgled. Through the little window, he saw stars in the clear night sky. I've left home, he thought, trying it on for size. "Hello, my name's Adamson. I've left home. I live with a friend." If home was the house you grew up in, he'd never had one. If it was your parents and brothers and sisters.... He didn't like his sisters except to play games with them. True, he'd jump in a river to pull them out if they were drowning. Once he'd steered Stella home when she fell off her bike and chipped her front tooth, and he'd picked innumerable splinters from Inkblot's feet. She was a splinter magnet. Was that Home? Was it Love?

All week, he helped his mother pack and clean, then went to Sal's to sleep. On Thursday, they took Bella the dog to the airport to be shipped in a crate to Italy. Friday, a man came to take both cars; George had arranged the sale. He stood next to Victoria in the driveway watching a thickset fellow and his son get in the blue automobiles, wave, and drive away, leaving them carless in America. She looked blank; she was detaching. He'd seen this before. Saturday, the taxi came to take them to the Ramada Inn. Adamson helped with suitcases and hugged his sisters. Victoria had a list in her hand. "Is the garage door locked? Girls, do you have everything? Isabel, where's your bear? Did you pack that doll in the bathroom?" The taxi driver waited as they trooped through the house once more. Victoria was businesslike, no more drooling over abandoned drapery. The house was as empty as it had been nine months before when they'd bought it. Like a bloody whirlwind weekend, he thought. Eventually they got into the taxi.

"Not coming, sir?" asked the driver.

"No, I'm leaving home," Adamson said.

"Oh, darling," said Victoria, biting her lip.

"See you at Christmas." He poured himself into the backseat window. The infernal, aggravating females in his life were lined up in the back seat like dolls. "Save some spag for me, Inkblot," he said. He couldn't think of advice for Stella and beamed at his mother. "Argy-bargy," he said and imitated Inspector Clouseau. "Don't forget to call me on the 'fern,' madam."

"You have the hotel number? And Daddy's number?"

"I have all the 'fern' numbers, madam. Kindly remove yourself before I 'ave to remove you myself." He pecked his mother on the cheek. She smelled of hair spray. Her hair was lacquered into a stiff helmet that flipped at the ends. She squeezed his wrist.

"Call us tonight," she said.

"Bye, Adder," said Stella. As nicknames went, that one wasn't bad.

"Au revoir, bon voyage," he shouted, stepping away from the taxi. "Your check is in the mail." Wardheimer was polishing Golden Boy, watching the farewell.

"Moving to France?" Adamson heard the driver ask as they pulled away. Another successful detour of meaning, he thought. They waved through the back window till he couldn't see them anymore. Wardheimer walked across the street.

"Call us if you need anything. You have the number."

"Right you are, sir," said Adamson, thinking: unlikely. He walked to Sal's, and Paulette called as he entered the kitchen.

"Want to do something tonight?" she asked in a perky tone. Usually she had to care for her brothers and sisters.

"Yeah," said Adamson.

"I'll come around six, and we can figure it out," she said.

"Hot date?" said Sal, leaning in the doorway.

"Don't know," said Adamson. "Could you give us a ride to the movies?"

"Sorry, I'm booked. Lisa at seven. You need a driver's license, son." Victoria and George had both given him driving lessons but there hadn't been time to complete the process. Too bad they hadn't left him a car.

"Does Paulette have a license?" asked Sal.

"Dunno. Her cousin was teaching her."

"Maybe Dad would let you use the station wagon. Then she could drive you to the movies." Sal lowered his voice, "I suggest a drive-in." Adamson called Paulette back.

"Do you have your drivers license?"

"Yeah. You got a car?"

"Uh," he looked at Sal, "maybe. Want to go to the drive-in?" Later, Lou winked at Adamson as he handed Paulette the keys. She was wearing a sleeveless black blouse and blue jeans with a sharp crease ironed down the front of each leg. He longed to trace the curve of her lovely bicep with his thumb. They drove in Lou's Chevy station wagon to the Bedford Drive-In. He paid. She parked and hooked the speaker to the driver's side window. They looked at each other and laughed. "Popcorn, madam? Fizzy drink? Small-medium-large?"

"Split a popcorn. And I'd like a small Coca-Cola, please," she replied.

He bounded to the refreshment hut, drumming his fingers on all available surfaces. Adamson to Alistair, I'm in orbit. I'm dating at a drive-in! I'm driving, well, being driven, and I'm Parent-Free! Come in, Alistair. Life is good!

The movie was *Butch Cassidy and the Sundance Kid*. As the screen lit up with coming attractions, he let his arm swing over Paulette's shoulder, and she scooted close, hugging the popcorn. She rested her Coke on the dashboard. They were well into the story of America's most charming outlaws when he remembered he should phone his mother.

"Where are they staying?" asked Paulette.

"The Ramada Inn in Concord. Or is it the Sheraton? Bloody hell! I left the number at home."

"Don't panic." She placed her hand on his forearm. "Is it the Ramada or the Sheraton? Think."

He closed his eyes. "The Ramada. It's definitely Concord." She handed him change.

"Go use the pay phone."

"I don't know their room number."

"Ask by name. Adamson, sometimes you are such a baby."

"Whaaa!" he bleated and slid out of the car. The pay phone at the Refreshment Hut was out of order. They directed him to the admission gate, to which he walked backwards so as not to miss Robert Redford and Paul Newman being pursued by the Super Posse. "May I use the phone, please?"

"Pay phone's at Refreshments," said the cashier, cigarette hanging from his mouth.

"They sent me down here."

"They shouldn't have. Can't tie up the line."

What, the President might call for show times? he thought. "It's an emergency!" he said. As the cashier pushed the phone toward him, a chain of ash fell across the dial. The cashier blew the ash, which flew in Adamson's face. He asked directory assistance for the number. It was quarter to ten. He grabbed the cashier's pencil and wrote the number on the edge of the day's tally sheet.

"You can't do that!" cried the cashier, pulling the paper away. Adamson dialed before he forgot the number.

"Just a moment," said the hotel receptionist. "No one answers, sir. Would you like to leave a message?" Where were they, painting the town red? How much fun could you have with an eight-year-old and a twelve-year-old in tow?

"Tell them Adamson called. Ask them to ring in the morning." He left Sal's number in case Victoria had lost it.

"Some emergency," said the cashier.

"Too bad you can't find work that suits you," said Adamson, "like grave robbing."

In the car, he wanted to kiss Paulette but she was engrossed in the film. Not till they got to Sal's house did he realize that she had taken a bus to Lexington and needed a ride home to Roxbury. Sal and Lou were out on dates. Neither he nor Paulette had given thought to how the evening would end. Too bad he didn't have a motorbike.

"There's loads of people out. If the bus doesn't come, I'll hitchhike," she said. That didn't seem right. "I guess I could spend the night." She glanced at the couch.

"Take my bed, I'll sleep up here," he said. He found extra sheets in his chest of drawers. Thanks, Mum, he thought. Upstairs, Paulette was on the phone.

"Tell Mom I'll be home by lunch... I'm stuck here... Oh, shut up!" She smiled. "I don't mind sleeping up here. I don't want to put you out of your bed."

"I don't trust Sal, or Lou." He imitated Sal creeping up on the couch, rubbing his hands together and licking his lips. She agreed to take his bed. She borrowed a T-shirt of his, which she looked fantastic in, right out of Playboy. He made himself a bed on the basement floor. He'd almost drifted off when she whispered his name. He kneeled next to the bed. "You all right?"

In reply, she slipped her arms around his neck and drew his lips to hers. He kissed her and climbed into bed. She was warm as toast. They kissed and touched each other for a long time. When they were still at it after half an hour, boiling like pots on the stove, he whispered, "I can't take it much longer."

"You're so sweet," she said. Then she caressed him. A minute later he stumbled in the dark, stubbing his toe on the chest of drawers, trying to retrieve one of the little condom packets Sal had given him. His toe hurt like crazy. He turned on the light. No visible damage. She kissed his hurt toe. Then she kissed his knees and his belly button and his chest. He kissed her beautiful shoulders and when he touched both her breasts, she rolled back onto the bed and pulled him down into her arms. She nuzzled his bicep, his collarbone, his neck, and by the time she found his lips again, his bruised toe was completely forgotten.

JUNE

He lay in the hammock strung across two oaks in Sal's back yard, studying a photo from *The Boston Globe* with the caption, "The Miniskirted Nun." It had run on the AP wire and on telly. I could have taken that picture if I'd been there, he thought. Demonstrations against the Vietnam War were happening every day on campuses across America. He mustn't put himself in a position to get arrested but he hadn't forgotten the demo at Harvard. Would there would be demos at Bridgeport? The next time he heard about one, he'd load up with film and go but keep out of the fray. He'd ask Paulette to keep her ears peeled.

Ah, Paulette. What a man he'd become in the past few months, having sexual adventures with not one but two lovelies. He felt a twinge of guilt about not missing his family more but took a deep breath and it passed. Victoria had sent letters and postcards, inquiring if he was all right or needed money. He missed Stella a fraction more than he'd anticipated. She had only signed her name to a postcard. Victoria said Stella "had taken to Italy like a fish to water," which probably meant she'd discovered drinking and boys.

Their departure had been confusing. Victoria had been at the emergency room when he'd called the night before they left. Inkblot had cut her finger in the bathroom at the hotel. Bleeding, X-rays, and stitches but nothing broken. Girls, attention-getters, every last one. Adamson hadn't had a chance to be lonely. There was Sal and Lou and Paulette and even Wardheimer had left a message. Perhaps Hannah had been recruited to fix dinner. She had rallied after being dumped by Sal. He'd seen her at the pharmacy and she'd said she was now dating a volleyball player from Framingham High. "Olympic material," whatever that meant. She looked flushed, maybe high. It was hard to tell.

With graduation approaching, he bought his cap and gown. He'd already dabbed a peace sign in pink frosty nail polish on the top of the mortarboard. There would be no sobbing goodbyes for him for the high school he'd attended for only one year. He'd found it antiseptic, with its wide, modern hallways, tidy, crewcut teachers, and patriotic slogans pasted on the walls, like, "Lexington 1776: Birthplace of American Independence." On the first day of school he'd leaned over to the lad next to him and asked, "What happened in 1776?" Not his bloody fault he hadn't studied American history! So it was their Battle of Hastings, except they won. Good riddance, Lexington. Hello, Bridgeport.

He was snoozing when Sal tipped him out of the hammock. "It's Wardheimer again," Sal said.

Wardheimer's voice buzzed like a bluebottle through the receiver, "We would like you to come to lunch after graduation. We are going out to Orpheus Steak House near Natick. Will you come?" Adamson's eyes zipped back and forth like a cuckoo clock.

"Yes, thank you," he said, after running out of ideas to decline. "See you at graduation." What was it about Wardheimer? He couldn't put his finger on it. A lonely old foreigner who thinks I'm a lonely young foreigner, full stop. Better take film to graduation. Someone might protest something. The phone rang again. This time it was Wallace, the guidance counselor, wanting to see him *today*. He wondered if there was there a form he hadn't filled out. As he strolled through the high school, past the junior varsity jocks in the cafeteria, he already felt like a graduate. Sod on them, he thought. All year, they'd tormented him for his long hair and paisley shirts, but he was graduating and leaving and they were doomed to lives of receding fame and matching hairlines. No fat like muscle turned to fat, he thought, and vaulted the last four steps to Wallace's hole-in-the-wall.

Wallace shut the door behind Adamson's chair and took a breath as if to speak but instead looked up at the ceiling. Involuntarily, Adamson looked up too. Was there something up there? "There's a problem with your graduation," said Wallace. He handed Adamson a letter from the Associate Principal notifying Adamson that he didn't meet the graduation requirements.

"What?" was all he could say. He was on his feet before he knew it but the tiny room made him feel claustrophobic, so he sat down.

"I'm here to help you."

"What am I going to do? They'll put me in the army! I'll be shooting men's heads off by the end of summer!"

"You're not going to Vietnam, son."

"How do you know? How do you know what's going on out there, locked in this shoebox? I can't even shoot a carnival rifle!" Wallace waited till Adamson slumped back in his chair.

"You're not going to Vietnam. You're going to…" He looked at his file. "… the University of Bridgeport. Repeat, 'I'm going to the University of Bridgeport.'" Wallace wouldn't continue till Adamson repeated the sentence. "Student Records wrote to your school in England, all your schools, to confirm your academic experience because you don't have a transcript."

"You don't need bloody transcripts in England! We talk to each other."

"He didn't get a reply," continued Wallace, "so in his infinite wisdom, he concluded you had no prior academic experience and were ineligible to graduate." Adamson sighed deeply. He was dealing with idiots. He threw a leg across the arm of his chair as if even sitting up straight didn't matter anymore. Wallace droned on. "I've spoken to Student Records, the Associate Principal, the Principal, and the head of records for the region. No help, but I have good news. *You are going to the University of Bridgeport.* They accepted you based on your current year's transcript and the promise of prior transcripts to come. By the time anyone realizes the transcripts haven't materialized, if they ever do, no one will care. You'll have a good record as a college freshman. Another reason to keep up your grades."

"I can go even if I don't graduate?"

"Not graduating is a technicality. You got Bs and Cs. How on earth could you pass Algebra II if you hadn't done Algebra I? As for having sufficient English credits, your English is fine, though your spelling is unorthodox, but plenty of men have become President of the United States who couldn't spell worth a damn. That's what speechwriters are for."

"What should I do?"

"Don't go to graduation; they won't have a diploma for you. Don't say anything to Bridgeport. If it comes up, give them my number, not the principal's, but it won't come up, trust me."

"Is it torture-foreign-students week?"

"It's bureaucracy, Adamson, armies of small-minded people paid to impede common sense. Avoid bureaucracies. Don't fear them, but find the gap and slip through. Get on with life. There will always be people to help you. Bridgeport is looking forward to having you. I suggest you get a summer job and avoid attention."

Adamson stumbled out of Wallace's office in a daze. He walked to town and stopped at Lexington Pharmacy for more "love packets." He'd never bought them himself. He was roaming the aisles when the cashier called out, "May I help you find something?" His head snapped around, hoping she was speaking to someone else, but the only other customers were a mother and daughter sitting at the soda fountain.

He'd have to pass the cashier to get out so he paused at magazines. She appeared at his elbow. "Perhaps the pharmacist can help," she said, nodding toward a man in a white jacket. "I'll be back in ten minutes," the cashier called and walked out. The pharmacist barely glanced up as Adamson mumbled his request. He placed a small blue box of Trojans on the counter. "One-eighty-nine," he said, ringing it up. Another hurdle vaulted. On his way out, Adamson saw a card on the bulletin board, "For Sale: Yamaha YL2 Motorcycle. Must sell: $300 or best offer." He jotted down the phone number.

The owner of the bike, Sam Higgins, was in debt and moving. He'd bought the shiny, gently used motorcycle from his cousin's boyfriend when he got a mechanic's job at Framingham Auto Palace, but he couldn't get to work on time, and they'd let him go. Sam caressed the gleaming chrome handlebars. Hated to part with it but his rent was due. "Got to have a pad for another month. No pad, no girls."

Adamson took her for a spin. No doubt, she was a beaut but he pretended to be unimpressed. "I'll call you next week," Adamson said, hands in his pockets. Sam, six and a half feet of gleaming muscle, towered over him.

"Next week's no good, man. Two-eighty, that's as low as I can go." Adamson counted to ten silently. "It's a real good deal," said Sam. Adamson fingered the fifty-dollar bills nestled in his pocket and shook his head. "Okay! Two-fifty. Cash money, right now." Adamson counted to five and smiled.

"You do have the papers?" he asked.

"She's mine, all right," said Sam, giving the Yamaha a caress, "but I can't take her with me." Adamson gave him five $50 bills.

"Where are you going?"

"Basic training," said Sam, then laughed at the horror on Adamson's face. "Motor pool, man. My brother's stationed in Saigon, he'll set me up real good. I ain't going to see action or my name's not Samuel K. Higgins." Adamson admired his bravado but Saigon was much closer to the action than he ever wanted to get. After signing over the title, Sam asked, "You got a license?" Adamson didn't. "You better get yourself a license. Police don't wanna hear about 'tomorrow.'" Sam gave him "the brother's handshake," which he fumbled.

Sal insisted on taking the motorbike out and when he returned Adamson was surprised to see Hannah jump off the back. Her hair, which used to be dark and curly, was now blond and straight. Was she back with Sal? "Dad wants to know how you're going to find us at graduation. Shall we meet at the flagpole?" He couldn't wheedle out of the lunch but he couldn't go to the ceremony.

"Sure. What time?" he asked.

She looked at him strangely. "After graduation. You'll be in the A row, and I'll be in Ws. That's why Dad said to check. By the way, this was delivered to our house." She handed him an airmail letter and went over to Sal, whose head was under the hood of a car in the garage. Adamson opened the letter carefully and rejoiced at a sheet of incomprehensible scrawl. Alistair! He put it in his pocket without reading it and parked the Yamaha under the overhang, which would provide some protection. No room in the garage with all of Sal and Lou's auto gubbins. He wished Hannah a good evening, poured a tall glass of orange juice, and went to his lair to savor the letter.

"*Dear Root,*" it began. Adamson trembled with delight. The nickname reflected his propensity for finding hidden chocolate.

Sorry not to write before, exams, Hong Kong, sailing, tough life, mate. My pater bought an old Chinese junk we're fixing up, actually, he is. I read comic books and hand him tools. Don't want to over-exert myself after the strain of school. No calluses for me, easy to avoid—so many flaming servants! We're coming to San Francisco July 12 to 17. Take the bus, show initiative! Otherwise, it could be a hundred years. It's just me and Pater, more's the pity (arf, arf). He's on business, worried I'll "get into trouble" meaning prostitutes and hashish. I mean, I am 18, old enough to go to war.

What the British Army doesn't need, Alistair Morris. I could be their secret weapon—"Chaos Erupts Behind Enemy Lines, MI6 Denies Involvement."

San Francisco Fairmont. Can't wait to order room service: "Sir, I'd like some grilled snails rare, if you please, and a codswallop of fathomswine. No fathomswine? What kind of place is this?" Hope you're having fun without THE FAMILY. Envy the ground you walk on. After boarding school, having the Mater and Pater around is wearing. Waring? Where's that? East of Wapping. Near Eaping? South of Eaping, closer to Tooting, out Waddon way. Blimey, you can see how we lost the Empire. See you at the Fairmont. Pater has lolly. Huff-huff. Snort. Drizzle. S-N-U-R-B, Alistair

He sighed. The sound of his mate's patter warmed him like crumpets at the hearth. He wasn't sure where San Francisco was but fire-breathing dragons couldn't keep him away. What a charge Alistair would get seeing him screech to a halt at the curb on his Yamaha! After consulting Lou's *Rand McNally Road Atlas,* however, Adamson conceded a long-distance bus might be more practical. How could it be over 3,000 miles to California? Almost as far as to England. What could there be between here and there? He re-read Alistair's letter. He didn't like the jokes about the military. What if Bridgeport balked? He imagined a horrible scene of his trunk on the curb, clothes strewn, university gates barred, then military cops in black boots throwing him into the Brig, then him wearing combat fatigues, subsisting on snails, trying to assemble a sodden rifle in a bamboo forest. He'd seen soldiers in Vietnam on telly. They looked miserable. The newspapers reported the Americans had started not-so-secretly bombing the next door country, Cambodia. It was insane. Wallace had said to keep his secret to himself. "I could consult a priest," he said out loud. I know I'm losing my marbles now, he thought, but the idea remained. If he absolutely had to tell someone, he could find a vicar or a priest sworn to secrecy or go back to Wallace.

It wasn't easy keeping the secret from Sal. He had to pretend he was going with them to graduation, and at the last moment, jump out of the car as if he'd forgotten something and yell, "You go on. I'll get there on the bike!" He hoped in the excitement of the moment they wouldn't look for him. He wanted to emerge casually on the other side of graduation. The house was quiet. The ceremony started at 10:15 a.m. and lasted a couple of hours. It was only five past nine. Could he get his motorbike license before lunch? He knew where the test place was because he'd been there when Victoria got her driver's license. She did fine till she backed over the curb. The test inspector liked her accent and let her try three times. On the third try, she passed. In the end, Adamson drove the motorcycle down to Motor Vehicles and picked up the Motorcycle Test Guide, which was good because there were terms he was unfamiliar with. He'd ask Paulette. At a sandwich shop on the outskirts of town where big lorries parked, he found a table near the window. The waitress chewed gum and had a pencil behind her ear, just like in the flicks. "Coffee?"

"Orange juice, please, and uh…" He wasn't hungry but it might be a long time till lunch. "Two fried eggs and brown toast."

"Hard or soft?"

"Pardon me?"

"Your eggs. Sunny side, over easy, or hard?"

"Not runny," he replied. America was one test after another.

"White or wheat?"

"Wheat, I think." The waitress paused as if there were another question but decided to use her own judgment. Probably "Marmalade or jam?" "Butter or margarine?" "Hot toast or cold?" So many choices in this country, everything was decision making. Twin bed, double bed, queen bed, king size bed, California king, waterbed, which bed would you like, sir? He hadn't slept well the previous night. He'd dreamed he was hiding in a dark basement, and a police officer with Sam's face put him in handcuffs. He closed his eyes briefly to rest. When he opened them, an orange juice, knife, fork, and napkin had been deposited.

Adamson watched two women working on a van. They would pause to wipe their hands and brows, point and talk, then one of them would lean deeply into the engine compartment with a spanner. Graduation Day. It didn't mean much to him. You don't graduate in England, you… He searched for the right word: Matriculate? Advance? "Leave school" was the accepted term. "Go on to university." He didn't remember a ceremony when the sixth-formers left. They simply looked happy at the end of Prize Day. His eggs arrived. It's a good day when strangers get your eggs right the first time.

"Everything all right?" The waitress topped up his water.

"First rate."

"Where you from?"

"England. My family came over last year."

"I love the way you talk," she said. "Say something else."

"Let's give peace a chance."

"My baby brother's over there. I pray for him every day." She leaned close to his ear. "Only three more months. I hate this damn war." Customers walked in and she placed the bill next to him. He finished his eggs and paid. Barely 10:30. To kill time, he drove his motorcycle toward Cambridge and stopped at a fresh fruit market near the rotary. "Get Back" was playing on the radio:

Get back, get back, get back
To where you once belonged
Get back, JoJo! Go home!

He chose an apple and counted out his pennies. "You need a job," said the cashier, collecting the change. "HoJo's is hiring short-order cooks." He looked as if he were trying to hear better, so she repeated it. "HoJo's is hiring short-order cooks." She spoke slowly with gestures, as if he were deaf. "Over there. HoJo's. Howard Johnson's. Ask for Wilma, the manager." He looked across the road at the bright orange roof with a blue-and-orange lettered sign and cars parked around it.

"What did you call it?" he asked.

"Ho-Jo's. Everyone calls it that. Twenty-eight flavors of ice cream. Great Indian pudding."

"Thanks," he said.

Wilma was stout and barely five feet. She assessed him with her hands in her apron pockets. The turquoise-and-white checked uniform fit tightly over her matronly bosom. "Ever worked in a kitchen?" she asked.

"Not professionally," he admitted.

"I got a college boy coming this afternoon for the kitchen job," she said. He wouldn't hire himself off the street either. "But I could use help in the dining room," Wilma added. "Can you carry a tray of dishes?"

"Like a waiter?"

"No, like a trained seal," said Wilma. Her tone was sharp but she produced a tray and put three ice cream sundae dishes on it. He waltzed around the empty dining room, returning successfully. Then she added two full glasses of Coke and a slice of pie. This was harder. He had to look where he was going and prevent the drinks from sloshing. She inspected the tray.

"What's $5.50 plus $8?" He answered. American money was easier than British with its "twelve pennies to a shilling, twenty shillings to a pound" long-division nightmare. Satisfied that he could add, walk, and carry dishes, she returned with two shirts and a form. "When can you start?"

"When would you like me?"

"Come back tonight. It's All-You-Can-Eat Fish Fry, you can train. Be here four-thirty on the nose. Dark pants, no jeans, uniform shirt. I'll give you the tie then. Bring the form back filled out. Two dollars an hour plus tips." She bellowed at a waitress wiping down a booth.

"How much you make in tips at Fish Fry?" The waitress considered the question.

"Twenty-five, thirty. It's a good night, lots of regulars."

"Well?" asked Wilma. He extended his hand and they shook on it.

At noon, he was standing beneath the high school flagpole, waiting for Hannah and family. Wilma of HoJo's had let him drink the Coke and eat the apple pie before he left so he wouldn't go hungry working there. Now he had transport, food, shelter, and sex. Before the first students burst out of the double doors, he heard cheers marking the end of the ceremony and drew on his cap and gown and strode forward. As the crowd streamed out of the school, he let it carry him back to the flagpole, and it wasn't long before he saw Hannah, Sal, and Paulette.

"Where were you? Where's your diploma?" Paulette asked. He gestured with his thumb to the knapsack.

"Got there just in time." He looked at her but she did not believe him.

"Adamson," she said.

"Later," he whispered. Her left eyebrow shot up. He loved the way she did that. "Really, promise." He kissed her quickly. Then her mother, cousins, brothers, and sisters were by her side and then introductions. He began shooting pictures. Hannah appeared.

"I didn't see you walk," she challenged. Her mortarboard was askew.

"The As fly by, my dear, it's always that way." He, Hannah, and her sister, Esther, squeezed into the back seat of Golden Boy. He was sitting behind the driver's seat and Wardheimer's eyes occasionally looked at him in the rearview mirror. Hannah chattered. Esther sat silent in the middle. The Orpheus Steak House, inside Natick Mall, was disconcerting. You walked into the mall as if to buy tennis shoes, and suddenly you were in a wood-paneled, clubby restaurant with fox heads and hunt scenes on the wall.

"I'll take the fox, please, well done," he whispered to Hannah. He looked to see if she got the joke but she seemed pale and dazed. He wasn't fond of steak, big slabs of bleeding flesh hanging off your plate. Victoria had pointed out that a piece of meat meant for one person in America would last an English village a whole week. His mother had lived through World War II deprivation, when foods like oranges and sugar and eggs were rationed or unavailable. She said she'd gone ten years without tasting an orange.

He ordered a filet mignon. It came with a jacket potato and salad bar. Best of all, it sat in a dainty lump on your plate without threatening to overtake the Free World. When he went to the salad bar, Hannah was clutching the edge, taking deep breaths, looking green.

"Need some fresh air?" he asked. She nodded. He guided her to the door. At the table, he whispered in Wardheimer's ear. "Popping out for some fresh air, Hannah's keeping me company, be right back." He didn't wait for a reply. She was already in the mall, retching into a potted palm. He helped her out to the sunshine.

"What's wrong?"

"Kleenex. Water." When he returned, she was sitting on the curb in the shade of a tree. Her color looked better. "Too many uppers," she said, sipping the water, daintily wiping the corners of her mouth. Why would you need uppers on Graduation Day? Mrs. Wardheimer appeared, squinting into the sun like a mother mole.

"What is wrong?" she asked. He pulled Hannah to her feet.

"I'm fine, Mom. I'm so excited to be graduating."

Their food was waiting inside. "Everything all right?" asked Wardheimer, standing as his wife seated herself. To shift the focus, Adamson asked Wardheimer where he had graduated from. Wardheimer stared. It's not a trick question, Adamson thought. "I finished school in Berlin," he said, "then I went to the University of Heidelberg."

"Happy days," said Adamson.

"Not really," said Wardheimer and left it at that.

Adamson was relieved at pulling off the mock graduation. "Delicious spud," he noted, making Hannah laugh. She was coming back to herself, though she wasn't making much headway with her steak. Happy days at dinner for Snaps the dog, he thought. Mrs. Wardheimer asked what he planned to study in college and he said he wasn't sure, he enjoyed photography.

"Photography is useful," offered Wardheimer. "You can keep abreast of current events and make a living."

"I'm very interested in current events," Adamson said. He told them about the Miniskirted Nun. "It's been in all the papers. If I'd taken it, I'd have thousands in royalties."

"Some things are more important than money," said Mrs. Wardheimer. "Like freedom."

"My parents are very into freedom," said Hannah.

"It's high in my book too," he said. "When you've been to English boarding school, you value freedom."

"Perhaps you had a taste of persecution, or witnessed sordid behavior?" said Wardheimer.

"Don't know about sordid, but I shed no tears when I left." He didn't want to talk about boarding school any more than he wanted to talk about graduation.

"What are you going to study at university, Hannah?" he asked.

"She's going to study biology, aren't you, Hannah?" said Mrs. Wardheimer.

"I guess," said Hannah.

"What do you want to be?" asked Adamson.

"Be?" she said.

"What would you like to do?"

"I want to be a spy," said Hannah. "Like James Bond, but a woman. Fast cars, gadgets, missions, men to torment…"

"I expect it's important to be able to dissect frogs in that line of work," he offered. Mrs. Wardheimer laughed. She could be warm when she let herself relax but most of the time she seemed anxious.

"Marrying and having a family is a nice job too," she said.

"I guess," said Hannah.

He finished his steak and after two trips to the salad bar, still had room for a hot fudge sundae. Hannah's steak went in a doggie bag. She and her sister shared a brownie à la mode.

"Where can we drop you?" asked Wardheimer on the way home.

"My motorbike's at school," he said. "Thanks very much for lunch, most appreciated." Hannah walked Adamson to where he'd parked under a tree.

"Why don't you come to the reservoir tonight?" she asked. He looked confused. "Everyone's talking about it. Adamson, sometimes you're so vacant. Spotswood Reservoir. We're meeting at 9:30 to go skinny-dipping. Come get me at nine and I'll show you where. And don't worry, Paulette won't be there."

"How do you know?"

"Nine o'clock," said Hannah.

"What does skinny-dipping entail?" he asked, used to making a fool of himself.

"I'll show you." Another Hannah-scapade. Could be fun though.

It was almost four when Adamson remembered he was supposed to report to HoJo's so he called and gave Hannah his regrets. He could hardly button the shirt Wilma had given him. More of a man than she'd assumed, he thought. When he got there, the restaurant was bustling. Apparently All-You-Can-Eat Fish Fry brought people out. Wilma found him a larger shirt and gave him a sickly orange tie to wear. His job that night was to follow Helen around, watching her and learning where the food and supplies were kept. Though he'd scoffed at it in his mind, the job involved many skills such as being polite to screaming children and grouchy adults; remembering the sequence of ordering; learning the location of tartar and cocktail sauces, ketchup, mustard, bread rolls; pouring sodas; and balancing dishes on a tray while wiping the table with his other hand.

"Your turn," said Helen. "Take number three some water. They're regulars."

He marched over to the booth into which three large women had squeezed themselves and placed glasses of water in front of them.

"Adamson's in training," announced Helen. "Take their order." He tucked the cork-topped tray under his arm and pulled out his pad.

"What would you ladies like today?" The women burst out laughing.

"Adamson, it's Fish Fry. On Mondays, you say, 'Everyone having Fish Fry?'" said Helen. He repeated the question. The women nodded obediently.

"Gimme a Johnnie Walker Black on the rocks. Pete here'll have a Bud, and Caroline?" asked the biggest of the women. She was huge.

"Give me a Johnnie Walker as well." The women roared as if that were the punchline to the joke of the century. Helen explained the drink orders to Adamson and sent him to the bar. When he returned, he placed a little napkin in front of each woman and placed each drink on top of the napkin. When he'd finished, the women clapped. He blushed. Wilma in the fountain area gave him a thumbs-up.

"I'll be right back with your fish," he said, and the ladies howled again.

"They're good tippers," said Helen, "truck drivers or something." That's where he'd seen them before, earlier that day at the sandwich shop. They'd been working on their vehicle. The pair had walked in while he was talking to the waitress. Each time he brought more fish to their table, they conversed. Helen said he should make small talk but not neglect his other customers. Some talk made for better tips.

"I saw you this morning near the Department of Motor Vehicles," he said, refreshing their water glasses.

"Where did you say your parents went to?" asked the biggest one. His reply took several trips but by the end of the night they knew his life story and had also eaten more fried fish, French fries, and coleslaw than he thought possible.

"See you next Monday," he said, as they browsed the dessert menu.

"No, we'll be in California next week," said Huge Mary.

"I'm going to California next month," he said. As soon as he'd said it, he turned around to make sure no one had heard. It was bad form to discuss leaving on your first night. Mary and Pete wanted to know about his trip and he told them.

"How you getting there?" asked Pete, which was a funny name for her because of the three, she was the prettiest. He thought she ought to have a prettier name. She was large too but had a pixie-sweet face, winsome, he thought, and in his mind, he began calling her Winsome Pete.

"Bus, probably."

Huge Mary looked at Winsome Pete, who nodded. "We'll give you a ride, we go every month. Miami first, but if you don't mind helping out, the ride is yours."

"Is Miami out of the way?" he asked.

"Not the way we drive." Winsome Pete smiled her pixie smile.

7

JULY

Paulette fingered the candle on Adamson's tuck box, a small wooden trunk with his name stenciled on the top in black ink. At boarding school, it had held candy and prized possessions such as snake photographs and a Swiss Army knife. Now it served as a little coffee table. He nuzzled her and slipped his hand up the back of her blouse. When they were alone, she was usually affectionate but tonight she seemed distant. He put *Nashville Skyline* on the portable Phillips. Sal had him listening to Dylan, Jefferson Airplane, Jimi Hendrix, and Janis Joplin to help broaden him beyond the British blues. *Nashville Skyline* might set the right mood.

"We shouldn't feel tied to one other," said Paulette, all brown curls and fawn eyes. "You're going across country and I'm going to school in Vermont in the fall. We should feel like we can see other people." She detached wax dribbles.

"See other people?"

"Date," she clarified.

"Date?!" Like, another girlfriend? He felt as if he'd been clubbed. Dylan sang,

Oh, I miss my darling so
I didn't mean to see her go
But tonight no light will shine on me . . .

He was in agony and couldn't stop the tears. She wrapped her arms around him and cried too, but holding her made it worse. She was his girlfriend. He loved everything about her. He soaked one handkerchief and went to get another from the chest of drawers. His mother had ironed these handkerchiefs, and that thought set him off again. Every woman he loved was leaving. He curled up in a ball and grieved his murdered life.

They drank cocoa in the kitchen. He didn't usually drink it in the summer but he was desperate. Who else did she want? She was the best girlfriend, his only girlfriend. He'd kissed other girls and had loads of fantasies. And there was Hannah, but Paulette was his one and only real girlfriend. I shall never love again, he silently pledged.

"We'll always be friends. I didn't mean to hurt you," she said. But how can you hurt someone and not mean to? It had something to do with her identity, going to school, finding her own way. Bollocks. "We'll see each other at Christmas."

"Don't give me hope," he said. She tried not to smile and they almost ended up in bed but neither wanted to break open the delicate scab that had formed. At midnight, he drove her by motorbike to Harvard Square to catch the T home.

At 8 a.m. sharp, Huge Mary and Winsome Pete arrived in their yellow VW bus. Winsome Pete had a black eye but he didn't say anything. They stopped at the sandwich shop for take away coffee and donuts, then Adamson settled on the back bench with a large OJ and the *Road Atlas*.

With Paulette's coaching, he had acquired his motorcycle license and a driver's permit. "Pick your stretch to drive," said Huge Mary, who was driving them south on Interstate 95. Despite the trauma of the previous night, he was excited. Miami and San Francisco, the starters to his main course of seeing Alistair.

"You've done this trip before," he said.

"Oh, yeah," said Winsome Pete.

"When do we get to Miami?"

"In about thirty hours. We did it in twenty-five once."

"God," was all Huge Mary said.

"I've never driven thirty hours. I once sailed on an ocean liner from Liverpool to New York that took a week." No response. The *Road Atlas* revealed what a sprawling country America was. Roads, railways, cities and towns, lakes and rivers, and big blank spots in the middle. In England, you could never be more than ninety miles from the sea and the towns, especially near

London, were crammed next to each other. "Are we going through Bridge-port, Connecticut?" he asked.

"Passed it," said Winsome Pete.

"I'm going to college there," he said. The New York skyline appeared and Winsome Pete drove skillfully across a bridge in traffic. "Do you ever stop here?"

"Nope, we're truckers," she said. Deep in New Jersey, she remarked, "I like that bridge." He read the slogan written on the side of a metal bridge that looked as if it were made out of pieces of Meccano, "Trenton Makes The World Takes." Not much to look at in New Jersey so he curled up with his pillow on a blanket on the floor. He remembered car trips taken with his parents. He and Stewpot always shared the back seat riding home from Brighton after seeing his aunt and uncle and cousins. He liked sleeping in cars.

"Good soup here," said Winsome Pete, when he awoke at a truck stop. "Then you can drive." The women greeted a pack of gnarly men, who slapped each other on the back and nodded at Adamson. In a booth, Huge Mary ordered three soups and three grilled cheese sandwiches and the women drank coffee. A lady near the jukebox kissed one of the gnarly dudes and threw her head back laughing. He tried not to think about Paulette. He was grateful for the women and "new vistas," as his mother would say.

He drove them cautiously down to Washington, D.C. He wished they could stop but they were quickly across the river into Virginia. At Ashland, they paused for gas and Huge Mary made a phone call. Adamson walked a hundred yards down the railway tracks that bisected the little town. The setting sun cast elegant shadows on the side of a brick building. He photographed a passing freight train. They drove all night, stopping again for fuel. In the morning, he spied lanky palm trees and the breeze enveloped them like a warm, wet washcloth. Winsome Pete was curled up beside him on the floor. Huge Mary approached carrying a paper sack. "Rise and shine, hit the john. Hurry." Winsome Pete left the bus without a word.

"Not a morning person," said Huge Mary.

"Nor I," he said.

Back on the road, he sat in front sipping OJ while Huge Mary slept in the back. He marveled that someone he hardly knew had observed he never drank tea or coffee. People were always offering you tea if you were English. Bloody bilgewater.

They passed signs to Atlanta, Savannah, and Jacksonville. "We rose up fighting at Stonewall!" piped up Winsome Pete. "I will not be pushed around!" She said they'd been in a New York bar a week earlier, and the police had raided, not for drugs but because it was a hangout for homosexuals. "*Peaceful* homosexuals," she underscored. He'd suspected they were more than friends. "A cop tried to feel me up. That's when I got this," she said, pointing to her eye. "We were singing "We Shall Overcome" and we totally outnumbered the cops. They locked themselves inside the bar and there was a riot but we won. Christopher Street is ours!" She sang to the tune of "Ta-ra-ra Boom-de-ay,"

We are the Stonewall girls
We wear our hair in curls
We don't wear underwear
We show our pubic hair.

As they crossed into Florida, she pulled into an Esso station. "Home stretch. Rest stop." He sprinted for the men's room then guiltily walked down the road to a shop. The screen door banged behind him. It was crammed with fishing supplies, chewing gum, breakfast cereal, fizzy drinks, cleaning fluids, car wax, sunglasses, rifles, ammunition, crocodile handbags, and kitchen towels. It was like a natural history museum. He walked down one aisle and up the other. Selecting an orange drink from a cooler, he pondered a giant pink bun near a sign that read "Coconut Buns - Homemade & Delicious!" Outside, there was a beep-beep and he saw the bus idling. He added sunglasses and paid.

At Melbourne, Huge Mary steered the bus off the highway onto Route 1, a byway of seaside towns and beaches. Some were one-shop affairs with a few cottages; others had fun fairs, hotels, and seaside fronts like Brighton, except they had palm trees and sunshine. Eventually, they pulled into a driveway next to a bungalow in a grove of trees that sported upside-down bananas. How did they get them to grow that way? A long-haired man and a woman with a baby on her hip led them inside to a room with ceiling fans. Glass doors opened onto a large back garden with an inviting swimming pool. Frank the Host gave him a handshake more complicated than Motorbike Sam's.

"It's ready to move," said Gabrielle, the woman with the baby.

"Are you moving?" Adamson asked. Gabrielle's laugh was like a bird trill. She casually unbuttoned her shirt to feed the baby. No one was surprised by her naked breasts. Adamson helped them move stacks of black plastic blocks from Frank's VW in the garage to theirs. The garage smelled like a barn.

He wandered through the garden and swam, wondering if he'd ever own his own pool. Frank didn't look rich enough but they had a big cooker so perhaps he was a chef. Adamson took a nap in the hammock, dreaming of Paulette in a pink brassiere that he bit into. It tasted like coconut. He missed her.

None of the walls of the house reached the ceiling. In the shower, the only soap was Dr. Brommer's Liquid Peppermint Soap. The label quoted the Bible and listed dozens of uses, including cleaning spark plugs and brushing your teeth. As he replaced the bottle on a ledge, he came eye to eye with a lizard. "'ello, 'ello?" he said. The lizard stared unblinkingly. Frank and Gabrielle took them to a Cuban restaurant where they dined on chicken, black beans, rice, and platters of fried bananas, which reminded him of Victoria's banana fritters. When they came home, Frank lit a joint that he passed to Adamson. "Good stuff," Frank gasped, trying to keep the smoke in his lungs. Adamson took a toke and turned to Gabrielle, who was nursing her baby again.

"Oh, sorry," he said and rose to give the joint to Huge Mary.

"Hey," said Gabrielle and took a long draw before passing it. After they'd smoked, the artwork, the paper flowers, and a paisley quilt swirled around him and the overhead fan circled like an eagle.

"Three hundred a kilo, for sure," said Frank. Winsome Pete lay with her head in Huge Mary's lap and Mary stroked her hair like a cat's. He thought of the Cheshire Cat from *Alice's Adventures in Wonderland* and said to no one in particular, "A cat may look at a queen." As he fell asleep in a guest room, he thought he saw a giant lizard on the wall wink at him. He brought himself up to his elbows and winked back.

By half seven, they were on the highway again. Winsome Pete passed him a slice of mango, which tasted like flowers. They drove endlessly up Florida till they got to Tallahassee. Huge Mary took over when they crossed the Alabama state line. They stopped to eat sandwiches from the cooler and Adamson begged for a walk. "Fifteen minutes, no longer," said Huge Mary.

"I'll come," said Winsome Pete. Lush green shrubs grew on both sides of the road.

"What's that green bush growing everywhere?" he asked.

"King Cotton. Soon it'll be full of white puffs. Prettiest thing you ever saw if you never had to pick it," she said. He wished he had a cloth cap like the ones Southern men wore, emblazoned with Shell or Esso or the name of an animal, Bulls or Bears. They could be worn forward or backward. Winsome Pete padded beside him in a long skirt, sandals, and a straw hat. "I'd take you out on the Mississippi River if we had time," she said. "I went to college near Memphis."

"What did you study?"

"Music," she said, "but not the type they wanted to teach."

Back in the bus, he drew his finger along the shoreline of the Gulf of Mexico in the *Road Atlas* and found Mobile, their next destination, then he traced their route up through Jackson, Mississippi. They drove for hours and hours. He dozed in the passenger seat. The countryside seemed all agricultural, and the houses by the roadside were often ramshackle and sad as if lost in a bygone era. He awoke when Winsome Pete popped a tape into the player on the floor and music flooded the bus. It was almost dark outside.

"Are you ready for the King?" she yelled. "Are you ready for the Great Mississippi?" Huge Mary was sleeping in the back and cursed her partner's enthusiasm. Elvis belted out "Heartbreak Hotel" at top volume. Adamson couldn't help nodding to the beat. He'd always found Elvis' twang rather fake, but flying over the shadowy dockyards of Memphis and glimpsing the massive river below, he heard soul and courage in Elvis' voice, and he heard the connection to British blues. Elvis serenaded them all the way to Little Rock where Winsome Pete switched to Blind Willie Johnson and Elmore James, "the source of the blues," she said. James' "Dust My Broom" was a revelation.

They had a flat tire in Henryetta. He stood around uselessly as the women worked like synchronized swimmers. Whim-bam-whiz, tire was off. Whim-bam-whoo, spare was on, and soon they were back cruising. They checked into a motel in Oklahoma City, and the air-conditioning felt great. After showers, they walked to a Dairy Queen to eat. What meal was this? What day was it? The road had lulled him into a trance.

The next day they began before dawn. "This is the tough one," said Huge Mary. "Texas, New Mexico, Arizona, one burning hell after another." They baked as they drove west to Amarillo, grasslands turning to dry yellow plain. The women traded driving, and when they weren't driving, they rested. They seemed possessed. He would've found a cool motel. He was delirious by the time they pulled up at the Cactus Inn in Flagstaff, and he stood stupefied next to the bus as the women checked in.

"Howdy," said a voice out of the dark. An Arizona state trooper appeared, a giant with a toothpick in his mouth and a big black gun on his hip.

"Howdy," said Adamson. The trooper eyed the bus and the Massachusetts tag and asked Adamson where they were coming from. "Birthplace of Elvis Presley," Adamson said. The officer's features crinkled into pleasant valleys.

"You like country music or just rock 'n' roll?"

"I'm surprised to say I'm beginning to like country music," Adamson declared.

"I'm partial to Hank Williams myself. He gets in your blood." Adamson agreed as the trooper regarded the night sky. "Where y'all headed?" Adamson poured on the English accent and moved a few paces from the bus. He explained he was meeting his best friend in San Francisco. "That where you from? I thought maybe that was a Massachusetts accent. Y'all a little off route." As Adamson asked if it was always this hot, the motel office door opened, and the women returned to the bus.

"Howdy," said the trooper, obviously his opening line.

"Howdy, officer," said Huge Mary. "Get your stuff, Adamson, they got a swimmin' pool." Winsome Pete adopted a star-gazing posture next to the trooper.

"Do you think that's Jupiter?" she asked. "That's Venus so that one could be Jupiter. You must spend an awful lot of time beneath this beautiful sky." Pointing to another star, she said, "Betelgeuse is there, next to Orion's Belt. There's Cassiopeia, see the W? And there's the Andromeda Galaxy. We don't see stars like this in Boston. I expect you get used to the beauty." She moved closer. "Do you," she asked, "get used to the beauty?" She gazed at him with bedroom eyes and he stuttered. Seven feet tall, armed, and defenseless.

Huge Mary closed up the bus and with a wave they left Winsome Pete teaching the trooper about stars, a submissive tutor with a rapt student.

Watching Huge Mary swim laps as he bobbed in the deep end, he realized that not long ago he would have dismissed these women because he found them unattractive, yet they were kind, resourceful, and subversive. He liked his women petite and pretty, but these two had many redeeming qualities. Winsome Pete arrived and dive-bombed Huge Mary with her clothes on.

"How's our hulky friend?" asked Huge Mary.

"Counting his lucky stars down Highway 17," said Winsome Pete. She swam like an otter, rolling over and over then diving under water.

The next morning, Huge Mary let them swim before barreling through the high desert toward the Mojave. They paid the price with heat that would fry an egg on a rock. When he said he was dizzy, Huge Mary pulled into a truck stop outside Barstow, California. She said they had to avoid dehydration.

"Is this *the* Death Valley?" Adamson marveled, reading the menu's back cover. He thought that was a Hollywood fabrication. California in his mind was palm trees, orange groves, and movie stars in negligees, not semis on scorching highways. California: The Truck State. He found American license tags intriguing: "Minnesota: Land of 10,000 Lakes." How could one state have 10,000 lakes? How could one country have 10,000 lakes? "Missouri: The Show-Me State." Why not Massachusetts, whose people were very skeptical? "California: The Golden State." He thought it would be better named "The Beige State" because of the color of its mountains and grass. The sun dropped behind the western range but not before he glimpsed the knit-and-purl rows of orange trees. He thought orange groves would be like English apple orchards, with scampering lambs and the odd ladder leaning against a tree, not citrus factories.

They reached Berkeley at midnight and immediately unloaded the cargo. He was aimed toward a bed. When he awoke, a stoned-out youth counting glass marbles at the dining room table didn't look up when Adamson wished him good morning. No sign of the women. He heard shouts outside and grabbed an apple, his camera, and his sunglasses and went exploring. Beyond a Rexall drugstore on the corner, people were running. It was a veritable hippie marathon. Sirens wailed. A fire? He followed the runners to a park, where demonstrators chanted and carried placards. "Do not get arrested," echoed the dual advice of his father and his guidance counselor, but he had to see.

He followed the crowd through the gates of the University of California Berkeley. The campus was bigger than Harvard's. It had Spanish-looking buildings with red tiled roofs, broad lawns, and big leafy trees. Standing on a hillside, he watched police lines form. Someone yelled through a megaphone, then he heard the familiar breaking of glass, then some pops and smoke began to rise amid the crowd. People were running toward him and soon his eyes were stinging. He wanted to photograph but couldn't open his eyes. Nearby, he heard sticks hitting bone and screams, and he hurried as fast as he could away from the sounds. Tear gas was everywhere. Repeated crack-cracks sounded like gunfire. It was a hell zone.

"Help!" cried a voice. Squinting, Adamson found a young man cowering under a picnic table. "I got stung, I'm allergic. Help me man, please, I'm gonna die." Adamson helped him up. He did have a big swelling on his arm. He said he lived on Allston Way in "Big Green" and directed Adamson off campus. Armed soldiers in jeeps drove along the street. I am not going to war, he thought. I'll go back to England. I am not carrying a gun.

They found the bright green house. The man sobbed when he saw it. Probably high. A girl was playing guitar on the stoop, and in the living room, a naked couple on the sofa fed each other oranges. Adamson followed the young man upstairs and watched him gobble some pills before throwing himself on a mattress on the floor. "I woulda died out there, man, thanks." He closed his eyes and Adamson shut the door behind him.

He cursed himself for not noting the house address where he was staying. After wandering an hour through the off-campus streets, he finally spied the Rexall sign and sent his thanks skyward. Winsome Pete and their new host were smoking but he declined the joint. The sight of the police loading tear-gassed students into armored wagons had been sobering. "Come on," said the host, "you gotta be stoned in Berkeley." Winsome Pete asked if he got gassed and brought him a wet washcloth, some water, and a cheese sandwich. Eventually, he took a few tokes and told his story. It seemed almost amusing in the safety of the living room.

The next morning, Huge Mary dropped Adamson's duffle on the sidewalk in front of the Fairmont Hotel. The Fairmont was a palace! The doorman looked disapprovingly at the bus. "Peace, brother," Mary said and clapped his shoulders. This was California. Actually, it was all California: the trucks, the women, the police, the weed, the misty bay, and the Fairmont, one hundred percent California.

"See you at All-You-Can-Eat Clams," said Winsome Pete. As she hugged him, she whispered, "I put a treat in your bag." After he waved goodbye, Adamson marched into the lobby where the white and gray marble floor reminded him of a chessboard. After inquiring at the front desk, he waited and watched a woman in heels with two miniature poodles tip-tap across the lobby. An elderly man read a Russian newspaper.

"Right, mate!" He spun around as Alistair strode toward him, trying to look serious. They embraced, swung apart grinning, and slapped each other on the back. Alistair's face was slimmer. He wore a black V-neck sweater, button-down shirt, and beige trousers like a businessman. His dad was on the phone in their room. The fifth floor suite was stupendous. It overlooked the city, a tall white tower, and the beautiful bay.

"Not bad, m'lad," said Adamson.

"You look more..." Alistair searched for the word, "... experienced!" They both launched into air guitar versions of "Are You Experienced?"

"Henry," said Mr. Morris, "my word, you've grown. Sorry, always hated when adults said that to me. What was I supposed to do, shrink? How's America?" After Adamson filled them in, Mr. Morris said, "Italy? Goodness. Now, Alistair, you've got money and a key. I'm meeting the chap from Formosa at noon. Take Henry—sorry, you said you preferred Adamson, I'll get it—to lunch. Dinner here at seven. Adamson, this is your home while you're here. I'll have them send up a camp bed or you can sleep on the sofa, your choice. No drinks from room service, young man," he pointed at Alistair. His hand was scarcely off the knob before Alistair was on the phone.

"Double gin and tonic and a large orange juice." Alistair brandished a book entitled *Swinging San Francisco*. "Let's go see the hippies."

"Woof," said Adamson, and he and Alistair broke into a round of cathartic barking, just like old times. The doorman, all smiles now, directed them to the Haight but when they saw an old-fashioned streetcar, they jumped on it and whooped down California Street to the docks. Ships were loading cargo. At Pier 17, a gray warship took on wooden crates. A sailor on deck caught Adamson's eye and saluted. Adamson pivoted in panic, striding back the way they'd come. Alistair yanked on his sleeve.

"Pardon me, weren't we going this way?" Everywhere Adamson looked were uniforms and battleships. His heart saw the ships and tried to flee his body. Alistair took his arm. "Let's begone straight to the Haight." They boarded the N-Judah streetcar on Market and rode up the hill. Adamson's palpitations slowed and he took in his surroundings. When had he ever felt so out of control? "Better?" Alistair asked. Adamson nodded. O levels? Lost in London on his motorbike? Nothing came to mind. Alistair steered them to a homely neighborhood of incense emporia and corner shops.

"This is it?" asked Adamson. They'd already been panhandled twice. This was where the hippies gathered in '67 for the Summer of Love? It didn't hold a candle to Carnaby Street in London. He followed Alistair into a poster shop, stepping over two drunks sprawled on the sidewalk. Alistair bought a Hendrix black light poster and Adamson examined the pot pipes. They bought donuts from a bakery next door and ate them sitting on a wall outside the shop. Alistair launched into "San Francisco," and one of the winos yelled, "Shut up!"

"No sense of history," Alistair observed.

"How was school this year?" Adamson asked.

"I did very well. Several friends are top-notch scholars."

"What about your O levels? How did you cheat on those?" Adamson was surprised at his own indignation. Since when did he care about rules?

"You jest?" retorted Alistair, licking his fingers. Adamson told Alistair he'd had a horrible year. "I thought you had girls, girls, girls? And cars?" Adamson conceded that the girl part was very good but the school part was awful. Alistair wasn't convinced. Adamson confided his problems with graduation.

"If I get kicked out of university, I'm cannon fodder," he said. Alistair looked away. "Bored, are you? They could put me on one of those battleships, mate, and stick a rifle in my hands, me, a bleedin' nincompoop, and say, 'Go shoot some Chinese waiters, we'll see you in a year!'" Adamson was shouting.

"I'll tell you about 'Nam," yelled one of the winos. "Poontang, baby. Dollar buy you anything, except your way home." The wino got shakily to his feet. "Got a smoke?" Alistair produced a box of Players Filter Tips. "Whazzis?" the wino said, accepting a light. "Looky here." The wino pointed to his foot in a sandal. It was mangled. "I blew off my toes in Khe Sanh but I ain't in Viet-goddamned-nam no more." Adamson recoiled. "You gotta keep the big toe, otherwise they take your whole foot. Four months, man. I went out of my friggin' mind." The wino grabbed Adamson, pulling him close. "Blow your foot off, blow your brains out if you have to but don't go."

"Keep the pack," Alistair said, brushing off his trousers. "You won't find advice like that on Fleet Street, mate. Let's go. Don't worry. Come to England, we'll take care of you."

"I'd be a wanted man."

"You'd be alive."

Adamson borrowed a jacket and tie for dinner though he needn't have. They went downstairs to the Tonga Room and Hurricane Bar in the cellar of the hotel, a Polynesian-themed extravaganza decorated with an actual sailing ship—masts, sails and all—and a five-piece band floating in a "lagoon" that was once the hotel's indoor swimming pool. It was wild. Mr. Morris let Alistair order a Singapore Sling. Adamson had a pineapple juice that came with a wedge of real pineapple and an umbrella stuck in the top.

Mr. Morris was in "Import/Export." He imported loads of different things but Alistair liked telling everyone his dad "was in women's underwear." When they drank a toast, Alistair always said, "Here's to ladies' knickers." Mr. Morris teased Alistair, listened to his boisterous lies, which he didn't believe, judging by the winks he gave Adamson. He wished his own father was more like Mr. Morris, easygoing and confident. Mr. Morris never chewed his cuticles. For an instant, Adamson missed his family, imagining them around the candlelit table listening to tall tales about the South Seas. The room glowed in the lamplight. Everywhere were carved Polynesian statues and frondy tropical plants. Victoria would like it. He'd send her a postcard. Then he remembered that Inkblot would be kicking him under the table with her clodhopper shoes, Victoria would be flirting with the waiter, Stella would be sulking in the bathroom, and his father wouldn't even be there—out of the country on some secret mission. The restaurant would refuse Victoria's check or credit card and there'd be an embarrassing interlude with the manager.

"… drive to Sausalito tomorrow," Mr. Morris was saying. "I have to go to Haywood in the morning but you lot will be sleeping. I'll hire a car and we can cross the bridge. People live on houseboats like in Amsterdam." Mr. Morris lifted his glass in Adamson's direction, and he felt wanted.

Turned out, Sausalito wasn't much except for a bunch of hippies living in paradise, so they drove farther up the coast to Point Reyes Seashore Park.

He was expecting a seaside town but it was a desolate sandy beach with tall cliffs. A sign said, "Falling Rock—Stay Away," but that was hard because embedded in the cliffs were millions of fossils. Wild gray surf broke on the shore. Adamson took off his sandals and ran knee deep in the icy foam. Alistair joined him and soon they were both soaked. Mr. Morris strolled down the beach.

"I'm freezing!" said Alistair, sitting in wet sand. The Pacific Ocean was huge, and Alistair told him there was nothing till you hit China. This stretch of park was called Drake's Beach because Sir Francis Drake had landed there for five minutes in 1579 and staked a claim for Elizabeth I. Adamson imagined Drake's galleon rolling into view, land ahoy, matey. "Water's full of sharks, you know," said Alistair. "We eat 'em raw for dinner in Hong Kong." Raw shark, right. Adamson scooped water into Alistair's face and a fight ensued. He was a head taller than Alistair, who could only win a wrestling match by cheating, and Adamson soon had him in a half nelson kneeling in the water. Alistair came up gasping, spitting salt water. Adamson held out a hand and pulled him to his feet, their eyes glinting from exertion and fresh air. He flung an arm around his friend's shoulder and Alistair did the same. Sometimes it was enough to be alive. Mr. Morris was a dot down the beach. They ran in the surf and threw driftwood out to sea and skimmed flat stones. At his feet, he found a stone with a fossilized insect that he slipped in his pocket.

After breakfast the next day, Alistair suggested the Castro. "A quaint village, full of surprises." Adamson wasn't shocked by the leather bars and transvestites. When he was sixteen, he'd go to Soho in London on solo voyages on his motorbike. A growth spurt made him look older and, pretending to nurse a beer, he'd witnessed the full cross-section of sexual parings.

"Care for a drink?" Alistair asked. Without waiting, Alistair led the way into a bar with a ferocious leather-studded bouncer at the door. After Adamson's eyes adjusted to the dark, he realized he was arm's length from two lumberjacks kissing. A man in a dog collar trotted their way. Alistair bought a round of drinks, and Adamson noticed Dog Collar beginning to touch Alistair. When a leather-clad biker type parked himself nearby, Adamson quickly finished his OJ and retreated to the sunshine. Outside, he examined leather jackets on a vendor's stall till Alistair re-emerged. "What happened to you?" he asked.

"Not my scene, mate," said Adamson. He was surprised to learn it was Alistair's. Alistair slipped behind the stall. Adamson followed him. "I don't care, you know," Adamson said.

Alistair rolled his eyes and fluttered his eyelashes. "I'm a man of the world, you see."

"Like, gay?"

"More like, bi-," he said.

Adamson refreshed his memory, recalling Alistair's friends at school. Was Ali's macho bravado all a cover? He supposed Ali had to hide himself at boarding school to avoid the inevitable shaming, but was he, Adamson, only a prop in Alistair's real life, a "pretend" best mate to make him look "normal?" Surely not.

Alistair held up a jacket threaded with silver chains. "Fancy yourself in chains? Never mind, I like this one for myself." He tried it on. It looked good so he bought it.

"This one's more my speed," said Adamson, picking up a black leather trench coat, a Long John Silver look, though he couldn't imagine wearing it in straight-laced Lexington. Could work for band appearances though. He saw himself striding on stage at the Boston Tea Party. Except his band was on break. He put the coat back.

"Oy-oy." Alistair drew Adamson's attention to a pair of women in chiffon dresses, sashaying arm in arm down the sidewalk. They watched them pass and admired the women's twitchy rears.

"Counterfeit," said Alistair.

"Really?" said Adamson. "They look real to me." Though he had to admit, few of his female friends would waltz around in party dresses and swoopy hairdos on a Wednesday afternoon. Another pair of women, dressed as Adolf Hitler and Charlie Chaplin, directed them down Geary to the Sutro Baths. The ruins of the Victorian-era bathhouse now hosted seagulls and a few beachcombers. A woman on the seawall used a metallic reflector to soak up the sun's rays. In a secluded spot, Adamson took out a joint, part of the farewell gift from Winsome Pete.

"My son," said Alistair, sniffing the joint like a fine cigar, "I'm shocked and delighted." Alistair lit the joint and they passed it back and forth. Adamson could now hold the sweet smoke in his lungs. Alistair had no problem as he'd been smoking cigarettes since he was eight. The ocean rolled before them like an immense creature. Suddenly a man shouted and pointed out to sea. The beachcombers looked up. Was someone drowning? The young woman went to the water and held up her arms like an archbishop.

"Whales! So beautiful!" she exclaimed. Her face, framed with pale curls, was radiant as a Madonna's. What Adamson had taken as animated waves were, in fact, animals out to sea, breaking the surface in graceful leaps and plunges. He extended his hand to the woman, "My name's Adamson."

"Lara," she said. They watched till the whales were gone, then Lara took them to a nearby soup kitchen in a church where she was some sort of official. She said the Reverend Jim Jones would be speaking shortly. "He's very dynamic. Stay, at least for the music." She sat with them as they ate free lasagna and salad in a room full of hippies, black families, and loads of children. A smudge of sauce remained near her mouth.

"Here," he said and pointed to the corner of his own mouth. Her eyes had flecks of gold and green, sunshine in a forest. Her shoulders were freckled. She rubbed her mouth but missed the spot. He took a napkin and wiped it. She smiled with dazzling teeth and said she'd see him upstairs.

"A luscious bit," pronounced Alistair after she left. "I'll skip the service. Church never brought out the best in me." Children of all hues played ring-around-the-rosie. People were carrying their dishes through a swinging door into the kitchen.

"I think I'll stay," said Adamson. During the service, he didn't know any of the songs but the singing was exuberant. Finally, the minister took the stage.

"Children of God," began Reverend Jones, "I cannot redeem you, God cannot redeem you, but with God's help, you can redeem yourselves. Bring me your tired, your poor, your huddled masses yearning to breathe free. Yearning for freedom from prejudice, from the bondage of a capitalistic, mechanistic society that grinds you up and spits you out. God wants you to practice the teachings of our Lord and Savior Jesus Christ and be healed! Jesus wants us to live together, black and white and brown and yellow and red, brothers and sisters in freedom and harmony, free of the threat of nuclear war, free from the manacles of American consumption, free from the compulsion to murder our yellow brothers and sisters in the East. We must prepare for the coming revolution! God, Jesus, Yahweh, Muhammed, Jehovah, Buddha want us to be free..." So it went for a solid hour. Then the infirm staggered to the stage for the laying on of hands. People with cancer, people in wheelchairs. He couldn't quite see but it looked as if one woman had vomited a tumor, at least that's what they said it was. The lame were cured on the spot and a blind woman got her sight back. As the gathering broke up, Lara reappeared. "Would you like to meet him?"

Up close, the Reverend was not as tall as he seemed on stage, but he was muscular and vigorous with dark hair. He wore black sunglasses like the men who guard the President. When Reverend Jones shook his hand, Adamson felt a surge of electricity up his arm.

"Adamson came for the dinner and stayed," said Lara. "The Reverend has to wear these glasses because his gaze is so intense, he might hurt you." Jones held onto Adamson's hand as if taking a psychic reading.

"We have a farm up in Ukiah where we can be safe," said Jones. "If you need to disappear, for any reason, we'll help you." Adamson felt as if Jones had taken an imprint of his soul, and the words stayed in his mind, "If you need to disappear…" He could still feel Jones' grip long after he was released.

"How was it?" asked Alistair, watching telly in the dark while eating crisps. "Thought you might be whale dancing with Lara Doone." Adamson had hoped so too but after he'd met Jones, Lara vanished. "Teddy Kennedy drove off a bridge, drowned his girlfriend, and forgot to call the police, naughty bugger." The telly showed Ted Kennedy holding his wife's hand, surrounded by children. "Moving when fams stick together, isn't it?"

On their last day, they went back to the beach, Adamson in hope of seeing Lara, Alistair because he liked to paddle in the water. No Lara but in a cafe near Golden Gate Park, the Moon landing was on telly. Houston Control intoned the progress of the lunar module, and the place exploded in proud cheers when it touched down. "Beer on the house! God bless America!" yelled the owner, an Italian with an anchor tattooed on each bicep like Popeye. As the astronauts bounced on the Moon gathering rocks, Adamson felt awe. The Moon was as far from home as men could go, yet they commanded the whole world's attention beneath the inky cathedral of space. Of course, the astronauts were mere visitors. *He* was a colonist.

"'ere's to 'istoric occasions and 'olidays in sunny climes," said Alistair. He and his dad would soon fly back to Hong Kong. Mr. Morris had already queried Adamson on how he was getting home. Adamson had enough money for the Greyhound bus but that would leave him skint. "Why not ask Whale Girl if she can find you a ride?" Alistair suggested. Brilliant idea! They went back to the Peoples Temple and waited outside for the evening service.

As Alistair blabbed on about Chinese women, Adamson felt uncomfortable. "You don't have to keep up appearances with me," he said. He looked Alistair straight in the face. Though he'd wondered how his friend could love a man "that way," he knew Ali could charm anyone. "A mate's a mate," said Adamson.

"Lion heart!" growled Alistair but his eyes were bright and vulnerable.

Using a chalky rock on the sidewalk, Adamson drew a picture of an astronaut stick figure raising a flag near a lunar module. Then he drew the Earth and a figure with a smile and a drink, and joined the Earth to the Moon with a dotted line. Alistair took the rock and drew another figure next to the drinker, wrapping them in a fast car. He drew a balloon above the astronaut and wrote, "Invincible!" Adamson took the rock back and wrote in a balloon above the car, "All right, mate!"

When Lara arrived to open the doors, Adamson asked about getting a ride to the east coast. She said she'd ask around. They patiently stayed through dinner and were starting to lose hope when she returned with a young man carrying a guitar case. Adamson wondered if he was part of the evening's entertainment.

She introduced him as Raymond. He was from Canada and was heading east and could take a rider. "I have to stop in British Columbia to see my mom but her husband's an alkie, we won't stay long, he's not my dad. You got gas money? Adamson replied affirmatively. "Great. We'll leave tomorrow. We can get to my Mom's in a day." Adamson found Lara in the kitchen and thanked her. She gave him a chaste hug and the Peoples Temple phone number. The heartbeat in her neck was as light as a bird's.

"I've got two tickets to a rock concert in Upstate New York if you're interested," said Raymond, as they left the dining hall. He pulled the tickets from his wallet. "Won them yesterday," he said, lowering his voice, "in a poker game. Three days, $18 bucks each. There'll be free food and we can camp out. I have a tent." Adamson had never been to an outdoor rock concert. The tickets were emblazoned with a bar, a star, and a crescent moon, one for each of the three days, August 15, 16, and 17. They read, "Woodstock Music and Art Fair."

AUGUST

In a mammoth, American-style drive-a-thon, they made it up to the Canadian border and beyond to Raymond's mom's house. They found his mother Lucretia recovering from being flung against the toilet. She had stitches in her head, and his stepfather was incarcerated in the Chilliwack jail. Raymond had warned Adamson that they might not find a "happy families" scene, but this crisis required a lot more than a quick hello and goodbye. Adamson fixed dinner night after night, and Abbott, Raymond's younger sister, regaled him with tales of pop stars and telly shows. Raymond made calls to Child Protective Services, the police, lawyers, and the bank, and tried to tidy up their messy lives.

Lucretia's husband had bought a new Land Rover in her name and run up bills all over town. They found a ton of pricey fishing and hunting gear in the back of the vehicle and laid out the rods, wading boots, coolers, rifles, and bullets next to their terrace apartment. A neighbor passing by asked, "You selling this?" as he picked up a fishing rod and feigned casting. "Give you forty dollars cash," he said. By evening, they'd sold the lot.

Lucretia went back to work the following week and Raymond helped her get a restraining order. Her husband wasn't allowed to come within 100 feet of her or Abbott. He and Adamson took the Land Rover back to the car lot. "You don't owe a thing," Raymond told her. He had threatened to sue the company for accepting a fraudulent signature. His mother looked ashamed and squeezed a balled-up tissue. "I'll be going soon," said Raymond. "I didn't plan to stay this long." Adamson knew Raymond felt guilty.

"Can't we do something fun before you go?" asked Abbott.

"Like what?" said Raymond, chucking her chin.

"Like fishing?" she asked. Raymond suggested instead showing Adamson Sasquatch. They drove up to Ruby Creek on the shore of a lake and hiked through the pine forest to a clearing where a statue of a Neanderthal stood.

"So Sasquatch is the Abominable Snowman?" asked Adamson, reading a plaque.

"People have taken real movies of him," said Abbott. Adamson looked wide-eyed and let his mouth gape open. She tried hitting him with her Barbie and they ended up all playing tag. When they collapsed beneath the trees, Abbott stretched out her head in Raymond's lap and put her feet on Adamson's knees. Lucretia took their picture. "I wish you'd stay forever," said Abbott. Raymond twirled her hair as she twirled Barbie's.

"You could come back east, Mom," Raymond said. Lucretia said no, she liked British Columbia and Abbott liked her school, a fact that Abbott disputed.

"I can't always run," Lucretia said. "I have friends here now. I'm not taking him back." Adamson caught Raymond's eye and sent an encouraging glance. They climbed a stream bed where they tried to catch fish with a net. Adamson caught a little frog but let him go.

That night, they mapped their route on Maple Leaf 1, the Trans-Canadian Highway. They had about three weeks till the concert. Right before they left, Raymond argued with his mother. She tried to give him some money, which seemed like a good idea, but Raymond refused it and stormed out to the car. When she held out the Canadian twenties to Adamson, he took them. Abbott was crying. Adamson picked up Barbie.

"All I care about is my hair," he squeaked, "and my handbag, and my slippers, and my…" He flew Barbie into Abbott's ponytail, "…my Abbott! I'm stuck!" Abbott untangled Barbie and looked at him seriously.

"Don't be silly, I'm upset."

"All the more reason to be silly. Let me be frank," he said, pumping her hand. "Hello, Frank, nice to meet you." Raymond honked outside. "Look, he's only angry because he loves you and he feels bad about leaving you both." Abbott toddled out in her nightie and Raymond hugged her though the car window but didn't say a word for half an hour.

He seemed to be working something out as he concentrated on the road. The mountains, distant in the morning, began to loom above them. Surely they weren't driving over those, Adamson thought. At the Revelstoke General Store, they bought canned beans, hot dogs, fruit, milk, cereal, and chocolate, and Raymond put up the tent. He had a useful set of pots, plates, and spoons, and they were able to put together dinner. Though it was ten at night, the sky was light because they were so far north. Raymond pulled out his guitar and sang a song that tapped into Adamson's feeling about loss and leaving.

In South Carolina
There are many tall pines
I remember the oak trees
That we used to climb…

Adamson walked down to the river. The air was maddeningly fresh, full of hay-sweetened updrafts from the valleys and icy downdrafts from the peaks. Here he was, eighteen, breathing in the scents of pine and rock in the Canadian wild. That night, they were awakened by falling trash cans. Their tent was zippered against the cold. In the morning, the campsite was littered with trash, and the car was scratched where a bear had tried to find food. The wild was exceedingly close.

They drove through Glacier National Park. Adamson had seen hills before, the Malvern Hills in the Cotswalds and the White Mountains of New Hampshire, and he'd marveled at the peaks in New Mexico, but these Rocky Mountains were like the castles of giants. Perhaps God lived here, he thought, causing a lump in his throat. On a grassy plain, bison were grazing. Bloody bison! Then the broad, bright blue-green waters of Lake Louise came into view, surrounded by a fortress of mountains. At lake's end, snow reached almost to the water. "That's the Victoria Glacier," said Raymond. "They've pulled saber-toothed tigers out of that."

Adamson asked if you could walk on it. He was pretty sure Alistair had never hiked a glacier. Raymond was dubious because he'd heard it had bottomless crevasses. Adamson followed Raymond into the original Lake Louise Lodge, which smelled of leather and woodsmoke. In the restaurant, Adamson treated them to sandwiches, juice, and Crunchie bars. After lunch, they walked down the road to Chateau Lake Louise, built during the grand era of railway barons. Adamson was reluctant to enter.

"Who's to stop us?" said Raymond. "We've got money, at least, you do."

The Chateau reminded Adamson of the Fairmont, fancy restaurants, gift shops selling Canadian blankets and silver key rings. In a rose garden, guests drank wine and tea and watched hikers walk the lake's perimeter. Raymond and Adamson decided to follow the hikers.

Eating their Crunchies, they approached the astonishing turquoise water. The path toward the glacier rose into a pine forest, enveloping them in shadow, bird calls, and occasional hoots of tourists echoing across the lake. They walked for thirty minutes but the glacier seemed no closer. The sky had clouded over while they were in the woods and the temperature was dropping.

"We'll go to the campsite and pitch our tent," said Raymond, but it began snowing before they reached the car. In August! The old lodge had only one single room vacant.

"We'll take it," said Raymond, "we can toss for who gets the floor. At least we'll be warm."

"I can give you a mat for the loser," said the obliging man behind the desk.

Adamson paid the twenty-six dollars. The snow was sticking and the guests twittered near the windows as the innkeeper lit lanterns. Their perfect summer day had transformed into a snowy wonderland. A little girl about six stood near the window, nuzzling and stroking her black-and-white stuffed tiger cat. Adamson thought about Inkblot and Stewpot and Abbott. He got postcards and stamps from the front desk and wrote one card to his sisters, using their proper names, one to Paulette, on which he included kisses, and one to Hannah, to whom he somehow felt he should say hello.

Raymond was playing guitar by the fire. As usual, the females flocked to him. I should have learned guitar, Adamson thought, makes you magnetic. If he had an English accent *and* played guitar, though, he'd never have any solitude. Raymond was a veritable catalogue of songs about every city, state, province, mountain range, river, and type of automobile in North America. All afternoon and through the night it snowed, making the snowfall on August 2, 1969, the heaviest at Lake Louise in eighty-four years. During the party at the Lodge the following day, the innkeeper dispensed hats, gloves, and coats from the lost-and-found bin. Whisky flowed freely, and a snowball battle between the Lodge and the Chateau ended badly for the Chateau but well for the Lodge because its denizens were treated to champagne, caviar, and petit fours in the Chateau lounge, where everyone sang "Blue Canadian Rockies." Raymond took requests and lent his guitar to other musicians. On August 4, the sky cleared and the temperature rose. Soon, it was almost summer again.

Coming down the mountain was disappointing. The grandeur slipped away like a mirage till they were on an ordinary highway to Calgary. Adamson took the wheel through Medicine Hat and across the Saskatchewan line. They camped on a narrow lake and in the morning, he took his first canoe ride with another camper. Forest rose on both sides of the lake, and the huge Canadian quiet was broken only by the sound of paddles and a bird that cried like a baby. A haze of mist floated above the water.

They drove across the flatness of Saskatchewan, through Moose Jaw, Regina, and Moosomin, and Raymond sang to keep them awake.

"Where do you actually live?" asked Adamson. "Where's your stuff?" He thought of his dresser and handkerchiefs in Sal's basement.

"I live in my car though I have places I can stay."

"Friends?"

"Yeah, girlfriends, friends of girlfriends, friends of friends of girlfriends."

"You know how to keep a network going, don't you?" he said.

They ate and showered at a truck stop. In the booth next to Adamson a man was intently writing a letter. Without introduction, the man cleared his throat and began reading his letter out loud.

Dear Sister Elaine,

I hope you will come to your senses and realize there is no place for priests and nuns in the political scheme. You are at a crossroads. There is still hope for mending your future but if you follow in the footsteps of numerous other dissidents & give up your vows and your church & commit yourself to Pagan ideology you will..."

He turned the page.

"...fall into a rut! If you have merely put your toes in the water, you are still on firm ground! Give up your evil Companions of DC9—& be penitent & contrite and take Mary Magdalene's example; it is not easy but your future

can be re-shaped & the world will finally forgive & work with you if you are contrite and of Good Faith and realize you did wrong.

Sincerely, Ernest Wright, Anti-Demonstration League

"Well?" Ernest's black eyes bored into Adamson.

"Who's it to?" Adamson asked. Ernest passed him a news clipping. It was the Miniskirted Nun. She was wearing knee-high leather boots and a long pearly necklace. She didn't look like a nun. She looked like she'd be fun at a party, and she didn't look contrite. Her name was Sister Elaine Certeu, a Catholic nun of the Order of Loretto. The caption read, "Demonstrators protested a Dow Chemical Corp. recruiter at the University of Notre Dame. (AP)"

"AP, that's the Associated Press. They licensed the picture," said Adamson. "They're a big syndicate."

At the word "syndicate," Ernest winked as if they were both in the know and he stuffed the letter into an envelope. He licked many stamps and pasted them on the front and back of the envelope with a big show. The stamps were variations on the same theme: "Help stop American Trade with Communist Countries." "Help Radio Free Asia Stop Communism." "Asia's Freedom and ours depends on The Truth."

"I'm very interested in the truth," said Ernest.

"Hard to find," said Adamson.

"Not if you have Jesus Christ in your heart," said Ernest.

Raymond swung into the booth, his wet hair slicked back. "How's the uh... cash? Full breakfast or toast and coffee?"

"Full breakfast," said Adamson, amused to be the banker. Ha-ha. And his father never thought he could do much with numbers.

They passed through Portage la Prairie and Winnipeg, then Ontario, and headed for Thunder Bay where Raymond knew a girl. They had to pull over when black smoke poured from the engine compartment in the back of the beetle. The internal combustion engine was a mystery to Adamson. Raymond poked around but more black smoke spewed forth so they tied a white T-shirt to the antenna and waited. A Royal Canadian Mounted Police car glided to a stop almost immediately, and an officer in a smart red jacket and a peaked hat stepped from his mount, which was a Plymouth Fury.

Before long, Mabella Towing hauled them into a gas station. The owner was working on his own VW bus. Raymond reached his friend Maggie by phone and she agreed to come fetch them. The garage owner thought they might have thrown a piston but called later to say they were in luck, it only needed a new head gasket, two hundred dollars American. Raymond said he'd only paid $300 for the whole car but Adamson said he'd contribute because they needed wheels to get home. The owner said he would drop the bill to $175 if they could wait a few days.

Adamson said they should use the time to raise capital. He was, after all, the bank manager. Maggie worked as a hairdresser in a shopping center where they were hiring day laborers for $4 an hour. In three days, they'd replenished most of the repair cost.

Each evening, they returned to Maggie's apartment worn out from digging and mulching. They'd shower and eat, then she would show them around Thunder Bay. Maggie had long jet-black hair. Adamson had fallen head-over-heels for her. She was part Indian, the most fascinating girl he'd ever seen, even more than Paulette, but she was Raymond's girl so he kept his desires to himself. Adamson asked her loads of questions about Thunder Bay, being a hairdresser, Canadian Indians, and anything else he could think of to give him an excuse for staring at her. She had dangly silver earrings and always wore blue.

Thunder Bay had a massive island at the mouth of the harbor, known as The Sleeping Giant. "Once upon a time," Maggie told them, "God rewarded the Ojibway with a silver mine, which we could mine forever as long as outsiders never found it. The Sioux, noticing our silver, yearned to know the source and sent a spy. It didn't take the spy long to find the mine on an island in the bay. On his way home, he stopped at a trading post and some Europeans got him drunk and convinced him to show them where it was."

Maggie lit a cigarette, took a few puffs, and handed it to Raymond. She never finished one. "A storm rose as their boat approached the mine entrance, and when the storm had passed, the Europeans had drowned, the Sioux spy was raving mad, and where there had once been a wide inlet there lay a huge island in the shape of a sleeping warrior. God had punished the Ojibway by turning our Chief into stone."

The breeze blew Maggie's hair across Raymond's face. He brushed it away and stroked her shoulder. At the flat, Adamson heard Maggie and Raymond whispering in their room, then grunts and bed squeaks. He was hard with excitement then sick with jealousy. Was Paulette missing him? Was Hannah?

On the third night, as they ate dinner like lumps in front of the telly, a reporter next to a big house described a shooting in California. Shootings happened all the time in America; police shot students and Black Panthers, the KKK shot civil rights marchers, husbands shot wives, and nutcases shot strangers.

"It was Sharon Tate, she was in *Valley of the Dolls*," said Maggie, weeping in distress. Adamson didn't recognize the actress. Raymond asked if she was in *Petticoat Junction*. "Shh!" Perhaps Maggie knew this Sharon Tate personally, Adamson thought. The story was a particularly grisly murder of film stars and their friends. Sharon Tate had been very pregnant, and both she and her unborn baby had been stabbed to death. Why would anyone do that? When Adamson tried to take a goodbye picture, Maggie hid her face in Raymond's shoulder. She was still torn up about the dead movie star. A nutter was being questioned, the leader of a horrible California gang.

Having started with plenty of time, Raymond and Adamson had only three days to drive a little over a thousand miles to Woodstock. Piece of cake as long as the car held up. Adamson hoped the festival would yield opportunities for pictures to sell. Famous people like the Rolling Stones would be strolling around, Raymond promised. Adamson looked forward to relaxing after the transcontinental drive. He imagined a grassy hillside spotted with people picnicking on blankets, puffy white clouds overhead, music through the loudspeakers, William Wordsworth sort of days.

Through Sault Ste. Marie, and the beetle was running fabulously. The Canadian Parliament in Ottawa reminded Adamson of the Houses of Parliament in London with its Big Ben tower, green roof, and cathedral structure. He had no idea the French had settled in Canada; he thought of it as British, part of the Commonwealth. Raymond said the French had tried to take over America but the Americans gave them the boot so they went to Canada.

They got lost in Montreal and ended up in a Greek neighborhood. As they passed three girls giggling in a sidewalk café, Raymond convinced Adamson it was time for a respite. Two hours later, Raymond was singing his third set, they'd had complementary dinners, and one of the girls, Marguerite, sat in Adamson's lap, teasing him about his schoolboy French. She lived nearby with her brother, and they spent the night on her living room floor. She sent them off early with a paper sack of bread and cheese and gave Adamson a long goodbye kiss.

"I had no idea Canadians were so compassionate," Adamson remarked.

In comparison to the Canadians, the U.S. border guards were all business. They thoroughly searched Raymond's guitar case and their luggage. As a precaution, Adamson had hidden the last two joints in his wallet before leaving Montreal. As they bounced through Adirondack Park in the final stretch, their spirits soared. "Let's have a smoke to celebrate," said Raymond. Adamson lit a joint and they smoked half. Raymond warned him to keep his eyes open for cops at the festival. The traffic slowed ahead and police lights flashed, trouble. The cops were waving people over. Adamson saw a officer lean into each car window.

"Cripes, think he'll smell the weed?" he said. Raymond instructed Adamson to eat the roach. It tasted like burnt wood. He quickly took the last joint from his wallet and chewed that up too. Horrible, but it was gone.

"Can't believe you did that."

"You told me to," said Adamson.

"I didn't expect you to do it. No driving for you today, you'll be stoned out of your gourd." Raymond pulled up alongside the officer. "Good afternoon, sir," he said. The officer stuck his head into the car, an inch from Raymond's face.

"Would you boys like to buy some chicken? We're selling fried chicken for the Saugerties Police Benevolence Fund."

Raymond looked at Adamson. "Chicken?"

"Yes, please," said Adamson.

"Two chickens, please," said Raymond. The officer waved them through. They inched down the road, Adamson balancing two plates of fried chicken, potato salad, and sliced tomatoes on his lap, and singing,

Knees up, Mother Brown,
Knees up, Mother Brown,
Under the table we must go,
Ee-aye, Ee-aye, Ee-aye-oh . . .

Then the cars stopped altogether. Raymond jumped out to get information.

"We have to walk the rest of the way. Traffic's backed up to the gate." Adamson pulled his duffle from the car and asked how far. "Ten miles," said Raymond.

"Ten miles? That's a bleeding forced march!" As they eyeballed their gear, a blonde passed by and gave Raymond a lit joint.

"Peace, man," she said and continued walking. Bloody chick magnet.

"Oy-oy, none of that," he said to Raymond, snatching the joint and snuffing it out. We've had quite enough of that for now."

"Speak for yourself," said Raymond.

Adamson was all for leaving the tent in the car, but Raymond said he smelled rain. In the end, they took the tent, the sleeping bags, food, the guitar, and Adamson's camera bag and left everything else. Fellow travelers helped them carry the gear, and in this kindly spirit, they made it to Woodstock.

But what was Woodstock, he wondered as they surveyed "the gate," a mangled wire fence on the ground. There were no ticket takers, just a torrent of people walking over a hill and into the woods. Where was the stage? Adamson was feeling sedated and confused.

"Listen!" Raymond was at attention. "I can hear it." Adamson could hear music coming from somewhere. "Let's pitch camp," said Raymond, "then we'll find the stage. Man, this is going to be great!" A girl carrying a baby and holding the hand of a blond toddler passed them. She was so close he could smell her spicy perfume. It was like a scene from immigrants of old, an influx of hungry, hopeful people. Adamson stood watching the flow, snapping pictures, till Raymond called to him. You could get lost here, he thought.

They pitched the tent in the woods before it began to rain. They'd missed the opening acts but caught the warbly strains of Joan Baez, one of Raymond's favorites. Couldn't get anywhere near the stage; there were thousands of people, maybe tens of thousands. Raymond said he'd never seen so many people at a concert and he'd been to Monterey. As they crawled into their tent that night, people were still arriving.

He didn't sleep well on the damp, hard ground and he was still half-stoned when he woke, but when he surveyed the woods, he felt grateful.

Many people didn't have tents or sleeping bags and lay curled up in wet piles like refugees.

The music started again late morning. Raymond said he was going to make it to the stage, and Adamson watched him wind through the sea of humanity. He preferred to roam and take pictures. The sun came out briefly, and naked men and women frolicked in a muddy pond. They seemed to have a good time. A bearded swimmer holding his little girl flashed the peace sign as Adamson took their picture. He meandered the edges of the crowd, if you could call them "edges." Someone announced that the Governor had proclaimed Woodstock "a disaster area," and Adamson had to agree: mud and trash everywhere and still, people were arriving.

He followed a line moving toward the concession stands but couldn't get near. They'd had yogurt for breakfast and finished the chicken so he wasn't hungry. Inside a teepee, a young man was thrashing and a girl was trying to calm him.

"I'm psychic, man! I'm psychic! Poughkeepsie! Poughkeepsie!"

"It's cool, man, dig it and relax," said the girl. "It's acid, you'll come down."

Was that tripping? Adamson had heard about it but it didn't look fun. His head was still turned around from eating the weed.

"Poughkeepsie! Don't hurt me!" shouted the boy. The girl tried to soothe him but a doctor had to give him a hypodermic to calm him. The girl smiled at Adamson.

"We could use some help talking people down, man," she said.

He snapped her picture. "Sorry, I'm not the Florence Nightingale type."

It took Adamson hours to reach the stage. The Grateful Dead was playing, not his favorite band but he found a good vantage point and took pictures of the crowd and the stage. No sign of Raymond. I mean, it was a city, not a place you could *find* anyone. Despite the mud and rain, people were dancing, singing, tripping. He had never seen anyone actually having sex but as he passed close to a sound truck, in the gloom of the truck bed, he saw the bounding of a man's bare bum and the grimy soles of a girl's feet.

When it began seriously raining, Adamson slogged back to the tent. It was getting dark, he was hungry and thirsty and could barely see. More than once he trod on a hand, a foot, even hair. This is way too much humanity, he thought, as he slipped and bruised his elbow while protecting his camera. Inside their tent, by flashlight, Raymond was serenading a girl with long red hair sucking on a cherry lollypop. Oh, great, Adamson thought. "Sorry," he said. Cherry Pop had pulled her skirt up to her thighs and was gazing dreamily at Raymond.

"This is Rose," Raymond said. He wasn't really playing his guitar so much as caressing it, a poor substitute for Rose's thighs.

"Wanna catch up with us?" asked Raymond, holding out a blue pill. "Mescaline. Very stoney, nice colors, beautiful," he smiled at Rose.

"I don't want to be shouting my head off," said Adamson.

"We'll stick together," said Raymond. "It's up to you." Adamson took the pill with the dregs of some flat Coke. Rose laughed and rumpled his hair.

"I love the way you talk. Say something else." Adamson sang all the verses he knew of "I Am the Very Model of a Modern Major-General," and by the second time through, was beginning to feel a bit tingly, a bit extra-specially zippy. It was still pouring outside, but it was hot with the tent flaps closed so they opened them. He stuck his hand out and raindrops bounced off his skin like little rubber balls. How wonderful, he thought. Raymond played guitar and Adamson used Raymond's comb to comb Rose's copper hair. He knew how to brush long hair because he'd seen his mother do it a thousand times to his sisters. You started at the bottom and held onto the hair higher up so if you ran into a snag, you wouldn't hurt her. Adamson combed the ends so gently Rose didn't realize he was doing it until he was halfway up her back. When the rain stopped, music began again, filtering through the dark. Holding hands, they took Rose down to Raymond's hangout near the sound tower. Two women whooped as they saw someone they recognized. Extraordinary, he thought. Perhaps people will never stop coming, perhaps the concert and the city it spawned will flourish forever. Holding hands with Rose, this made him happy.

Once again, the journey to the stage took hours. The mescaline amplified the sound and lights and Adamson heard himself saying "Oh, wow!" over and over. It was as if the hallucinations were happening to someone else, a pleasant, dense young Englishman named Adamson. Raymond seemed perfectly unified: capable, clearheaded, trustworthy. Thank God for Raymond, he thought, as the crowd roared its approval of a country rock band. Raymond had made friends with a couple camping at the sound tower to the right of the stage, and they somehow made a spot on the framework of the tower for the three of them to climb up and hang onto. Though he was only six feet off the ground, Adamson looked down as if he were Gulliver and marveled at the Lilliputians below.

When Sly and the Family Stone came on, the crowd near the stage began dancing and surging forward like a massive jellyfish. He nodded his head gently to the music, afraid that vigorous movement might rock them off the scaffold. A dozen people or more had climbed higher on the tower, but Raymond's periodic "It's cool, man," encouraged Adamson to more or less relax. In the deep night, you couldn't see as much as feel the mass of people. Sly picked up the pulse, magnified it, and passed it back to the crowd. The drugs and music kept them awake. Adamson didn't remember how they got back to the tent but he hugged his camera bag like a lost friend and fell over the edge of fatigue into sleep.

It rained again that night. By morning, they were all soaking wet. The sleeping bags were wet, his clothes were wet, his hair was wet. They went looking for food but the concession stands had been demolished. Helicopters buzzed overhead, ferrying musicians to and from the stage. Raymond, Adamson, and Rose were surveying the remnants of the concession area when a truck began dispensing sandwiches and hard-boiled eggs. A bag landed at Raymond's feet, which was lucky because the crowd swarmed the food truck and the supplies were gone in minutes.

Raymond went back to the stage to see The Band while Adamson went to find a loo. After an agonizing hour-long wait for his turn in the Port-O-San, he trained his camera on the crowd using his longest lens. He snapped a woman, arms lifted to the sky, bare from the waist up, soaking up the energy of the people around her. He shifted to the right and spied a woman with an Afro, her arm around the waist of a brother, swaying to the music of Joe Cocker's "With a Little Help from My Friends." She looks like my Paulette, he thought. Then the woman turned and put her arms around the man's neck and kissed him, and shock ran through Adamson. That is my Paulette. No, surely not... As if fate took a hand, the woman looked toward him and Adamson's finger automatically clicked the shutter before she turned back to the music. He clutched his camera, one man among thousands, appalled, breathless. It couldn't have been Paulette, he thought as he trudged back to the tent for the last time. He unzipped the flap. Raymond and Rose writhed naked on the muddy sleeping bags. "Excuse me," he said, grabbing his camera bag.

"What's going on?" asked Raymond.

"I'll write you a letter," he said, crawling out. A big gray cloud was moving over them. Raymond scrambled out, buttoning his jeans.

"What happened?" Adamson felt worse after Raymond assured him it must have been someone else.

"I'm going home," said Adamson. "I'll find a ride. Have a great time. It was very, very cool, man." He shook Raymond's hand and gave him a piece of lens paper with Sal's address on it. "Call me. I have pictures." Rose emerged from the tent.

"You're not splitting because of me?"

"Yes, my little morsel, it's all your fault." He pinched her bum. She squealed.

"What about your stuff?" said Raymond. Adamson had his film, everything else was replaceable. He couldn't think of anything in his duffle bag that he couldn't live without.

"Bring it to me if you're in the area." He tied a torn tarp around his camera bag when it began raining and crawled under a truck during the worst of it. Loads of people were leaving, he had plenty of muddy company on the road. When he stuck out his thumb he got a ride, though it took two hours to clear the standing traffic. He didn't want to talk to his travel mates, three men and a woman in a flatbed heading for Springfield, Massachusetts. He curled up with his camera bag and let the truck carry him away.

A succession of hitches got him to Cambridge. By nine that evening, he was in front of the Fresh Pond HoJo's. Wilma stood at the cash register. Was it Fish Fry night? Reflected in the glass door, he looked like a mountain man. Helen was all over him, tutting at his appearance, ordering him a double grilled cheese. As he inhaled an orange juice, Wilma stood over him like a tombstone.

"Ever get to California?" she asked. "Woodstock, bunch of hippies." She laid a check on the counter.

"Everyone was quite nice, actually," he said. The new girl behind the counter was making a strawberry shake using too much syrup, so it came out red instead of pink. Helen corrected her. For the best milkshakes, one squirt of fruit syrup, two of chocolate. Fast film for the best shots. Comb a girl's hair from the ends. He'd once combed Paulette's hair into a cloud of fluff that she'd patted down to decent proportions. The woman at Woodstock had big hair. Whether or not it was Paulette, she'd never be his girlfriend again. Helen placed the botched milkshake in front of him.

"Hate to see mistakes wasted."

"I'm dying of a broken heart," he said. Checking for Wilma, Helen put two straws in the milkshake, pushed one his way and took the other for herself. They drank eyeball to eyeball until reaching the noisy bottom.

"Want to work tomorrow?"

He was supposed to be in Bridgeport but surely a day or two wouldn't matter. Helen told him to come at eleven. He liked her even if she was just a middle-aged lady.

At Sal's, everything was the same. Bed, chest of drawers, handkerchiefs, records, picture of Paulette, one of him and his sisters. Sal and his dad were out. The cat crept downstairs and curled up on Adamson's chest. Their eyes closed. He dreamed his pockets were full of film. A camouflaged soldier named Abbott defended him from a bear attack. He hiked through the mountains, across an amber field, and bathed in a icy turquoise lake. He emerged and swam toward Maggie, sitting on a rock at Thunder Bay, wind blowing her hair, silver earrings turning in the pink dawn. He woke to the warm weight of the sleeping cat and clomping upstairs in the kitchen. His eyes fluttered and he fell asleep again.

9

SEPTEMBER

Bridgeport, Connecticut, was not as he'd imagined nor how it appeared in the college brochure. Instead of a coastal village with lush lawns and a yacht-dotted bay, he faced a gritty industrial metropolis. The campus was wedged between an interstate and a public housing complex. His roommate, nicknamed Mole within days, lived beneath a mound of dirty clothes, empty Vienna sausage tins, wet towels, newspapers, and beer cans buzzing with flies. Adamson surveyed the wreckage when he returned from Organic Chemistry. He couldn't tell if Mole was in the pile. He poked it with a ruler and it stirred. When Adamson returned with coffee, Mole was asleep on top of the sheets, mouth open.

"Mole," he said. No response. "Mole!" Adamson shouted. Mole wiped drool from his chin. "I brought you some coffee. Don't you have class? Why do I have an eight o'clock class on Monday morning and you're still sleeping?"

"You're serious, man," said Mole, taking the coffee.

"I am not!" he said.

"What are you majoring in, veterinary science?"

"Zoology," said Adamson, defensively. "I happen to like animals."

"I'm not declaring a major till I have to," said Mole.

"I thought you had to declare?" Adamson felt as if he'd been tricked.

"Not till you're a junior."

"What classes do you take?"

"Can't remember. Something Monday afternoon but it's not important." Mole pulled on his jeans, spilling coffee on his T-shirt without noticing.

"How do you know it's not important?" asked Adamson, desperate to understand the arcane rules of American universities.

"I think it's Soc."

"Sociology I? I'm in that. It's interesting. We're going to study sex habits."

"Good, fill me in," said Mole.

"Don't you have to go to class because of the draft?" Adamson asked.

"My dad's a Brigadier General. I'm not going to 'Nam," Mole said and slunk off to the bathroom. Adamson kicked Mole's stuff out of the way. At boarding school, some boys got better treatment if they were from prominent families, but he thought the draft was cut and dried, infallible. How could Mole not go if called? Strings could be pulled, but which ones? Did one's father hand someone an envelope of cash? Did you call your congressman? Somewhere in the system, someone interfered with the process of Mole being put in uniform and substituted someone named Adamson. In front of the mirror, he tried out, "My father's a Dynamic Electric engineer; I'm not going to 'Nam" but it sounded ridiculous. He pictured a master sergeant spitting on the floor and smacking him in the chest with a set of fatigues.

Adamson cranked open the window to liberate the flies. Someone knocked. A curly-haired young man with a joint tucked behind his ear stood in the doorway tossing a roll of masking tape in the air. "Michael Sullivan, at your service. Thought you could use some help. May I?" he asked, holding up the tape. "Come on in, Les." Another young man from down the hall entered. Adamson stood. It was getting crowded. Michael and Les pushed Mole's clothes and debris to his side of the room. Starting with the top of the window, they ran a line of tape down the center of room and across the floor to the door. As they finished, Mole entered and dropped a wet towel on Adamson's bed. "Uh-uh," said Michael, taking the towel and dropping it on Mole's. "From now on, your stuff goes on that side of the tape."

"Who are you?" asked Mole.

"Michael Sullivan, third floor, sophomore. I recommend you have all this on your side by tonight." Michael threw an arm around Adamson's shoulder. Michael, Les, and Adamson walked to the beach to smoke the joint. It wasn't a nice beach, but it had sand and waves that lapped the edge and boats on the horizon. If you squinted, it could look idyllic. Adamson had seen Michael with the football players but had been too busy to make friends.

"How did you know?" he asked. Michael responded that he was community-minded. That afternoon, Adamson skipped Soc. and English. The guys took him off campus for moussaka, which was like Shepard's Pie with savory custard on top instead of mash. Best grub he'd had in ages. He learned "nobody" ate in the cafeteria, which explained why he could always find a table. The food was mediocre but a meal card gave him unlimited access. He asked Michael how he afforded to eat out.

"Free market economy," said Michael.

"Biggest weed dealer on campus," said Les.

"Keeps me out of trouble," said Michael. After lunch, Michael took Adamson to the projects where he tutored boys in the afternoons as part of the Black Panther Community Program. Residents waved as they crossed a shabby playground. The boys, twins Darrell and Peter, and their friend Ali, were third graders. Michael administered gentle punches as the boys swarmed over him while he reviewed their homework. They assumed Adamson liked the same treatment and he was ducking blows when Darrell and Peter's mother barked at them. Adamson grabbed a comic book and began reading aloud. Soon all three boys were curled around him like puppies. He could feel Darrell's crinkly hair against his arm as the boy peered at the pictures.

Adamson excused himself from Michael around eight. He had Advanced Algebra (a re-do of Algebra II for his math requirement) and American History on Tuesdays and Thursdays, both of which were challenging. Mole had moved his stuff but the room was depressing so he took his books to the lounge. He caught the end of *Laugh-In,* not getting all the jokes but liking the silliness. When a show about a country sheriff and his deputy came on, he opened his math book. He hated formulas and focused on a single one to at least get something right on the test.

After half an hour, he switched to history. He read about the seeds of the American Revolution, which he hadn't known about till he went to Lexington High School. The Founding Fathers seemed like a bright lot, especially Jefferson and Hamilton. Franklin was a hoot. Washington seemed like a plodder, though Adamson conceded he must have had something going for him to be offered the position of king, which he humbly declined. The lounge emptied as Adamson answered his history questions.

When the news came on, an analyst reported on Ho Chi Minh's successor. Adamson cracked his organic chem book and shuddered.

Alkanes *are hydrocarbons that contain only single bonds. When carbons double back on one another to form a ring, they are called* **cycloalkanes**.

Organic Chem was a big mistake. At registration, a man had told him to declare a major and gave him a list to choose from, so Adamson chose Zoology because he liked animals. He saw himself answering questions, quieting anacondas, and sexing parrots. The man had given Adamson a curriculum. The Organic Chem professor was a grad student who advised him to "study hard and he'd soon catch up" but it was fruitless.

Since we generally don't care about the non-reactive portions of molecules, organic chemists often use the symbol **R** *to represent alkyl substituents.*

Adamson would have liked to use the symbol **R** to represent the whole bleeding wallop.

He'd expected the same pressure as high school but his professors didn't care if he came to class as long as he did the work, and imagine, his Soc. teacher had invited them out for beer on Friday afternoon! They had to do in-depth reports in English, but the professor, an attractive Canadian, said they could form teams and do it jointly. Another student had asked Adamson if he wanted to team up. No one bossed you, you were your own man or woman. Some students had jobs and cars; some, like Michael, were involved in social action. What's my agenda? Adamson thought.

❅ ❅ ❅

His mail held a postcard of the Bridge of Sighs in Venice from Stella.

Dear HA! she wrote, using one of her less objectionable nicknames for him.

They marched prisoners to dungeon death across this bridge—thought you'd like it. School is good, small, we take Italian. I now know the difference between the Italian for 'grapes' and 'local brandy' (long story). How's university? Ciao, Stella

He penned a response during English class.

Dear Stella,

Got your postcard. Enclosed is a picture of my friends Maggie and Raymond, taken when we were stranded in Canada (long story). University is better than boarding school and a million times better than high school. I have new friends (and no bratty…

He stopped and scratched out the snide remark.

…and a roommate named Mole. Dorm is nice, you can eat when you want, go to class when you want, basically anything. Hear from Alistair? Didn't think so. He's probably working as Chief Taster for Beefeater's Gin.

Adamson paused his correspondence to jot down the class assignment.

Not been drafted yet in case you're wondering. How's Italy? Been pinched on the bum yet? Keep up the flag. Adamson

He added his signature squiggly troll figure.

❊ ❊ ❊

Soon he was failing Organic Chem and Math. His professor suggested a tutor but he lost the name. Michael asked what kind of tutoring he needed and showed up the next day with quadratic paper, sharp pencils, and half a joint of Colombian. "For when we're done," he said. They used Michael's high school text because Adamson's grasp of the basics was thin. By the end of an hour, he was reacquainted with Real Numbers. "Cs make degrees," said Michael, lighting up. Adamson accepted Michael's help three times a week and in exchange, he bagged half-ounces and substitute-tutored at the projects when Michael was away. He was often away to New York City on "shopping trips."

The collaborative English paper, "White Visions of Slavery," went well. It started with Jefferson (because Adamson had leftover notes from American History), explored Henry David Thoreau, and ended with Walt Whitman. The piece wandered, admittedly, but they read most of *Walden Pond* and *Leaves of Grass* and produced the right number of pages with footnotes and a bibliography that wasn't forged. They both received an "A" and the professor read segments to the class.

One morning, early, Adamson woke to a loud knock. "Phone!" A jock had answered the hall phone. The dorm was divided into social sections: the Freaks, who smoked weed; the Jocks, who drank beer and threw up in the showers; and the Vets, who drank, smoked, and could be crazy enough to earn a wide berth.

"A-Man!" Adamson recognized Sal's voice.

"Salamander!" he said. Sal invited him to a big party at U. Mass Amherst the next weekend, insisting he come. The directions were to take the Massachusetts Turnpike to Amherst and come to Lewis Hall, but Adamson's motorbike had been untrustworthy of late.

"Go to the radio station then," said Sal. "Ask them to announce you need a ride to U. Mass." Sal dropped his voice. "It's going to be a trip, man."

By Saturday, Adamson had two offers and chose the one with the most people to save money. The Datsun was uncomfortable for four long-legged souls, but gas and tolls cost only $2.50! He found Sal's room in Davis Hall.

A girl sat on the floor counting something and when she turned Adamson was shocked to see it was Hannah. Her hair exploded out of an elastic band in a puff of red curls and she jumped up to hug him. I think she's landed, he thought. He could tell she was different and before he could find out why, beers were popping and *Give Peace a Chance* was blasting through the room. The real party would be held off campus at a friend's house. When they arrived, incense was burning, candles flickered in Mexican pots, and beaded curtains partitioned the rooms. The scent of some exotic dish wafted from the kitchen. Hannah was mixing mashed beans and spices in a huge bowl. She put him to work crushing more cooked beans with a potato masher. He reported how well he was doing in English and how poorly in Math and Organic Chem. "I'm not the scientific type," he said. "You look happy, though." The room was empty but for the two of them.

She moved closer to him, and he could smell the scent of cloves. "I'm involved with Jane," she said quietly. Her eyes gleamed. "It's a secret organization that helps women get safe abortions."

"Oh," said Adamson, wondering how she'd fallen into this pickle pot. She continued.

"I had to get an abortion this summer." His gut flip-flopped like a fish on land. "I don't know who the father was," she said, matter-of-factly. He felt as if the air had been sucked out of the room. Should he apologize? Give condolences?

"What happened?" he asked. All he could think of was a butcher shop. "I thought you were on the Pill?" She cast her eyes down to the kitchen counter. "Weren't you?" She rocked her head gently side to side.

"I missed a few … I didn't think it would matter." She looked at him and rolled her eyes. "Someone put me in touch with Jane in Chicago."

"Who's Jane?"

"Not who, what. It's an organization. They arranged for my abortion and took care of me. It's illegal." She nudged an escaped curl from her face. "It's a lot, being pregnant and needing help. You feel desperate."

He wished he had been around to help and at the same time was so relieved that he wasn't. Hannah was his first love, sort of. Mad as a hatter but lovely in her way. He put his arm around her shoulder.

"Members of Jane train women how to do abortions." He didn't like how this was going. "You don't need to be a doctor to do the basic procedure, you just need training. So I volunteered."

Gruesome images flashed through his mind. The word "abortion" was often accompanied by the words "back alley," and alleys, he knew, were not safe places. "We've started a Boston group. I do pre-care and post-op. I've decided to switch to Pre-Med and go to medical school." Hannah, who made Cs in high school, now involved in an illegal abortion ring, was going to swot to become a doctor? She took the mashed beans and added them to her big bowl. In the living room, a grinding guitar solo was playing along to a chorus of *"It's 1969 … it's 1969 …"* but in the kitchen he was trying to grip a new reality.

"Does Sal know?"

"No one knows but you. It would jeopardize the action. You mustn't tell anyone." Had he been an almost-father with this kooky girl? Of course he wouldn't tell. He wasn't averse to illegal activities. The boundaries were arbitrary. Smoke weed? Illegal. Smoke cigarettes? Fine. Kill your neighbor because you don't like him? Electric chair. Kill a Vietnamese peasant in his rice paddy? Double thumbs-up. Dental surgery to remove a rotten tooth? Okey-dokey. Surgery to remove an unwanted fetus? Imprisonment.

"You must be busy, what with classes and … other activities." She radiated assurance. He wasn't convinced he'd want her setting his broken leg, but at least she wasn't shaking and gray-faced, throwing up on the pavement.

Hours later, they were all on a Magical Mystery Tour, Adamson's first LSD trip. Sal had solemnly distributed tiny "windowpanes" of cardboard after dinner. Adamson laughed at the half centimeter of cardboard. Like this would do much. Actually, it was quite strong. First, his sense of perspective shifted. Things appeared closer or farther away. He spent what felt like hours running his fingers up and down the top three stairs.

"Did you get off?" Hannah asked him. He'd discovered that the world was divided into things you could eat and things that you couldn't. Upstairs he and Hannah explored a room full of Middle Eastern objects: photographs, a Turkish rug, enameled vases, and brass candlesticks. He felt he could read the Arabic script in a framed scroll and that he was a Sultan traveling by camel through the desert at night. In an oasis with rustling date palms, he dreamed he kissed a cloaked maiden.

"Adamson," Sal loomed above him. "Come see the moon." Sal led Adamson, who walked gingerly down the stairs and out to the porch where a few friends were sitting and lying down. A monster moon had risen in the sky over the hills of western Massachusetts. "Purple Haze" was playing on the record player. A young man with a guitar strummed along. He thought of Raymond. People were still arriving, seeping through the front door, bulging out of the back, finding love nests in the bedrooms, dancing in the dining room, eating tortilla pie on the stairs. Hannah was playing pat-a-cake with a child. The guitarist sang Jose Feliciano and Janis Ian. Sal was charming twins, one on each arm, shades of Alistair, or at least the Alistair he used to know. Suddenly, Sal rose. "Hey!"

Adamson, coiled in a porch glider, looked up in surprise at an enormous Afro encircling the head of an angel. The Angel was surprised too and kissed him.

"I didn't know you'd be here," said Paulette.

"I didn't know you'd be here," he managed to echo. Speaking was difficult. His mouth didn't work. He saw the word "here" trail away in a cartoon bubble. Sal chatted as if nothing unusual was happening. Paulette wore a black coat to her ankles with a miniskirt. He wanted to ask her a question but it took him what seemed like hours and then sounded too loud.

"Was I where?" she asked, dragging on a joint.

"Woodstock," he repeated.

"Why?" she asked. His photograph had been too blurry even under a magnifier to identify the subject.

"I saw you," he said, "with a brother. Your hair was … big." She blushed. He loved that, the Egyptian sunrise creeping up her throat into her cheeks, making her brown eyes shine gold. "Well?" he asked. If he kept his words minimal he could handle a conversation. Otherwise, they were like flying fish floating away, distracting him. She was here and he wanted to visit, not trip out over candlesticks and tissue boxes.

"There are two black students so we got together."

"Classes?" he asked. She put her hands together to make a steeple.

"Majoring in journalism. The other students are very smart."

"So are you," he said, proud to get out three words. Maybe the LSD was wearing off.

"Let's dance," she said, pulling him to his feet. The acid made him creep because he kept wondering if the floor hurt when he walked on it then he remembered wood was inanimate. But was it really? He'd seemed inanimate most of his life. Didn't people call him "wooden" sometimes? Perhaps wood felt our steps and took offense at muddy boots and dogs' nails. "What's wrong?" she asked.

"Tripping," he managed to say.

She rolled her eyes. He nodded. Nodding was fun! He nodded his head to the beat then danced that way all night. Even when Paulette gave up and threw herself on the sofa, Adamson continued doing "The Dog," thinking of toy dogs sitting in car back windows, nodding to the rhythm of traffic. At one point he was dancing with Hannah and Paulette and they were all doing The Dog. Then the whole room was doing The Dog and he knew he could be a trendsetter.

He danced for hours. Paulette got him to drink some juice and he fell asleep in her arms, singing along to "All You Need Is Love." He didn't sleep so much as nod the night away. When he awoke, they were on the floor covered in a blanket, and someone was singing in the kitchen. Sunshine poured in the windows, mist lay on the mountains.

He washed his face, still jittery, but he could speak without balloons forming and walk without wondering how the floor felt, and ignore the molecular structure of objects. He was a bit sorry, for experiencing a revved-up molecular world was exciting and expansive, but it was tiring. Sometimes, a cup is just a cup.

Sal toured him around the campus and he saw the pond, the head shop, the student union, and the radio station. Though only a freshman, Sal was a top dog, getting them free sandwiches and beer at the pub and a free joint at the radio station.

"You should be in the diplomatic corps," said Adamson. Sal was majoring in computers. He coiled himself with long snakes of dotted printer paper. Pity, Adamson thought, he could have made a good living with his hospitality skills. How many companies would hire a computer programmer?

Adamson walked Paulette to her bus back to Vermont. Outside the bus station, he pulled her behind a sign and kissed her. He asked when she'd come to visit him. She broke off the kiss but didn't seem unhappy. "I don't know," she said. When her bus door whipped open with a hydraulic wheeze, he shook her hand.

"Lovely doing business with you, madam, come again," he said in his most obsequious Monty Python tone, and she waved goodbye through the window.

He found himself a ride through the radio station, sleeping most of the way back. He'd been stunned when Sal told him he took acid three or four times a week. Suppose it affects people differently, he thought. Waiting for Adamson in his room was the torture tome, *Organic Chemistry*. He had over forty pages to read and three experiments to rough out before 8:00 a.m. the next day, and it was already past eleven. He stayed up till two, read most of the chapter, and roughed out one problem. He wasn't confident he'd done it right, and sure enough, when he got to class, he was completely lost.

"How's the tutoring going?" his professor asked. Adamson sighed. "Why are you in Organic Chem? What's your major?"

"Zoology," he said.

The professor looked puzzled. "You have a lot of science in front of you. Do you know that? Vertebrate and invertebrate biology, genetics, endocrinology, paleobiology, marine symbiosis. Are you sure you're prepared, Mr. ...." The professor glanced at his roster, "... Mr. Henry? Or is Henry your first name?"

"If I drop Zoology, will I be expelled?" he asked.

The professor laughed. "Good God, no," he said. "And it's not too late to withdraw. People change majors all the time. You'd have to talk someone into taking you into another class to get your money's worth, but you could do that." Adamson breezed through English and Soc. in the afternoon, knowing the die was cast: he'd drop Zoology and walk, no, run away from Organic Chem. He would try to sign up for Photography instead. Why didn't he sign up for that before?

After a sandwich with Les at the Student Union, Adamson returned to his room to wrestle with math. At midnight, he went to the lounge for something to drink. He couldn't find the light switch and felt his way to the fridge. An orange coal lit up the corner and Adamson smelled a cigarette.

"They'll pound you if you get caught smoking in here, mate," he said, and got his OJ. Looking over in the dark, he saw one of the vets, the one who roomed near the phone. The vet grunted in amusement.

"Pound me?" he asked. Adamson closed the fridge. It was dark again though light filtered through the glass panel from the hall. He'd detected a lost animal look when the fridge door was open and tarried. Safer to stay than leave, he thought, though he couldn't say why. Flopping down on the sofa, he drank from the carton. He held it toward the vet who put his hand out. Adamson got up and took it to him. The vet, who smelled of alcohol, tipped it back and drank. He's going to finish it, thought Adamson.

"I've got another," Adamson said, lying. The vet drank till it was drained, then put his cigarette out in the carton with a hiss. "I'm Adamson."

"Adam's son," said the vet slowly. "What's that make me?"

"Drunk?" said Adamson. The vet laughed and lit another cigarette.

"They ain't gonna pound me."

"You vets do what you like, don't you?'

"You got that right. Ulysses," he said, and stuck out his hand. Adamson shook it, giving Ulysses his best Paulette double-brother over-under clasp.

"How long have you been back?" asked Adamson, gingerly.

"Don't know," said Ulysses.

"Army?" he asked.

"Smoke?" Adamson took a cigarette to be companionable and let it burn down without puffing. Ulysses didn't notice. He told Adamson he got drafted out of Newark. He'd never been anywhere, then he went to boot camp, then "straight to hell." Adamson could see Ulysses clearly now. He told Adamson about the Tet Offensive and a hamlet where he'd seen hundreds of Vietnamese women and children killed. "I never wanted to go to 'Nam and I sure never wanted to shoot babies and women. Crapping white assholes couldn't tell a Vietcong from a Mama-san. They didn't care." He joked about finding the remains of a smoking USO chopper while on recon.

They picked up the survivors, a sax player and three dancing girls in red miniskirts and white go-go boots. "That was 'Nam," he said, "one crap trip after another."

Adamson woke the next day tasting tobacco. Returning from brushing his teeth, he saw the resident assistant talking to two men in suits. "Adamson," the RA called, "these men want to talk to you." Great, he thought. They discovered I didn't graduate. Adamson asked them to wait in the lounge while he dressed. Mole was asleep in his pile as usual.

"Take a seat," said G-Man Number One. Adamson had the sense to wait and see how much they knew before turning himself in. G-Man Number Two mumbled his name and flashed a badge in a leather case with a crested insignia, but whipped it away too soon for Adamson to grasp who they were. Some government police. G-Man Number One got down to business, handing him a photo.

"Do you know this man?" Adamson stared.

"It's my old neighbor, Wardheimer." Adamson was light-headed with relief. Perhaps it wasn't about him or his transcript. Perhaps Wardheimer was missing. "Is everything all right?" he asked. Hannah hadn't said anything on the weekend. The G-Men ignored him. They had their own agenda. G-Man Number One asked the questions, G-Man Number Two wrote in a black book. They asked about "the nature of the relationship," and when was the last time Adamson had seen Wardheimer; what they'd talked about; whether Wardheimer had ever asked him to mail or hold packages. The answer to all these questions was no till Adamson remembered that, yes, Wardheimer had once asked him to take a parcel to the post office. The G-Men exchanged glances and leaned forward. There was something sinister about them, their insistence on anonymity (flip-flap of government IDs notwithstanding), and their creepy interest in Wardheimer who had his faults but was just a stranger in a strange land. They wanted to know about the parcel: when, where, how heavy, the address, any special markings.

"I'm sorry," Adamson said. "There was nothing strange about it. It was a brown envelope about so big..." he demonstrated. "... going to London airmail. I didn't ask what it was. He was my..." Adamson almost said, "my girlfriend's father," but caught himself. "He was my friend's father. We rode to school together."

"Did Mr. Wardheimer ever evidence a sudden increase in income? Extravagant family trips or special purchases, like a boat or a car?" Adamson thought of Golden Boy the Cadillac, and the thwock it made when you closed the door.

"No," he said, "none I can recall."

OCTOBER

She came in through the bathroom window
Protected by a silver spoon...

WPKN played the whole of the Beatles' new album, *Abbey Road*. It was flipping fantastic, Adamson thought. Mole was gone, a victim of mononucleosis. So far Mole was the only person in his dorm to succumb, though five others on campus had caught it. Adamson reveled in having his own room and turned up the volume.

In front of him was the withdrawal paperwork for dropping Organic Chem. He'd never been so sure of anything in his life. Though it meant he'd probably never be director of the Whipsnade Zoo, he could still own a pet shop or travel to snake-infested habitats as a photographer. Like a gong, the thought had struck: major in photography. At first he thought he shouldn't because he was already a good photographer but Koch, the photography master, said he could get better if he studied. He could try movies, Koch had said. Work more in color. Get experimental. Learn photojournalism. Adamson didn't want to experiment; he was more the "frame and shoot" kind of chap, but he'd awoken in such good spirits after talking to Koch, it was as if someone had drawn aside a curtain and revealed a land of uncharted wonders: his life, and the knowledge that he could do with it what he wanted. He hadn't told his parents. What did they care, caught up with their lives in Italy? As long as he stayed in school, he could direct life to suit himself.

As a reward for filing the withdrawal forms in triplicate, he'd gone to Sears to buy the new album. Passing Zovey's Ice Cream, he'd waved at someone from English. The gate of the Warner Bra and Girdle Factory was open and a truck was being loaded with boxes. Four black men threw boxes to one another as if they were basketballs. Adamson wondered how much a box of bras and girdles weighed. At Sears, he cruised through women's apparel and rode the escalator to the second floor. "B" for Beatles, *White Album*, *Revolver*, and there it was, *Abbey Road*. On the cover, the Beatles were walking on a zebra crossing. Paul was barefoot. John had a great shaggy mane of hair and beard and a white suit. He looked like a lion. Adamson didn't have a favorite Beatle. He had favored all of them at different times but right now, he identified most with John the Rebel and Peace Activist.

He worked on his English paper while listening to the album. Afterward, he met Michael at the Black Panther Center for a meeting on tutoring. A woman a bit like Paulette was making snacks for the kids. Adamson wished he had a girlfriend. He was still moping when Michael and Lester came by on the weekend.

"There's a teach-in on Indochina this afternoon. Come on," said Michael. Lester was chewing his hair. Adamson hated that. Inkblot used to do it, disgusting habit.

"Don't think so," he said. He was trying to read *Slaughterhouse Five* but kept getting distracted. Michael flopped down on one bed, Lester on another.

"What's happening?"

"I need a girlfriend," said Adamson.

"Three o'clock at the Student Center. Nothing like revolutionary girls," said Michael.

"Won't they be…" Adamson searched for the right word, "uncompromising?"

"On the War, very, but willing on the home front," said Michael.

"Bring your camera," said Lester. "Girls like having their photo taken, especially by an Englishman. Perfect opener."

Adamson didn't feel confident in the intimate-relations department. It wasn't the intimate part he was nervous about, it was the banter, the repartee, hunting the quarry, the come-on line. You couldn't come right out and say, "Hello, you're attractive, mind if I poke you?" No, you had to get to know them, buy lunch, appear interested, worm your way into their affections. He liked when one of them asked him out. That way, he knew she was interested, at least in talking, and when he talked to her, he could work out what might come next. "Maybe you could introduce me to … "

"Some promising candidates? My pleasure," said Michael.

Multiple sessions were happening at the teach-in. Adamson was quickly introduced to Bee, coordinator of the teach-in, a cheerful bosomy girl with frizzy hair. She took him to the different sessions: "History of Indochina," "Facts on the Draft," "Posters and Publicity," and "Demo Tactics." The best-looking women were in History so he began there. Bee spoke to each of the session monitors, which made his photo-taking official. In fact, Bee assumed he'd provide her with copies and give the best shots to the campus paper. Why not? he thought.

He liked the look of an anemic blond, thin as a rail, with wide Twiggy eyes. He took her picture and she gave him a watery smile. The session leader was one of the history professors, Ratner. He didn't look much older than the students. Ratner began with geography and terrain, then gave a quick tour through Vietnam's colonial history, the Frogs, Brits, and Yanks. He dwelled on the Viet Cong's leader, Ho Chi Minh, who had been against the colonials from a young age. Ho had left Vietnam at twenty-one and sailed on an ocean liner to Paris, where he worked as a photo re-toucher. That drew Adamson in. Ho had tried to speak about the plight of Vietnam to President Woodrow Wilson, who was on tour promoting his League of Nations, but was rebuffed. Soon, Ho became a French Communist and a Soviet agent, and over the years, he had many aliases and though he claimed to be celibate to enhance his revolutionary reputation, he'd had several wives and concubines. In 1929, he'd organized the Indochinese Communist party and ten years later, he founded the Viet Minh, an acronym for the Vietnam Independence League.

"From this he derived his *nom de guerre*," said Ratner, "Ho Chi Minh— meaning 'Bringer of Light.'" Ho had just died in September. Adamson wondered how this would affect the course of the war. As if reading his mind, Ratner said, "Ho's dream was to unify Vietnam under his flag. Any settlement means accepting a permanent partition and forfeiting the dream. Ho was clear on this, and we shouldn't expect his successor, Le Duan, to deviate." As they switched rooms, Adamson noticed Blondy tuck her hand into the back pocket of a bearded upperclassman. Taken.

He went to "Facts on the Draft," and after taking a few shots, planned to leave the room but it was difficult because the place was packed. He sat cross-legged on a desk shoved in a corner. The speaker talked about the procedures followed by the Selective Service. It gave him the creeps. He began perspiring.

"I am not going to Vietnam, I am not going to Vietnam," he repeated to himself.

"Half a million American soldiers are in Vietnam today," the speaker announced, "but you don't have to be one of them. You have options. You can request alternative service because of moral or religious beliefs..."

"Or get your ass to Canada," yelled one of the students.

"Or South America," shouted another.

"That's right," said the speaker, "but leaving the country is a legal violation I don't recommend without understanding the repercussions."

"A Canadian wife and kids!" shouted another voice. Adamson didn't want to hear about the draft but he didn't think people should heckle the messenger. The speaker pointed to a chart. "You can join the ROTC. I know that sounds crazy but you reduce your chances of going to Vietnam. Likewise, if you volunteer for any branch besides the Army, you'll be less likely to carry a rifle."

"Whose side are you on?" asked a student.

"Come December, you may find yourself with a low lottery number. Then you'll want to know what you can do." Silence. "Stay in school and get a student deferment. If you're graduating or out of school, join your home state National Guard if you can get in. It usually takes some political pull but if any of your parents are on the state Democratic or Republican committees or have relatives who are politicians, use it. You can get married and have a child and try for a head-of-household deferment." Snickers at this. Blondy gave her boyfriend a kiss. "Or join the ministry, any legitimate ministry. Or transfer to a seminary. Seminary students and ministers, priests, and rabbis are exempt from the draft. You can leave the country but you can't come back. And you can fail your pre-induction physical. People try all kinds of tricks, including being high, raising their blood pressure, and creating 'tracks' on their arms. It's a risky proposition but if you've tried everything else, you should give it a go. Get the name of a sympathetic doctor. I have a list of reasons why people have failed physicals in the past if that's of interest." He dispersed a handout.

"How will the lottery work?" asked a young man.

"It's supposed to make the draft fairer," said the speaker. "But they may do away with most student deferments." The students got even quieter. Adamson felt nauseated and pushed his way out of the room. In the hallway, he tried to take deep breaths. He was almost panting. He took a couple of photos of the wall to steady himself. I am not going to Vietnam, he repeated, I will go back to England.

The "Facts on the Draft" session had been dominated by males, but "Posters and Publicity" was predominantly female. The upcoming Moratorium demonstration would mean big demos all over the country, including Boston Common, which he might go to. He smiled at a girl painting a peace dove on poster board. Students were painting a banner from sewn-together bedsheets that read, "U Bridgeport says STOP THE WAR!" The lettering was neat but it lacked pizzazz. Soon he was on his hands and knees adding peace symbols, birds, butterflies, and a few lizards.

"Are you going to Tactics?" asked the main poster girl, Karen. That sounded like an invitation. At "Demo Tactics," Bee introduced him to a bearded fellow with a wise face and an older woman who looked as if she'd survived more than a few demos. The man started off talking about the Mobe, the anti-war mobilization committee planning the October Moratorium. He said they were hoping to get five million people around the country to participate.

"Activities are happening in every major city and on almost every campus in America," he said. "Teach-ins, candlelight vigils, prayer services, peace rallies. America opposes the Vietnam War. Next week, teachers, union members, factory workers, lawyers, clergy, mothers, and grandmothers will stand up to show their support for peace. I've spent six weeks traveling this country, talking to people about the Moratorium. In small towns, big cities, farmland, prairie, it's all the same. America opposes the War, and Richard Nixon is going to hear from us as he's never heard before!" The speaker had started soft-spoken and ended with his voice and fist raised. The lady, whose name was Canada or something, also spoke.

"How many of you have been gassed before?" A few raised their hands. Most didn't. He remembered Berkeley. "Carry some handkerchiefs soaked in vinegar in a plastic bag," said Canada. "If you get gassed, use them to breathe through. If the cops grab you, go limp. You'll be less likely to get injured with passive resistance. Before you go, remove any jewelry that could get pulled off causing injury." Karen reached to her earlobe and removed a large hoop. Canada and Wise One discussed the Boston demo, how many were needed for security, how many for publicity, and ways to get positive media attention. Adamson snapped pictures of the speakers. After the session, Wise One introduced himself to Adamson as Ralph Milstein.

"Are you coming to Boston next week?" Milstein asked. Adamson nodded yes. "Good. We can't trust the straight media to report the truth. I suggest shooting for scope as well as story. Ideally, you can get both in the same shot. That's the one we want on the front page of *The Boston Globe* October 16." Adamson thought about the Miniskirted Nun, how she'd cropped up everywhere. Her picture caught the contradictions and passion of the times in which even nuns were forced to act on conscience. What city desk editor could resist a miniskirted nun? "Come to the stage when you get there," said Milstein. "I'll make sure you get a press pass. Are you any good?" Milstein added, as if it were a joke.

"I'm good," said Adamson.

Adamson and Karen shared a grinder at Zovey's. She was a second-year nursing student from New Jersey, against the war but compassionate for the soldiers. She wore a pink sweater and said she might volunteer after she graduated.

"For Vietnam?" He was incredulous.

"No, Coney Island."

"Where's Coney Island?"

"Where you from again?" She pushed the rest of the grinder his way.

"Merry Old England," he said, hopeful.

"Don't they teach geography?" she said.

"We memorize kings and queens, milady," he said. He'd learned about battles, charters, political movements that swapped sides, the red and white, roundheads and royalists, Church of England and Catholics. The importance of the English Channel, hills, dales, moors, ancient stones, and rivers.

"Never go wandering alone on the moor in case of fog," he said.

"What's a moor?" she asked.

"You want some more? Silly girl, you haven't finished what's on your plate!" After he walked her to the dorm, she slipped in without giving him her phone number.

Moratorium Day was spectacular. He rode up to Boston with Michael, Les, and three other students in a 1959 Chevrolet. One of the side windows was broken, but it was a clear New England day and scores of other protesters were driving up I-95, cars bedecked with signs. They left the car in Cambridge and hitched a ride across the river to the Common. Doctors and medical students in white coats stopped passersby to sign postcards calling for President Nixon to withdraw the troops. Throngs of students, children, and ordinary people converged on the open lawn where he'd once played Frisbee. It was like Woodstock without the mud. He got his press pass, which also allowed him free beverages at the press table.

Throughout the day, he tried close-up shots, mingling masses, juxtapositions of specific protesters and signs, portraits of passionate speakers, but none of the shots said, "We are rolling for Peace!" That was how the crowd made him feel. None of his shots made him tingle as he had speeding up the highway with protesters in front and behind, to the left and right. Adamson climbed the grandstand behind the stage for a better look at the crowd while shooting his last roll. The Common was full and the sun cast long shadows. A skywriting plane had drawn a peace sign. Adamson gauged the shot and took three in quick succession.

Since transferring to Photography I, he had access to the department darkroom. He didn't like darkroom work, all that pouring, dipping, fishing, and waiting business, but you could save a bundle on development costs as well as see your shots quicker. When the timer rang, he turned off the infrared and turned on the gooseneck lamp. The shot with the peace sign was beautiful. So were some others, but the peace sign spoke. He immediately took three copies to Milstein, and Milstein said he'd try *The Globe,* the *Herald,* and *The New York Times.*

"What about *Boston After Dark*?" Adamson asked.

"This is a great picture," said Milstein, wagging his finger. "Unless their photographers got the same shot or better, this is the one." Milstein dashed out the front door with coattails flying, reminding Adamson of Alistair. It was the coat. Alistair always flew around in a gray winter coat with a deep vent in the back that gave the perception of wings. Adamson picked up his mail, an aerogramme from Alistair as well as a letter from his mother, an issue of *Esquire*, and junk from the university. Adamson savored Alistair's letter in his room.

Hail Western Lad!

What of thee? What a tale I have. See enclosed (illegally) tiny photo of Luscious Lily, who monopolizes my time outrageously, interfering with my A level swots (English, History, Geog.). Met her last year when we shared the same tutor. She's at St. Clare's, 5 miles down the road. Have perfected midnight drainpipe escape. All right, stole the back door key, satisfied? Several rendezvous.

I haven't heard from you but once. Are you drafted? I didn't write to you but you know I'M A ROTTEN SOD LETTER WRITER! The Pater says hello. He'll be in New York next month and said he'd call. He won't let me come, some barf about studies. All right, you won't write if I don't write so here it is.

Pring! A.

Alistair's sexuality confused Adamson. He said he was bisexual, which presumably meant he still fancied girls as well as men? It seemed complicated, but Adamson could see Alistair sneaking out at night. He could be exaggerating but Ali was an risk-taker.

Victoria's letter was newsy: His father's work was very hush-hush. The pay was good though, and not much travel. Inkblot was in fourth grade.

Stella has been riding around town on the back of an Italian boy's Vespa. His name is Mario and he has a gaggle of friends. They buzz up the hill in a swarm to collect her and buzz back down to the square to hang out. His father owns the local ice cream shop. She's doing well in school and learning Italian.

I bet she is, he thought. The image of his sister with a smooth Latin number made him feel strangely protective. He shook his head to dislodge the idea. If anyone could take care of herself, it was Stewpot. Victoria asked him to come for Christmas and said they'd send a ticket. Not bad, Christmas in Italy. During school he could forget he had no family, but not when his friends packed off for the holidays. He'd moved a lot of his stuff from Sal's basement, and Sal's father might decide to rent it. Victoria included a P.S.: What would he like for his birthday? He'd be nineteen on October 26. Nineteen was when they could force you to commit unspeakable acts in the name of "patriotism." A girl in English class had recently recited a poem by an Englishman who fought in World War I called "The Death of the Ball Turret Gunner."

"Would you like a copy?" she'd asked, dropping a mimeograph on his desk.

From my mother's sleep I fell into the State,
And I hunched in its belly till my wet fur froze.
Six miles from earth, loosed from the dream of life,
I woke to black flak and the nightmare fighters.
When I died they washed me out of the turret with a hose.

He and Les were watching the late news when they announced the date for the draft lottery, December 1. The lottery was new. Numbers from 1 to 366 would be drawn from a barrel, each number corresponding to a birth day. The order of the draw would determine who would be called up first. Student deferments might only be good till the end of the semester. Adamson knew this was fairer than the system allowing rich blokes to avoid the draft by staying in school indefinitely, but still. No more deferments?

A commercial for the new Ford Thunderbird came on. "Soaring into the '70s far ahead of the rest... A new flight of Thunderbirds! New in beauty. Size. And aerodynamic grace."

"My pop has a Thunderbird," said Les. "He won't let me drive it."

In an update on the peace negotiations, a defense undersecretary announced robotically that the anti-war movement was undermining "America's search for peace."

"Have you lost it?" Adamson shouted at the telly. "Peace, where are you? Get out of that 'ole, you scurvy weasel. They think Peace is a bloomin' Pekinese under the sofa." The story-of-the-week wrap-up was the Manson story again. Nutter Charles Manson had been arrested for the stabbing murder of the actress and her friends in California. He thought of Maggie, her hair blowing in the wind off Thunder Bay.

Adamson planned to sleep in the morning after the Moratorium but was awoken early by furious pounding. He opened the door expecting to see Tweedledum and Tweedledee from the FBI. "Prepare to be amazed," said Milstein, holding up *The New York Times*. "Read the tiny type." Adamson focused. Blimey! It was his shot! "And the icing on the cake…." Milstein produced *The Boston Globe*, A section, page two, another print of his peace sign in the sky.

"Are they paying?" Adamson asked.

"$450 from *The Times* and $250 from *The Globe*. We hope you'll make a contribution to the movement," said Milstein.

"All of it?" Adamson asked.

"We hoped you would," said Milstein.

"I'll give you some," Adamson said.

"You'll be coming to Washington next month?" asked Milstein, "for the March Against Death?"

"How did you sell it to both papers?" asked Adamson.

"I can sell anything I believe in, and I want to stop the carnage. Believe in something and other people will too." Milstein shook his hand. It was barely eight o'clock. He couldn't go back to sleep. He was too thrilled. He definitely believed in stopping the carnage. God knows he was healthy enough to be drafted. Could he fake psychosis? If not, he'd have to leave the country. He didn't really want to return to England, to that gray flannel straitjacketed life. Despite the trouble of learning the ropes in America, he realized he no longer wanted to leave. Could he hide out at Jim Jones' farm? He could think of worse fates than Armageddon sermons and communal dining with Lara. He wrote Jones a letter, care of Lara, asking about specifics if he needed asylum.

After Soc., Adamson went to the darkroom to make some prints. At Professor Koch's insistence, he'd been experimenting with light and shadow. Artsy-fartsy stuff wasn't his thing, but Koch convinced him that even journalistic photographers needed to know how to make the most of a shot. He'd decided to do what he was told. He was more skilled than the other students. Koch was only in his second year of teaching but Adamson wanted to learn whatever skills he could even if he didn't need them, like filmmaking. He was almost finished developing when someone knocked.

"Just a minute." The sign on the door told the knocker the lab was in use. He turned on the regular light. "All right, come in." A big girl from Photography class walked in and greeted by him name, throwing her stringy hair over her shoulder. She wore a tight yellow sweater.

"Hello," he said. He couldn't remember her name.

"Fantastic shot in *The Globe*," she gushed, standing too close to him. He shifted down the lab table but she followed, mumbling about a lucky break. When he tried to leave, Sweater Girl shut the door and leaned against it smiling. Cripes. He asked what she was working on.

"Romance studies," she said, not moving. Would he have to plow through her? He assessed her size but she was pretty big and he didn't want a tussle. "Let's take a look on the light table, shall we?" he said, yanking her away from the door and throwing it open. She laid out a half dozen black and whites of bodies intertwined unrecognizably, pursed lips against bark, thighs around tree trunks. "Nice textures," he said.

"Really?" she asked, running her finger up his arm. He felt a jolt of desire but thought, hell, no. Not in the photo lab. Not with Sweater Girl. True, he'd been feeling lonely but in a flash of wisdom, he knew he was one of those men who wanted to like the ladies he poked, preferably be in love, at least find them attractive. While his member was willing, he was afraid of Sweater Girl. Why was she...? The blasted newspapers.

Her lips were grazing his neck. "You're warm," she said. His prints were lying on the bench behind her. He broke free, grabbed them, and lit for the door. Locked. "I don't know what you want, but this isn't funny."

"Can't we just be friends?" she said, slinking up to him again. Psycho, he thought.

"Marilyn, your medication is overdue. Lie down immediately," he said in his most authoritative Monty Python doctor voice. Sweater Girl looked momentarily confused but obliged by lying on the lab floor. She adjusted her sweater demurely.

"It's Charlotte, not Marilyn."

"As I said, Marilyn, I must treat you immediately. Close your eyes and keep them closed." She giggled and kicked off her shoes and closed her eyes as Adamson eyed the fire escape. "I will treat you personally," he said, opening the window.

"What are doing?" she asked, sitting up.

"We need fresh air," said Adamson. "Close your eyes, take deep breaths. In, out. In, out. You must relax before I begin The Treatment," he tried to make his voice sexy. "Soon I shall ask you to remove your sweater." Sweater Girl took deep breaths and seemed to relax. He picked up his prints and stepped quietly out of the window onto the fire escape.

"Toodles," he said and climbed down as fast as he could, running all the way to the Student Union, where Michael bought him a celebratory OJ. Adamson felt safer in the bubbly crowd of the pub.

✳ ✳ ✳

Sal came down to visit that weekend, and Adamson showed him around campus. On Saturday night, they built a bonfire on the beach. The Long Island Sound had a slick of oil on the surface as usual. City trash regularly washed up on the shore, but it was still a beach and it was on the edge of campus. Michael brought marshmallows and hot dogs, someone else brought macaroni salad, and he and Sal supplied beer and OJ. They stuck sticks through the hot dogs and roasted them. Quite good in a charred sort of way. He was aware Americans liked their meat well charred and thought it must be an acquired taste. Michael's plan for the marshmallows was elaborate. You put one on a stick (this was a very shish kaboby picnic), you roasted it in the fire till it was melty and charred, then you sandwiched it between a wholemeal biscuit called Graham and some chocolate. The chocolate marshmallow sandwich had a mumbly name that everyone knew. Nurse Karen put his together after he burned his first two marshmallows to cinders.

"Here comes a boat," said Les, pointing at the water. "A couple of 'em. Hey!" An armada of small motor boats headed toward shore. Les grabbed the first boat's rope and at least a dozen people jumped out. One sailor's arm was in a makeshift sling.

"Bust at Yale!" said Napoleon. "Police have blockaded the campus exits. We had to escape down the Sound!" Another motor boat drew up next to it.

"Better get you all under wraps," said Michael. He was quick, that Michael. Might be President one day. The campfire picnic became a rescue convoy, one group staying to help the boat people disembark, the others whisking the new arrivals into dorm rooms and dry clothes. Within an hour, twenty-five people and two boats had been sequestered. Adamson and Sal had one Leonard Miffs bunking in their room. Leonard was a physics major with a fondness for hashish, which he shared. He'd been to England several times. His father was a visiting scholar at Oxford, and he knew some of the places on the River Thames that Adamson loved, like Caversham and Lechlade. They stayed up late, listening to music, smoking, and talking. The New Haven police had to make do with confiscating the boats, having been unable to find any of the Yale escapees. The Tale of the Yale Flotilla became Bridgeport lore. I'm an eyewitness to history, Adamson thought.

The next morning, he took Sal to Zovey's for brunch. He wondered why Sal wasn't making hay to get back to U. Mass, but Sal seemed content to drink coffee and read the comics. Adamson excused himself to study. Sal said he'd come say goodbye later. After reading and highlighting a while, Adamson sucked up the last of Leonard's hash and fell asleep to Jeff Beck. His room was dim when he awoke, and he was disoriented from the hash and the nap. He thought he heard a whisper. Then a giggle. He called Sal's name and sat up. Another giggle. Surely Sal hadn't let Sweater Girl in? A shadowy lump moved.

"Who's there?"

"Surprise!" Sal turned on the lamp and lumps jumped up. Hannah. Michael. Paulette! He sat up in bed blinking like Mr. Magoo.

"Happy birthday, Adamson!" Hannah handed him a present. Paulette, gorgeous as ever, sat demurely at the foot of the bed and offered him a small box. He'd tried to forget that his 19th birthday was coming up. Sal's job had been to distract him. The Yale Flotilla was a bonus diversion.

The lounge was decorated with streamers and balloons. Food was spread out on the counter. The refrigerator was stocked with drinks. Hannah and Paulette had driven down that morning with chili and rice and a big chocolate cake. Michael and Les had spread the word. Adamson had never had a surprise birthday party before. Hannah even organized musical chairs to the new Hendrix album, *Electric Ladyland*. Bril! Paulette landed in his lap on the third round. "My place!" she yelled, wriggling into a small space on the sofa.

"I was here first, missy!" he replied. Her face was inches from his. She smelled as sweet as violets. She fluttered her long lashes and kissed him sensuously on the lips.

"Ooooo!" cried everyone else on the sofa.

"Happy birthday, Adamson," she said and smiled her old smile. He was encouraged enough to try to get her to stay the night, but she put her forefinger on his lips to silence him. He gave her the fossil he'd found on Drake's Beach. She examined it, rubbed it in her palm with pleasure, but she followed Hannah to sleep in the girls' dorm. He would never understand women, ever.

The next day, he'd reserved an 8mm movie camera to do his video assignment. As an impromptu birthday gift, Paulette, Sal, and Hannah met him on the beach for the shoot. Hannah and Sal played out a Prince Charming-Fairy Princess scene that ended up with Sal throwing the Princess into the Sound, after which Paulette kicked off her shoes and danced a story. At first, Paulette's dance was a slave narrative involving toil and whipping and an escape to freedom, then she turned frivolous, flitting like a butterfly, twirling her scarf like Isadora Duncan. Sal and Hannah huddled wet on a log. Adamson moved in and out with the camera, letting her dance into frame and disappear. He liked movies where people disappeared mysteriously from the picture. When she dropped to the sand, Adamson stood above her and slowly knelt down. Her whole face and hair filled the frame. She kissed her fingertips and pressed them against the lens, never breaking eye contact, not even once.

NOVEMBER

Adamson had been fairly indifferent to news till Milstein showed him how the news was constructed by reporters, photographers, editors, wire services, politicians, diplomats, public relations men, and activists, and encouraged him to pay attention. Some news was tripe. Paul McCartney wasn't dead. McCartney himself had laughed, flexing his feeble Liverpudlian biceps for the camera, yet the story persisted because crackpot news made money, like Manson or the vet who hijacked a plane to Rome.

Adamson was studying the newspaper at the Student Union when Michael flopped down in a chair, uncharacteristically morose. He confessed that his New York supplier had been busted. He asked Adamson if he'd substitute tutor at the Panther storefront that afternoon.

"I can be there by four," Adamson said. He was trying not to skip class. Some professors graded only on exams and papers but a few gave points for attendance, and he needed all the points he could get. The new university president, a former Marine, had announced an expulsion policy for students who didn't keep a C average or better, which Milstein said was illegal. Adamson sped to the Panther storefront after Soc. and a stern woman pointed to four boys and thrust a math book in his hands.

"You're not the dude," said Big Ears.

"I'm the dude's friend, he couldn't be here."

"He got busted," said Pug Nose.

"Jail?" asked Sleepy, lifting his head from his arms.

"He's not in jail," Adamson said, "I saw him this morning."

"He going to jail," said Pug, the best connected. They discussed how much time Michael would serve, the time their fathers and brothers were serving, and asked whether Adamson had served time. Not unless you include boarding school, he told them, and turned to their homework, but they wanted to know how boarding school was like jail. He told them about the rotten food, the uniforms, and the rules, including fagging, corporal punishment, and mandatory church, rising in their esteem until Pug announced, "You done *hard* time."

Having qualified himself, Adamson focused them on equations. He was delighted that when he checked the answers, they'd got all the problems right. He wished he had lollipops and said so. They begged so loudly that Stern Face exploded in blue language and they returned to sullenness. Adamson didn't like witnessing spirits broken so he asked Big Ears, aka Alvin, to lead them on an extra credit question and sprinted to the corner shop. Black men stood around the door but parted to let him through. He must appear as an alien, he thought, while paying for five chocolate bars. Perhaps a green cyclops. Stern Face was angry but the candy was gone by the time she'd finished lecturing on "the slavery of junk food." Then she chided the boys, "The Man taking down Brother Bobby and you all taking candy from a white boy, hmm!"

"You should of bought her one," whispered Pug. Stern Face was talking about Bobby Seale. Adamson had seen the news on the Chicago Eight trial. The Chicago Eight were a group of protest leaders who'd been arrested at the National Democratic Convention in Chicago the previous year. He remembered watching the police clubbing protesters on the telly shortly after he'd arrived in America. It had been an odd welcome. The trial judge, a white man, had outrageously ordered the only black defendant, Black Panther Bobby Seale, gagged and bound in court, and had separated his case from the other defendants.

Preparations were underway for an even bigger anti-war demonstration in Washington, and Milstein got Adamson a press pass. Sal wanted to ride with him from Bridgeport to D.C., and they teamed up with Michael and Les for the five-hour drive. Michael had been laying low, attending class, and hanging out instead of going into the city. The Moratorium March on Washington was scheduled to begin Thursday night and run through the weekend with the big march on Saturday. They'd crash at Les' friends' apartment in D.C.

"Ready to get your head bashed in?" Sal asked, wearing a black-and-white striped jersey like a football referee's. Adamson had several vinegar-soaked washcloths in a plastic bag and borrowed a Super 8 movie camera from the Photography Department. He'd made four movies so far: Paulette dancing; Sunrise on the Sound; a romance staring Les and Karen the Nurse; and a short documentary about a worker at the Warner Bra and Girdle Factory, inspired by Warhol's movies. Warhol trained the camera on his drugged-out, transsexual friends and let them cavort, shoot up, and gab for hours. They were silly movies but he liked the idea of turning on the camera and letting it run uncensored and that's how he planned to document the Moratorium March. If it was good, it could be his end-of-term project; if not, he'd return to the Bra and Girdle Factory for Part Two, listening to the seamstresses talking matter-of-factly about "stretch factor, buttock ride, and cup stress."

Five minutes into the journey, Sal distributed blotter acid. Adamson put the pane in his pocket. He didn't want to be tripping when Constable Watson clobbered him with a blackjack. He asked Michael if he ought to drive and trip but Michael assured him he drove better tripping than straight. Interstate 95 was packed with buses and cars decked out for the demo. At a rest stop, Adamson switched places with Les, thinking that he would be better at reconnoitering. Sal and Les were quiet in the backseat. Halfway down the Jersey Turnpike, they discovered Les had chewed the middle out of the twenty-dollar bill set aside for tolls and food.

"I thought it was a snack," he said. They pooled their cash. Les was skint, Sal had five bucks, and Michael and Adamson had twenty between them. Since the tolls were ten each way, provisions for the weekend would have to come out of Sal's five.

Fortunately, cheese sandwiches awaited them at Mark and Mandi's in D.C. and he filled up on them. They walked down to a park near the White House where demonstrators had left signs upon which were written the names of dead servicemen and destroyed Vietnamese villages. "Alphonzo Park III," said one. "Emilio Juarez," said another, young lives reduced to signs leaning against a fence and destined for the rubbish bin. He imagined Alphonzo lying face down in mud, a big man like Samuel who'd sold him the motorbike. He saw Emilio burned to a crisp in a helicopter fire. Perhaps he'd played soulful ballads on the guitar to his companions. "When I died they washed me out of the turret with a hose," he recalled from English class.

This preliminary parade of signs was called the March against Death. Adamson let the camera run as people passed by, commenting on the signs. One girl laid pink roses. He caught her eye. She looked away. He pointed the camera in another direction and she smiled at his kindness. She thinks I'm a soul stealer, he thought. In the approaching darkness, he switched to his still camera with fast film, and they trudged back up Connecticut Avenue to the apartment. He photographed marchers reflected in the store windows of Elizabeth Arden. Remembering his mother's pots of make-up bearing the EA insignia that she'd smear on her face till it looked shiny and pale, he snapped a shot of the red door.

They watched the news about the March Against Death on the telly, demonstrators marching single file from Arlington National Cemetery past the White House, carrying the names of the dead. Mandi made them Chinese vegetables and rice. Adamson helped chop the veggies and watched her deftly handle the big round saucepan. After that, they lolled on the sofa and mattresses, smoking Michael's weed.

Adamson went out with Mandi to get ice cream from High's Dairy Store. Crossing P Street, they heard music from Dupont Circle. Though it was November, the night was mild, and girls splashed in the fountain. Young men played guitar and people crowded the four or five permanent chess tables illuminated by streetlights. Most of the seated chess players were black men. The air was scented with a fragrance of marijuana, patchouli oil, and autumn leaves. Mandi was a luscious girl with creamy-smooth skin, pendulous breasts (he'd noticed she didn't wear a bra), and a throaty laugh. Close to the music, she leaned into him. She was wearing only a cotton blouse and a granny skirt.

Suddenly he shouted, "Raymond!" and Raymond turned, acknowledging him with a grin. Soon it was all handshakes and backslaps. Raymond had just arrived from Detroit. He'd planned to crash with an ex-girlfriend but no answer. When they returned to the apartment with Rum Raisin ice cream, Raymond came with them. They sat up drinking jasmine tea, reliving the snowball fight, the bear attack, and digging shrubs till they dropped at Maggie's salon. They both sighed thinking of her.

"I didn't have a chance," said Raymond. "She'll only be serious with a Native guy."

"Her loss, mate," said Adamson.

In the morning, they marched with the crowd down Connecticut Avenue to the Mall, a long grassy area that stretched from the Capitol to the Lincoln Memorial. The Mall looked like a picture from his American History book. Marchers poured in. The organizers said 250,000, then 400,000. The police said 50,000, then 100,000. However many, it was a lot. After demos in Cambridge, Berkeley, and Boston, he thought this one was more like Woodstock. It was difficult to hear the speakers, supposedly George McGovern and Coretta Scott King. He could hear King's singsong cadence but not the words. Joan Baez and Judy Collins sang. Someone said Dylan was there, but it was probably a hoax. Dylan was like the Beatles, often rumored, rarely seen. Somebody from the Chicago trial spoke, but unable to hear, Adamson took a walk.

He established his visual landmarks—a political button stand in front of the Museum of Natural History and a bank of blue toilets—and pushed through the crowd. He'd shot some footage but feared it would be dull and jumpy. The plucky button salesman sold him a huge black-and-white button for a quarter. It said, "March Against Death, Washington, November 13-15—Vietnam 1,500,000—How many more?" He shot the grinning salesman in front of his wares. The crowd was mostly young white people though not entirely. He enjoyed some of the signage, "Long Island Mothers Against the War" and "Yippie Queers Make the Best Wives." The Yippies were funny, staging silly acts to make the Establishment realize how ridiculous it was. In Chicago, the Yippies had nominated Pigasus the Pig for President. Their leaders had thrown dollar bills on the floor of the New York Stock Exchange, creating an amusing, made-for-news riot of young capitalists diving for cash. They'd turned the Chicago Eight trial into theatre by wearing judges' robes and police uniforms to court. Sometimes the Yippies even poked fun at antiwar people.

The Natural History Museum doors opened and closed. He ought to listen to the earnest speakers or cheer long-haired men burning their draft cards, but the lure of dinosaurs was great. Alone in the hall of mastodons and stegosauri, he greeted them as old friends. Outside, demonstrators were trying to convince shady President Nixon and his generals that war was immoral and wasteful, while inside stood the immortal bones of creatures mightier than the biggest tank in the Mekong Delta. Eoraptor would shred you like shrapnel but Brachiosaurus and Diplodocus, the great grass eaters, were peaceful giants of the primordial forest. When Adamson asked if he could film them, the guard shrugged, and he panned from beast to beast.

When he rejoined his friends, Milstein was there. "Go to Waskow's tonight, shoot some pictures. It's a leftie commune, a real hub." Milstein scrawled the address. "Gotta run, Jane Fonda at 6, *Rolling Stone*." Adamson was hungry.

"Beans and rice at the apartment or potluck at Waskow's?" asked Sal. Mandi said they should try Waskow's first. It wasn't that far from the apartment. They climbed the hill to Wyoming Avenue, parched and famished. The front door of the commune was open. They waded through a crowded, wood-paneled living room and headed straight back to the kitchen. Luckily, they were first in line for spaghetti. As Adamson finished his second plate, he saw her. She wasn't wearing a miniskirt but he recognized her instantly and he wiggled his way next to her in a discussion circle. "I've seen your picture all over," he whispered. "I'm a photographer."

"Hello, I'm Elaine. Where are you from?" she asked. He told Sister Elaine the short version of his long life and how he was afraid of being drafted. "You're brave to come photograph the demonstration," she said. "Come to the vets' speak-out tonight." He didn't feel brave.

"What did you do to get your photo in the paper?" he asked. She said they'd broken into the Dow Chemical offices and seized documents. Then they published Dow's five-year plan that showed Dow would make millions in profits from selling murderous chemicals like napalm and nerve gas. A bearded man put his hand on Elaine's shoulder, and she squealed in recognition.

As she left the circle, Elaine said to him, "Dow advertises that they make life better but it's all lies." Adamson saw Dick Gregory and tried to get some pictures but the house was too crowded. He needed more space around his subjects. He preferred collaborating with people but he knew for news, you often had to take without asking. Some cultures viewed photography as "soul snatching." They do say "take your picture." He didn't believe this but the Roxbury lady who shooed him away from her kids did.

Adamson abandoned the party at the commune and traipsed back down the avenue. At the apartment, he found Mandi alone with Raymond, shoes off, playing guitar on a mattress in the living room, Mandi's hair disheveled, and no sign of Mark. Raymond, the old dog. Mandi gave Adamson directions to the speak-out but he accidentally ended up on 14th Street, which looked totally bombed out, shops shuttered and burned, sheets of wood hung in place of windows, and seedy characters smoking on the corners. He quickly made a right onto R Street as he heard footsteps behind him. He began running, loping up the west side of 15th until his radar ceased beeping. He found the church he was looking for and walked down into the lit basement.

The room was full of demonstrators with bandanas and buttons, women holding babies, grandfatherly and grandmotherly types in sensible shoes, and a platform on which sat three vets in sundry uniforms. One vet was clean-shaven and boyish. Another had a grizzly beard and wore an army jacket. The third, in wire-rim spectacles, was being introduced as a poet. His name was Terry. Adamson found a seat. He noticed that Terry's hands were shaking. Terry had been a medic in Vietnam for a year and half and was enrolled in med school at Georgetown. Mr. Grizzly asked Terry about the wounds he'd treated. Terry described gaping wounds, sepsis, amputations, misplaced gray matter, napalm and sulphur burns, ringworm, gonorrhea, and cholera. Then the boyish vet, a pilot, talked of how exciting it was to hit your bombing target, like in a game, but how horrible it was to see a fellow pilot's bomb-laden plane explode like fireworks. After a few questions and answers, Adamson left.

He realized Terry the Medic was walking behind him and paused to let him catch up. "I'm surprised you still want to go into medicine," Adamson said. Terry sucked on a cigarette and didn't reply, and they parted company at P Street. Elaine had told him the speak-out might help him clarify what he wanted to do. He'd heard from Terry that brains really were fleshy and gray, "like coils of worried wool." Adamson thought about the poet-medic all the way home. He thought of how the lowly medic wasn't technically allowed to perform the procedures he'd used to save lives. How he'd dutifully patched up soldiers only to have them return to battle and at times get obliterated.

❉   ❉   ❉

Back in class, Adamson played his movie with scenes from the White House, close-ups of dead veterans' names on placards, posters and banners, someone offering the camera a joint, the Mall, the button man, dinosaurs, Raymond playing guitar, Les, Michael, Sal, and Raymond stuffing themselves into the Beetle, and Mandi blowing kisses.

"What's he saying?" asked a stoned-out boy in sunglasses.

"The film is the statement," said Koch.

"Comes down to chicks," said Stoney.

"I think it's sensitive," said Sweater Girl, who still liked Adamson.

"Sensitive in what way?" asked Koch.

"About women, the war, people," she said, running out of steam.

"Ulysses? What do you think the war means to Adamson?" Ulysses uttered his usual one-syllable expletive, toothpick in the side of his mouth. He'd tried smoking in class but Koch put his foot down and Ulysses returned with an unlit cigarette behind one ear. "I know you're thoughtful, maybe the most thoughtful person in the room, certainly the most experienced." Koch had a way of pushing Ulysses that felt dangerous.

Ulysses sighed. "Adamson's a confused son-of-a-bitch. Half the movie's upside down because that's how he thinks, or maybe we look upside down to him, and dinosaurs are the only ones that make sense."

"And the war?" Ulysses wouldn't talk about the war. Another student said that Adamson was against the war but because he wasn't from here, it wasn't his war.

"It's not my war either," volunteered Sweater Girl.

When Adamson got back to his room, Raymond asked how the screening went. "*Spartacus* it ain't," Adamson said. There was a note that a Mr. Morris had called but no return number. Thanksgiving break was coming up, and Sal had finagled a house on Cape Cod and invited everyone to stay. After studying for an hour, Adamson went to help Michael and Les "pack some books," code for bagging weed, which meant Adamson could earn a bag for his trouble. A new supplier had prevailed on Michael to distribute, and the weed was destined for other institutions of higher learning, and Adamson's job was to bag half-ounce piles. After the Led Zeppelin record was over, he put on the *White Album*. When they finished, the room smelled strongly so they nonchalantly carried two suitcases up to a closet on the top floor, which Michael locked with a key.

After stowing his payment baggie in his room, Adamson checked his mailbox and found a letter from his father, a postcard from Alistair, and a letter from a post office box in California. His father's letter contained a ticket to Italy and a photo of his sisters in Venice, Stella looking glam and Inkblot a bit taller. Alistair's postcard said:

Hail HA!

Portsmouth by train for Xmas, 3 wks w/potty aunt + 5 cats—thanks a lot! Lily in the family way, all settled now thanks to my lolly but she's gone off me. Sticking to my own kind from now on. Sick of swotting. Save me, Ali

Portsmouth and cats, poor Alistair. They used to have fun at Christmas when Alistair came to stay. Thank God Hannah got an abortion, even if a wife and child could get him out of the draft. The third letter was from Lara of the Peoples Temple:

Dear Adamson,

We can help you disappear from your draft troubles at our beautiful community in Ukiah, north of San Francisco. Yours in faith, Lara.

He put the letter and her phone number with his social security card, green card, and passport. If he needed to escape, here was an alternative passport.

He wrote his English paper, due before Thanksgiving, and studied for a make-up math test. When he studied math, the numbers didn't stay on the lines properly. They danced around the page and did somersaults. They flip-flopped. It took Herculean concentration to keep them still and straight. Sometimes he thought he was hallucinating. He split a pizza with Michael and Les, picking off the pepperoni (spicy American shoe leather), and volunteered to go get chocolate chip cookies from Zovey's.

When he returned, two Bridgeport Police cars were parked outside the dorm. Inside, Michael was standing, hands behind his back, with a cop reading something to him. Another cop was placing a roach into a plastic bag with tweezers. They were on Adamson like fleas on a dog. Unfortunately, his pocket contained a few seeds and a tiny roach. Michael looked blankly at him. Les sat glumly on the bed. Adamson was handcuffed. The cops were testy, having searched Michael's, Les', and Adamson's rooms and turned up nothing. No sign of Raymond or Adamson's baggie. Students gawked as

Adamson and Les were pushed into the back of one car and Michael was taken away in another.

Adamson was questioned over and over about his involvement and clung to the same story: pizza, cookies, police. When asked if he knew Michael was a major East Coast weed dealer, Adamson honestly could say no. He said he had no idea where the detritus in his pocket came from. His wallet, keys, and shoelaces were taken and he was locked in a cell with assorted criminals. All night, men yelled, threw up, cursed, and steel doors slammed. In the morning, more questions. The cops said Michael and Les had told them "everything." It was his turn, then he could go. Adamson didn't fall for it. Upstairs, he was charged with possession of an illegal substance. He could post a $10,000 bond and was given one phone call. "Call your father," advised the cop.

Adamson knew his father couldn't help 3,500 miles away. He would've called Michael if Michael hadn't also been locked up. Lou probably wouldn't be home. "Call your parents. You're not the first kid to get busted for pot," snarled the cop. As Adamson flicked through his mental list of American acquaintances, he paused at Professor Koch. Koch probably smoked weed and might know what "posting bond" meant. He asked for a Bridgeport phone book but Koch wasn't listed. In the end, Adamson called the dorm. Perhaps someone could run and give Koch a message. It rang eight times before being picked up.

"This is Adamson Henry, who's this?" His heart was pounding. One call, the cop had been clear. The voice responded with an expletive. "Ulysses, help me." Ulysses was silent as Adamson begged him to tell Koch as soon as possible. Ulysses might be drunk and forget, Adamson thought when he was back in the holding cell. By late afternoon, no one had come. "Looks like you'll be our guest for the long weekend," said the officer on duty. "Tomorrow's Turkey Day and Friday's a state holiday."

He was taken with three other prisoners for showers. He could hear water running and the clank of plumbing. At boarding school, the showers were associated with unseemly activities. They stopped at a cage near the bathroom. "What your size, honey?" asked a person in the cage resembling, amazingly, Diana Ross of the Supremes. She flashed a smile and tossed her bouffant tresses. She leaned over the counter and looked him up and down, "You're a large, baby." She pushed a pile of clothes at him. Diana Ross wore a fitted version of Bridgeport's blue prison uniform. As he waited on a bench for the shower, Diana Ross flirted and sang out,

But Mama said you can't hurry love
No you've just have to wait
She said love don't come easy
It's a game of give and take...

One of the men spat at Diana Ross but she said, "See if you get my turkey tomorrow." He didn't want to know these people. Diana Ross shimmied, folding prison laundry, and placing it in cubbyholes by size. An inmate asked for a cigarette. "You can't smoke in here," she said, giving him the side eye after he whispered in her ear. The guard told the man to sit down.

"Adamson," shouted a guard, who prodded him back toward the holding cell.

"Bring back my clothes!" yelled Diana Ross. He didn't know what to do. The guard took the clothes. "Bye, honey!" she called. Upstairs, his wallet, keys, and shoelaces were returned. The guard pointed at a door on the other side of which sat Koch in a chair. He guided Adamson to the exit. In the car, Koch put the key in the ignition but didn't start it. They sat in silence. Adamson closed his eyes and allowed a wave of relief to pass over him. Koch patted his shoulder. Ulysses had done his job. Koch had come as soon as he heard and posted Adamson's bail.

"Not planning on leaving the country, are you?" asked Koch. Cross that bridge when I get there, Adamson thought. Everyone had left the dorm for the holiday except Raymond. He'd taken Adamson's weed and hidden out in the library.

❊   ❊   ❊

The motorbike gods were on their side, and they arrived at Onset, a little seaside town at the gateway to Cape Cod around lunch time. At Sal's cottage, a tiny elderly lady was sitting on the porch with Paulette. He hadn't expected Paulette and wasn't happy to see a handsome black man emerge from the house and drop into a nearby rocking chair.

"Good to see you," greeted the elderly lady with an accent. She presented her face to Adamson to be kissed and, as she was the same size and shape as his granny, he bussed her on the cheek. "You've grown so tall," she said. Paulette asked him to help take the turkey out of the oven, and in the kitchen she explained that the lady was Sal's roommate's grandmother, Marianna, who owned the cottage but lived in a nursing home because she had dementia. Sal's roommate was supposed to visit his granny regularly but Sal had offered to rent Marianna's house for $40 a month *and* bring her home for a visit whenever he could. Marianna was Cape Verdean. She'd settled with her family on Cape Cod years ago to work the cranberry bogs. She treated Sal and company as extended family. When she walked into the yard, Sal asked Clyde, Paulette's boyfriend, to keep his eye on her.

"Why can't he do it?" said Clyde, nodding at Raymond.

"Keep her in the yard. Make sure the gate's locked," said Sal. Adamson and Raymond were shown to an attic bedroom with two narrow beds and a small window overlooking the sparkling bay. They ate a sumptuous turkey dinner then walked the crescent beach. The village was like a miniature Brighton, with a little pier, a shuttered ice cream shop, a seafood restaurant, and gingerbread-style Victorian houses. Dogs and kids ran along the beach chasing seagulls, and motorcyclists drank out of paper bags near the pier.

What does she see in him besides massive shoulders? Adamson thought, eyeing Clyde. He was insanely jealous. Paulette was trying to get Clyde to splash in the water. She'd taken off her shoes and rolled her jeans up to the knees and was skipping in the shallows.

"No one wants to have fun around here," said Paulette.

"I do," said Sal, stripping off his shoes and socks and splashing her. She splashed him back. Adamson and Raymond took one look at the melee and in the ensuing water battle, Marianna ran in fully dressed. Paulette caught up to her and brought her back to shore. They hadn't brought towels to the beach and by the time they got back to the cottage, they were chilled to the bone. They got Marianna into dry clothes and Sal drove her back to the nursing home while Adamson made cocoa.

Hannah came the next day, looking beatniky in a black sweater and tight black jeans. Her hair was dark again, the way he liked it the best. She and Paulette cleaned the kitchen, which hadn't been scrubbed in years. He hadn't thought the two women got along but Hannah was a serious student now. He heard them laughing in the kitchen. Probably talking about me, he thought. He loved them both.

Clyde sat on the porch listening to a portable radio. Raymond was in the glider, composing a song. Adamson poked around the garden with Ron, who was telling him about M.I.T., the swotty college where he was studying computers and interning for the International Business Machine Company.

"Let me get this straight," Adamson said. "You get academic credit for helping them automate a typewriter for lawyers?"

"It started out for lawyers but it's gone beyond that," said Ron. "It's called Generalized Mark-up Language, GML, a combination of text editing, page composition, and retrieval. Say you've got an article on co-eds? Say the title is "Great Big Jugs. "Great Big Jugs" is text, and the appearance, say, sixteen point type, center aligned, boldface, is the presentation. GML manages the text *and* the presentation separately." Adamson said he didn't see the point of it. "The program automates the typist *and* the typewriter by storing codes as calls to stored formats that can be retrieved by other programs." Adamson was lost. "It's like typesetting, only the computer sets the type and communicates with other computers."

"Wouldn't it be easier to hire a typesetter?" Adamson asked.

"No! Take searching. Theoretically, we can search for all titles and headings containing the words, "Great Big Jugs," and the computer will spit out a list of books and articles with that specific text string in the title or heading."

"Like a librarian?"

"Exactly!" said Ron. Adamson asked why not use a librarian. "Because a computer can do it quicker, and with a computer, you could do the searches yourself!"

"I'd have to learn to use a computer."

"One day everyone will use computers, even kids."

"Poor mugs, locked in a freezing closet. That's not the future, it's the Dark Ages."

"One day, computers will fit in your pocket." Now Ron was talking fantasy.

However, since Ron was a certified math swot, Adamson asked his help on his take-home Algebra exam. Adamson's professor was trying to pass him with a D but it was a slog. Ron worked with Adamson, coaching him as they filled in the mimeo sheets while Hannah sat on the porch reading developmental psychology.

"You're transposing again," observed Ron. "Seventy-one is correct, but you wrote 17 in the answers. It's 71."

Hannah looked up. "Do you transpose often?" What did she mean? Ron said yes, he did, and he wrote his 3's and 5's backwards too. Adamson felt humiliated. It was bad enough that his numbers boogie-woogied without having it pointed out. Hannah looked at his answer sheet. "You might have a learning problem," she said. No kidding, he thought. "There's a pediatrics field studying this," she added.

"What can I do?" Adamson asked. He didn't want a lobotomy or anything. She said she'd ask her professor. He and Ron finished correcting Adamson's errors, and Sal came out with a joint, thank God. Sal asked Adamson if he'd like to share the house rent, along with the others, $12 dollars a month per person. Ron pointed out that the total was only $40 a month.

"Yeah, but I said I'd keep the electric on in the winter for the pipes, and there's the phone bill." Adamson agreed, and they toasted their beach house and named it Atlantis, for the "lost civilization." He gave Sal $24, which seemed like a lot of lolly as it passed from his hands but as he watched the sun drop behind the pier, he realized he could share the house with his mates, and he'd tell his parents and Stewpot, "I'm renting a beach house with friends."

On their last night, they played Monopoly. Sal wracked up property but Ron pulled ahead with a fortune in cash. Adamson didn't care for money or property. He liked the impromptu encounters of Chance and Community Chest that led to tax refunds or the Get Out of Jail Free Card. That would have been handy, he thought. Paulette turned on the little telly. She always read the paper and watched the news. He was washing dishes when Paulette shouted for Hannah to come right away. On the telly, a reporter stood outside a courthouse. "I think they arrested your father for spying."

"What?"

"I swear they said Wardheimer, definitely Dynamic Electric." Hannah called home, but the line was busy. Paulette grabbed the phone book and they stood listening as she tried to clarify with the TV station what had come over the wire. The phone answerer read something to Paulette who wrote it down. "Albert Wardheimer, an engineer at Dynamic Electric's Bedford lab, was arrested this morning and charged with espionage. He was arraigned in District Court and held without bond. The government alleges Wardheimer passed secrets through a network of Soviet spies based in London."

Hannah buried her face in her hands as if she couldn't burrow deep enough into darkness. She rocked herself and Paulette put her arms around her. The line at her house was still busy, likely off the hook. Hannah quickly stuffed her things into her bag but the zipper broke, then she was cursing and kicking the bag and sobbing. Adamson remembered the FBI and the package and felt like an accessory.

"Let me drive you home," he offered.

"I'm fine," she said. Then *Modern Endocrinology* fell out of her backpack.

"I'll drive you. You might go off the road. Raymond can drive my motorbike back, right?" As Adamson drove, he told Hannah everything. At her house, lights were on in the foyer and upstairs. Mrs. Wardheimer called down and Hannah left him in the hall. He got a glass of water. The Wardheimer story appeared on the front page of *The Globe*. Mrs. Wardheimer was composed when they came downstairs.

"My husband's a fool. It was his brother…"

"My freaking Uncle Fred!"

"His brother is the spy."

"He tricked Dad…"

Mrs. Wardheimer held up her hand. "Albert knew, we cannot fool ourselves." She turned to Adamson. "I am sorry he involved you." His brother, as far as she knew, was a successful businessman selling medical instruments in London. Hannah was crying again. Mrs. Wardheimer kissed Hannah on the top of her head. "Put Adamson in the guest room. Thank you for bringing my daughter home."

As Adamson rose from the kitchen table, he noticed the other story above the fold, "As Lottery Approaches, Apprehension Climbs."

DECEMBER

The Congressman reached into a jar containing plastic capsules and drew one out. The date inside the capsule was September 14. Adamson looked around the telly lounge. No one spoke. The slip of paper was fastened in the 001 position on a board listing numbers from 001 to 366, a slot for each birthdate, including leap year babies. The heading atop the board read, "Random Selection Sequence 1970." A state committee rep picked the date for 002, April 24.

"Jeez, I'm April 25th," said Les. He passed Adamson a carton of orange juice. The third capsule was December 30 and the fourth February 14. Happy freaking Valentine's, Adamson thought. Everyone in the room was tense, skewered by what was happening on the telly. As Adamson took a long pull of juice, the announcer said, "Zero Zero Seven: October 26." He choked, spitting juice all over his trousers.

"No!" he cried out.

"You?" asked Michael. On the telly, an assistant placed the date October 26 next to 007.

"I'm licensed to kill!" Adamson screamed before he ran to the bathroom and vomited his dinner. Did his parents have telly? Did they know he was doomed?

"Adamson!"

"What?" he cried out. He was panting, and Michael was shaking him by the shoulders.

"You're a freshman, Class of '73. You'll get a student deferment. You're not going to Vietnam, and in four years the war will be over."

"They can get rid of deferments!"

"And you could get shot tomorrow." This happy note was offered by Ulysses standing in the doorway, chewing on a toothpick. Adamson had thought about the danger of tutoring in the projects and oddly, this idea was a comfort. *I could die anywhere tomorrow.* Michael enumerated Adamson's options: go back to England; go to Canada; get a shrink to say he was mentally unfit. Adamson reflected on the vets in the church basement, the Miniskirted Nun, the bloke who led the teach-in on the draft. He, Adamson, had options that some, like the poet-medic and maybe Ulysses, may not have had. He would exercise his options. He could even marry and have a child. Or he could go hide out in Ukiah with Jim Jones. He did not *have* to fight in this senseless war. He had a low draft number and would soon be called for induction, but he realized, in a wave of relief, like the Pacific Ocean rolling ashore on Drake's Beach, that no matter what, he wouldn't go. He would not go.

※　※　※

Koch accompanied Adamson to court. He maintained his innocence, his lawyer spoke of his solid grades and good character, and after a few parlays in legalese and a fierce dressing down, the judge found him guilty of marijuana possession and gave him a year's probation. If he stayed straight, his record would be clean. His lawyer had to go to the bench to get permission for Adamson to travel to Italy at Christmas, and the judge remind him that the Italian police would let him "rot in dung" if he were caught with drugs. He went out with Koch for a sandwich when it was over.

"Let's not do this again," said Koch, whose wife had been unhappy that he'd put their house up to cover Adamson's bond. "What about a thank-you photo?" Koch suggested. "She'd like one of those romantic ones on the beach. Bring it to dinner tomorrow night."

Adamson printed a copy of his favorite photo, Paulette reaching for a dusky sky at Onset, signed it, and put on his best caftan shirt. When Koch opened the door, Adamson glimpsed a pair of streaking toddlers who hid under the dining table, giggling in their bath-damp nakedness. Their mother appeared with pajamas in both hands, blond hair escaping from a pigtail down her back. "I said he'd catch you naked." The dining table giggled. Madeleine, Koch's wife, was a part-time art professor. He'd seen her on campus but never connected the two because her name wasn't Koch. When Adamson said it never occurred to him that a woman would want to keep her own name after marriage, she lectured him on men's cluelessness, but he redeemed himself by showing the twins how to play cat's cradle.

Madeleine was a vegetarian. His heart sank as he'd been hoping for a nice roast beef and spuds, but the stuffed grape leaves and lentil stew were satisfying. He handed her the photo after dinner, wrapped in scrounged birthday paper. She held it close then far away, pronouncing it "quite good." As she put the girls to bed, Koch played *Blonde on Blonde* and washed the dishes while Adamson dried. Koch poured a couple of shots of brandy and raised his glass: "To Baby Jakob. Dylan's wife had a baby today."

On the way back to his room, Adamson picked up his mail and dropped off a postcard for Alistair:

Dear Ali Baba,

Math torture, history okay, photography fab. No sweetie but lovelies aplenty. Have own beach house on Cape Cod! Look on the map, mate—the crab claw of Massachusetts. Come for Easter. Happy Xmas—I'll be in Italy w/Stewpot, etc. Hope I see Gina Lollo-you-know-who. A.

His mail included a packet from his family: Victoria's postcard ("Wish you were here and soon you will be!"), a check for travel money, and a drawing of gondolas by Inkblot. Also a letter from Hannah that he put aside till after he studied. Exam prep was grueling, days of reviewing text that skittered across the page plus trying to decipher his own notes. Weed seemed to hurt his retention so he only smoked when visiting Michael, who'd got three years' probation and had cut out the dealing altogether.

Koch's grade was based on projects and attendance. There was also an assignment for continuing students: a series of twelve photos on a common theme, theme subject to Koch's approval. Adamson submitted "People On and Off Planes." During finals week there was a sit-in on campus to protest the My Lai massacre. He joined in blocking the steps of the Admin building till he recalled his probation, which was a good thing because a handful of students were arrested for blocking traffic. Can't interfere with the holy automobile.

His first exam was math and it was horrible. Though he'd studied, the concepts wouldn't stick. He focused on problems he was confident in and wrote a note to his professor at the bottom of the exam, signing it, "Desperate for D." History was an essay and he'd absorbed the right stuff. Soc., which he liked, was part essay, part multiple choice. How could you not like a class with sex as a topic? English was tricky, an essay in which you had to tie everything together. He pottered along but ran out of ideas, then remembered the suggestion of an outline, and began again. Building a scaffold of ideas made remembering what he'd read easier, and he scribbled a list of books and excerpts he recalled. Visiting the list stirred his brain enough to keep writing.

He let out a whoop of joy at the dorm after finals, answered by whoops from all corners of the building. Michael and Les were out. Someone tossed him a can of beer. He didn't like the taste but it was better than nothing. He lay on his bed and read Hannah's letter:

Dear Adamson,

Thanks for your postcard. It came after a bad day in court. Dad's lawyer says he'll probably get five years in jail. Dad seems okay. (He liked your joke about the dungeon, by the way.) I've taken a leave of absence from school because I can't concentrate. I expected Mom to fall apart but she's fine. We've had lots of good talks. I'd always known she was a refugee but she told me she was also in a concentration camp. Uncle Fred has disappeared and may have defected to Russia. Don't pinch the girls in Italy!

Love, Hannah

P.S. Your problem with math and reading is called dyslexia. My professor says there's help so call me when you get back.

The airport departure lounge bustled with travelers. In a concession to winter, Adamson had bought a navy peacoat and added socks to his sandals, which was good because the plane was cold and he was exhausted. He landed in Rome at seven in the morning and connected to Venice.

"Venice International Airport" was an elaborately named shack at the end of a runway on the edge of a marsh. He'd expected gondolas in the distance or a straw-hatted geezer to carry his valise. Instead, he walked across ordinary tarmac to the shack. On the other side of Customs awaited his fan club. Inkblot bounced up and down like a rubber ball, Stewpot leaned languidly against the coffee bar, George waved as if Adamson hadn't seen them, and Victoria, his blessed mother, clutched her hanky and bit her lip. They were on him like a scrimmage, except for Stella, who kissed him continentally on both cheeks and slipped her arm through his as if she were Sophia Loren herself.

They drove home in an old Merc George had commandeered, amid blurry wet fields and female chatter. After an hour, Stella pointed at the windscreen and said, *"Vedi, eccola! I Dolomiti!"* He looked up to see clouds then realized what he'd taken as clouds were huge mountains topped with snow, so tall he had to crane his neck up. They were living in bleedin' Tibet! After the village square, the road began to rise and George turned into an iron-gated yard next to a pink house.

"Benvenuto a Via Mela," said Victoria. They'd all gone native. He had to admit the house was attractive, with black marble floors and rugs over which Bella the dog skittered in excited circles. The sitting room was simple with a sofa, chairs, and stereo, and they toasted his homecoming in the blue dining room. Inkblot toured him through the house, the bedrooms on the main floor, the finished basement where he'd sleep, and the attic. She took him through a vineyard in the back and they sampled the sweet leftover grapes on the vine. When he woke from a nap, it was dark out, and they took him to dinner at the Officers Club. After he went to bed, he woke in the middle of the night and explored the house at his leisure, stepping outside to take in the stars. He'd imagined his family living in an Army squat, not as colonial royalty. They even had a maid.

When he woke up properly the next day, Stella took him walking up Via Mela, a serious incline of rustic cottages and farmyards. "Maria lives down that lane," she said, pointing. "We'll stop on the way back. She's sixteen, her English is great. Her father raises Alsatians, German Shepherds."

"I know what an Alsatian is," he said, rubbing her head with his knuckles.

"I forget. Everyone here is either American or Italian. The Americans think we're quaint and the Italians are relieved we're not American so being English gets us extra credit." She wore blue eye shadow and green mascara and it looked all right. "I *love* it here," she said. "The kids at school are all military brats, used to moving. No more twin-sets and white picket fences."

"No more Minutemen."

"No plaid shorts and white leather prayer books, though I did see a G.I. in plaid shorts, but he was from Kentucky, they're hillbillies."

"I hope you're not friendly with G.I.s," he said.

"I have my admirers."

They walked up to a stone church called Madonna del Monte, with a clear view across the plain to the south. Stella explained that the Dolomite Mountains were the baby Alps. They smelled the scent of incense from morning Mass as they peeked in the open door of the church. Stella pointed to a side door and said it led to a bar where everyone went for a drink after church on Sundays. Catholicism, Italian-style. As they kept walking going uphill, Adamson told her about dorm life and Paulette and the bust. When she asked him to close his eyes, she led him forward into a tiny chapel with a few pews and a stained glass window. It was her favorite place, she said, a spot she came to think and write. He thought of what he'd do in a secluded spot like this.

"You be careful," he said.

"I'm safer here than I would be in the States. In Italy, if you molest a girl, her father, brothers, and uncles tear the man apart." He hoped he'd never be called on to do his brotherly duty.

George took them all for an afternoon drive along the foot of the mountains. Abutting the road were ancient stone cottages with worm-eaten wooden gates and lace curtains covering the windows. He spied children running in a courtyard and a woman feeding chickens. "Do we need a reservation for *Mezzamonte?*" his father asked. "We could watch the lights come up."

"Let's just go," said Stella. "I don't mind waiting. It's the most amazing view, Adamson. On a good day, you can see Venice and the sea." George aimed the Merc up the mountain. Victoria clutched her door handle around the switchbacks and said the Italian drivers were maniacs.

"Nonsense," said George, who was an able, though speedy, driver.

"George!" A sports car swished by. "They'll drive us off the road!"

"He'll be the one over the edge," said George.

"Cars do go off this road, Daddy," said Stella. "There's no railing."

"That's what makes it so fun," said George, squeezing Victoria's knee.

"Close your eyes, Mummy. I'll tell you when we're there."

Mezzamonte, meaning "halfway up the mountain," was an alpine inn with wide windows that took in the lowlands. Adamson could pick out farms, villages, and factories in the distance. A fire roared in the stone fireplace in the center of the dining room. When the waiter came, Victoria and Stella ordered in Italian. He had no idea what the waiter was saying but it sounded musical.

"The special is venison. I'm going to try it," said Stella.

"Oh, dear," said Adamson and everyone groaned. It was good to have one's humor appreciated. Stella spoke a few words to the waiter who responded with a crescendo of hand-circles. "It's baked over the fire and comes with gravy and polenta."

"Adamson might like the pan-fried trout," said Victoria.

"No, he should wait for Da Bepe's for that. They have the most exquisite trout," said his father. Since when had his family become such gourmets? Adamson let them debate and ordered roast chicken.

"*Pollo al forno per il mio fratello,*" said Stella. "*E insalata mista per tutti, per favore.*" The waiter bowed and left.

"Isn't she good?" said George. "You should go in for languages."

"I was going to be a spy but then I realized the spies are on the wrong side," said Stella.

"Every side has spies," said George.

"What are you going to be, Adder, now that zoology's out?"

"Since when?" asked his father.

"Since I dropped Organic Chemistry," said Adamson.

"Are you taking art, love?" his mother asked. She was arty and his father scientific. They'd always competed for Adamson's soul.

"I'm spending a lot of time on photography."

"Photography's more of a hobby though, isn't it?" said George. "It's not a real university subject."

"So what are you going to be?" asked Stella. Three pairs of eyes looked at him. Fortunately, a plane took off from the Aviano Air Base. His father said that Italy went with the Axis powers during the war, but the Italian underground had spies who worked these mountains for the Allies.

"You can't move anything on that airfield without it being seen from up here," said George. "Makes it strategic, but the fighting was fierce, brother against brother. There's still a fair degree of anti-American sentiment." It had seemed so peaceful on the drive up. They watched the runway lights come on. George explained that if you kept going up the mountain, you'd be in Austria by morning. If you went east, you'd be in Yugoslavia.

"Italian farmers hid Jewish families in their haylofts," said Stella.

"*Ci piace gli Italiani molti,*" said Victoria as the waiter took the salad bowls.

"*Grazie,*" said the waiter on behalf of his nation. Adamson locked eyes with Stella, who toasted him.

"To photography," she said. His sister had become very mature. Stella's friend Maria had stopped by to meet him. She was pretty with brown hair and brown eyes. She was studying for the equivalent of O levels and planned to study English at university.

"Maria helps me with my Italian," said Stella. "Mummy lets us take the bus together to Pordenone."

"And what do you do there, pray tell?" he'd asked. Both girls smiled. "Ogle boys, probably."

"Oh, no," said Stella, "they ogle us."

They went to Venice. Sister city Mestre's industrial sprawl was unimpressive but when they emerged on the other side of the train station, Venice stretched before them like a film set. Fog clung to the skirts of palazzos as they motored through the canals in a *vaporetto,* a water bus. A woman rinsing her boots at the canal's edge waved. By the time he'd lifted his camera though, the *vaporetto* had chugged on, and the lady was gone. They emerged from winding alleys into St. Mark's Square, which was partly flooded, and they had to walk on wooden planks to get from the covered gallery to the steps of the Basilica. Early Mass was over, a lady arranged flowers. It was business as usual in the House of the Lord. Stella guided him to the Pala d'Oro, the ornate golden altarpiece, which was adorned with enameled saints and encrusted with hundreds of rubies, sapphires, garnets, and pearls. It was hypnotic.

The food in Venice was great, especially the *gelato,* three little scoops of different flavors. Victoria wanted to visit the Guggenheim Collection but it was closed so they toured La Fenice Opera House instead. It was shabby on the outside but inside it was a red velvet and gold jewel box. On the Ponte Vecchio, Stella asked the leather goods man if Adamson could take his leathery portrait. The man posed proudly in front of belts and brief-cases, but what he really wanted was a picture cuddling Stella, who took down the man's address and promised to send him a copy.

Christmas Eve, he accompanied Victoria to the base. He waited in the Stars and Stripes Bookstore while she collected "Christmas bits," another way of saying, "I need to buy your pressie." An officer with brass on his chest and an airman in a flight jacket browsed magazines. Adamson tucked himself in a corner and flipped through *Everything You Ever Wanted to Know About Sex* (*But Were Afraid to Ask*).

Another Flight Jacket spoke quietly to the one reading Penthouse. "When did you get back?" "My last TDY. I'm AWOL next time. Da Nang? Forget it." Adamson didn't understand the lingo but gathered that they didn't want Top Brass to hear them, that wherever the airman had been, he held in complete disdain, and that a "chopper" had crashed, leading to deaths. His commander was trying to blame the crash on the "ARVN." Weren't those the South Vietnamese? Even in idyllic Italy, they were linked to the Asian jungle. Why *are* we in Vietnam? he wondered. Victoria's English voice cut through the air and caused the men to stare. Adamson snapped shut *Everything You Ever Wanted to Know* and opened *Operating Manual for Spaceship Earth*.

Maria's family invited them to Christmas Eve Mass, and he went with Stella. During the service, Maria cued him when to stand, sit, and kneel, and he was conscious of her father inspecting him.

"She likes you," said Stella, after they were dropped off. He made a face. "No, I mean, she *likes* you, God knows why." Before he could clobber her, she ran inside and locked the front door, giggling. This was more like the sister he knew. On Christmas Day, they opened pressies in pajamas. Italian television commercials were shown in a half-an-hour block before the regular programs. The commercials were sexy and funny, but the programs were impossible to follow. Victoria produced an excellent stuffed turkey, roast spuds *and* Yorkshire pudding, Christmas pudding *and* custard. Ink-blot found the fifty lira piece tucked into the pudding and wished that Adamson would stay. On Boxing Day, George took him over to his office to try and call Alistair in Hong Kong but a servant answered and said that they were all away. Perhaps Alistair's parents had gone to England for a change?

On Adamson's last day, Maria took him and Stella by train to Venice for an "insider's tour." She took them to the university where she hoped to study, and they lunched in the cafeteria. School was closed but the buildings were open. They went to Museo Correr, full of treasures of the City of Venice, then by ferry to the Glass Museum on Murano in the Lagoon. He loved seeing the glassblowers turn blobs of colored molten glass into tiny animals, and he bought a glass dog for Maria and a prancing green horse for Stella. Then he went back and got one each for Victoria, George, and Inkblot, and a lizard for himself. Victoria collected them from Pordenone station. At home, he handed his parents their gifts but they just stared at him. George sat on the sofa and Victoria sat unusually still next to him. Adamson gave Inkblot a pink glass kitten. No one said anything.

"What?" he asked.

"It's Alistair, darling," said his mother and she started to cry on his father's shoulder.

George had called Alistair's school and spoken to Matron. There had been an accident. She gave him another number in England to call. George had reached Mr. Morris at a hotel in Surrey. Alistair "had fallen, jumped, or was pushed" from a train six days ago. The funeral had been private, family only. Who was closer than us, Adamson thought. Alistair had spent every Christmas holiday with them. Apparently, he had become "involved with drugs," and somewhere between Central London and his aunt's house in Weybridge, had fallen from a moving train. His body was discovered by train-spotters. No witnesses. George asked about sending flowers but Mr. Morris had said he'd rather they not.

"What did they do to him?" stormed Adamson. "What did they do?" Stella was crying but he just felt angry. He told them about the pregnancy Alistair had confided and his pressure over exams. It was horrible, a vast horrible mystery. George found a family album with Christmas pictures in it and Victoria propped up one of Alistair in the little alcove in the living room. Stella fetched candlesticks and a vase of flowers and Victoria lit incense. Inkblot offered her new Barbie, who leaned against the photo, one arm raised in greeting, and Adamson added his glass lizard.

"We loved him," sobbed Stella. They reminisced about Alistair all evening, crying, laughing, crying again till the candles and incense burnt away. Victoria warmed some soup then took Inkblot and herself to bed, and George excused himself. Stella went to her room. On the other side of her door, she played her favorite Donovan song, "Isle of Islay," over and over.

How high the gulls fly
O'er Islay
How sad the farm lad
Deep in play…

If he were at the dorm, he'd play Procol Harem's "Repent Walpurgis." He could hear the soaring keyboards. He knew it by heart, the churning chords dissolving into sweet arpeggios, then all the unexplainable, unimaginable horror. He had no idea death would be so painful, a mistake without hope of repair. Things he'd left unsaid and undone. He beat the sofa, then his own hand with his fist, sobbing, the pain stinging him to his senses as he stared into the cave-mouth of grief.

Some time in the night, he woke in the cold living room and went down to his room in the basement where it was warm. Someone had turned on his electric heater hours ago. He went back up for water and looked in on Alistair's shrine. His best mate remained as he had been, as he would always be now, grinning toothily as he opened a wrapped present. In the picture, Adamson sat on the floor in the light of their Christmas tree. Stella was half out of frame, Inkblot held a teddy bear on top of her head, and Alistair, with sparkling eyes and devilish grin, was at the center of the picture and the center of their lives.

❊　❊　❊

Maria dropped in to say goodbye and said she'd light a candle for Alistair at church. After everyone left the room, she handed Adamson a box containing a small medallion. He'd never been given jewelry before.

"St. Christopher," she said, "for the traveler."

"I'll carry it always," he said, gamely.

"I thought you could wear it and think of me." He felt guilty. She must have thought he was a serious prospect when in fact he was just a lad on holiday. She pointed out that she'd put her address in the box and he could write, if he liked. She didn't let on if she was disappointed in his response and kissed him on the cheek. He watched her walk up the road and felt empty.

At the airport, George handed Adamson a copy of Asimov's *I, Robot* for the flight. In Rome, he bought some postcards of pretty girls for his friends.

When he boarded the plane for Boston, he followed a Greek family with five curly-haired kids. The stewardess taking the boarding passes was captivated by them. He was deep into *I, Robot* when he remembered he should take more photos for his project. He'd already taken two rolls of the terminal and on the night flight over but most of the shots were the same: people reading, eating, sleeping. Young people sprawled over boyfriends and girlfriends, middle-aged men shepherding families, and harried mothers. Nothing new, nothing exciting. Just ordinary, despicable life.

This being a day flight, he hoped for more variety of subjects. Adamson had perfected how to shoot people surreptitiously using the top viewfinder. On his first stroll, he visited the loo in First Class and shot the passengers as he ambled back to his seat, nabbing a professorial gent marking papers, the Greek family, and a playboy listening to the radio, picking lint off his well-tailored sleeve. In Coach, a fierce, attractive girl sitting next to a man stared his way as he passed. He had to backtrack to First to let the drinks cart through and when he passed her again, Tiger-Eye was staring out of the window, murmuring to her seat mate. He shot them both in profile.

By the time he got to his seat, he'd taken a whole roll. He reloaded. Sitting on the aisle, he could shoot passersby. Tiger-Eye passed him and ignored his smile. Most girls were attracted to a man with a camera. She didn't dress like a student or look Italian, maybe Spanish. He ordered an orange juice as the captain came on the loudspeaker.

"Ladies and gentlemen, welcome to TWA Flight 840, bound for Athens and Tel Aviv. Our cruising altitude is 33,000 feet and we'll arrive in Athens in about 50 minutes."

"Not Boston?" he said to the stewardess, who took his ticket and soon returned.

"You're on the wrong plane, sir. I'm afraid you'll have a brief stay in Athens. We'll sort you out when we get there." She handed back his ticket. He felt Alistair's presence, bent over in stitches, but he, Adamson, wasn't laughing. What happened, Ali? Fell was an accident. Jumped was suicide, surely not, he'd never do that, but pushed, that was murder. Where are you, mate? No answer. He thought about their adventures in San Francisco: Cocktails and apple pie for breakfast. Leather boys in the Castro. Drake's Beach. He blotted his eyes with the bev nap. The loudspeaker crackled.

"Ladies and gentleman," said a female voice, "kindly fasten your seat belts. This is your new captain. The Che Guevara Commando Unit of the Popular Front for the Liberation of Palestine has taken command of TWA Flight 840. We request all passengers adhere to the following instructions: Remain seated and calm. For your own safety, place your hands behind your heads." Across the aisle, the man already had his hands in position like a prisoner. Adamson heard whispers, "Hijacking!" He looped the strap of his camera over his neck and put one hand behind his head. With the other hand, he tucked the completed roll of film in his sock. Aladdin, Tiger-Eye's seat mate, strode down the aisle with a gun in one hand and a hand grenade in the other. Both weapons looked real. Everyone had their hands behind their heads. A child began crying.

I'm supposed to be eating Salisbury steak on my way to Beantown, he thought. He hoped he wasn't going to die. People didn't usually die in hijackings; mostly they ended up in Cuba. Tiger-Eye had mentioned Che Guevara, wasn't he Cuban? Her voice came on the loudspeaker again. "Make no move that would endanger the lives of other passengers." Aladdin roamed, looking for someone. He hammered on the toilet door in the back of the plane, threatening to shoot the lock off. The Professor from First came out with his hands up and Aladdin pushed him to the front of the plane.

"Among you is a passenger responsible for the death and misery of Palestinian men, women, and children, on behalf of whom we are carrying out this operation. This assassin will be brought before a Palestinian Revolutionary Court. The rest of you will be honored guests in a hospitable country." Aladdin interrogated the Professor in First Class. They could hear denials in English and another language. The Palestinians were angry and Che Guevara was their friend but who were they? He whispered a question to the Greek gent across the aisle.

"Refugees."

"From where?" Adamson asked. The man raised his impressive eyebrows in disbelief. "I'm English," Adamson said, as if to explain his ignorance of current events. Wasn't Palestine the Holy Land of years ago? The hijackers looked Middle Eastern, but they'd never discussed Palestine in his English or American History classes.

"You should know all about Palestine," whispered the Greek. "The British Mandate." As they overflew the Greek isles, passengers whispered about their destination. Would it be Lebanon, Syria, or Egypt? Surely the hijackers wouldn't shoot the pilot. They must have a sense of self-preservation. Adamson's arms ached and he lowered the least visible one but the girl next to him elbowed him to put it back up. Whispering, he learned that she'd been working in Rome.

"What do you do?" he asked.

"I'm a hydro-engineer in Tel Aviv." That was unexpected. She didn't look older than he was but she already had a Master's degree in engineering and had been in the Israeli Army. She lived on a farm called Kaboots. Her name was Sima. She told him water was very important to Israeli agriculture.

"Bit of a dry subject," he offered, but she didn't get it. Tiger-Eye approached and held out her hand.

"The film." She tugged at his camera strap. "Give me the film." As soon as he had the back open, she snatched the film and unwound it. "Is that all?" He nodded. Now he'd lied. The passengers were quiet. It took a lot of energy to keep their arms up. Aladdin paced. At least he wasn't a hothead. Tiger-Eye stayed in the cockpit most of the time.

"Don't draw attention to yourself," said Sima. The plane dipped and circled. Sima identified Lod Airport in Tel Aviv. Were they landing? "The Israelis would shoot them. We're going to an Arab country, probably Lebanon."

"Do you like living in Israel?" he asked.

"I can't imagine living anywhere else," she said. He suggested America. "What's America got that Israel doesn't? I've never been there but I've seen it in movies. It looks," she groped for the right word, "fake." He knew exactly what she meant.

"It's full of contradictions," he said. "For instance, the people are very religious but also money-grubbing and violent, but also," he thought of Sal, Paulette, and Michael, "very kind and generous." Then he thought of his vengeful university president, "except some."

"That's true everywhere," she said. He asked if that was true of Lebanon. She didn't answer. A fighter jet streaked by the window. Surely a hundred-plus passengers wouldn't be sacrificed for two Palestinian fruitcakes?

"Ladies and gentleman, I hope you are not too uncomfortable. Our mission will soon be complete. As I told ground control, we've kidnapped this American plane because Israel is a colony of America and Americans are giving the Israelis Phantom jets like the one you see outside the window." The fighter streaked away and was replaced by others.

"I think we're going to Syria," Sima said and closed her eyes. The Greek over the aisle crossed himself. As the undercarriage lowered, a woman began crying. Aladdin pointed his gun, "Be quiet. Nothing will happen to you." His voice was steady but it was like when the vampire in a film tells his victim, "Relax, no harm will come to you." They descended over beige mountains to a city marked by slim white towers, a dull fantasyland. Sima took his hand and squeezed it. Bump, bump, bump went the wheels as they touched down. At least they hadn't been obliterated in midair. That was a good sign. He knew it was naughty but as they taxied he reloaded his last roll of fresh film. The plane braked, jolting everyone.

"Stay in your seats," Aladdin commanded. Tiger-Eye barked an order. Aladdin reached into his backpack, still covering the passengers with his pistol. Leaning into the aisle, Adamson casually let his finger touch the shutter.

"I think he's giving out consolation prizes," he said.

"You have no idea," whispered Sima. Before he could think of a snappy comeback, everything happened. The pilot came on the loudspeaker telling everyone to disembark "Right now!" because the plane would explode. The Greek threw himself over the seat in front and opened the emergency exit. The man in front of Sima tried to do the same but couldn't budge it. Sima, exhibiting great strength, yanked the door open and disappeared. Adamson fell forward pushed by bodies behind him. He landed on the wing and slid to the ground. People spilled from the plane like silvery fish through a sluice gate.

"Get away from the plane!" someone shouted. Adamson ran until an explosion rocked him off his feet. He fell facedown on the runway, asphalt and blood in his mouth. Not dead yet, he thought. He flipped over on his back and shot the blazing wreckage, passengers running, smoke and fire. His eyes and nose stung. Where was Sima? An ambulance flashed across the runway. Some passengers were injured but most were only grazed and stunned as he was. They were herded into the terminal. Damascus. The last he saw of Tiger-Eye and Aladdin, they were walking down a hall with guards, chatting.

"Nationality?" he was asked. The guard told him to stand alone along a wall as passengers were sorted. He put his hands in his pocket and felt

Maria's St. Christopher medal. The selection process yielded Italians, Greeks, Americans, Israelis—and him. Sima stood with her compatriots but wouldn't make eye contact. Most of the passengers, including him, had lost their passports in the explosion. All of them except the Israelis were taken to the cafeteria and given a meal of meat and vegetables with flat bread and cups of tea. As soon as he could, Adamson slipped into the bathroom and secreted the second roll of film in his other sock. He didn't like that their hosts had separated out the Israelis. Chet, a Peace Corps volunteer stationed in Greece, who was returning from his grandfather's funeral, said there were ongoing hard feelings between Israel and the Arabs.

"What does that have to do with the Che Guevara hijackers?" Adamson asked.

"They're Arab refugees, displaced by the Israelis after the war. It's about land rights," said Chet. Chet's work involved helping local Greek governments sort out land reform. All the decent land was owned by three families and the rest of the people were serfs. Chet had majored in Economics at the University of Washington, which wasn't in Washington, D.C., but someplace near California. He was blind in one eye but you couldn't tell because his fake eye was really good. He'd wanted to go in the Army but the closest thing that would take him was the Peace Corps.

They were bused to an airport hotel. Adamson wanted to take a walk but they weren't even allowed in the lobby. He shared a room with Chet, who smoked nasty brown cigarettes. Adamson took a lukewarm shower and redressed in his grubby clothes. The mattress was lumpy, the room was stuffy, and Chet snored. He would have read if he'd had a book. Outside the sealed windows, he watched the green glare of the airport. Trucks rumbled down the airport road. He leaned his chin on the windowsill, his breath condensing on the glass. He could have called his parents but didn't. They would only worry and he didn't want to plunge back into their world or talk about Alistair. He fell asleep so soundly that Chet had to shake him to wake him up. An Alitalia plane would be sent to fetch them.

"Getting hijacked" sounded exciting but it was exhausting. His body felt sore and bruised. At the terminal, a guard tried to take away his camera but Adamson showed him that he had no film, and the guard backed down. They had to sit in one corner and couldn't go anywhere in the terminal. The

Israelis hadn't been at breakfast. He'd taken Sima's picture and would call the Israeli embassy as soon as he got home.

The flight to Rome was short and uneventful but they arrived too late for the TWA flight to Boston so he had to spend the night. A man named Marcello gave him vouchers for a hotel room and meals in the airport and some lira for incidentals. Marcello also helped him apply for a new passport, which the embassy would expedite and bring to the hotel.

"I will see what else we can do for you," said Marcello, glancing at Adamson's clothes. In his room at the Intercontinental, Adamson turned on the telly. It was the commercials half-hour, his favorite program. He should call his family. He should call Sal. On the telly, a lady in an evening dress stood singing on top of a white grand piano. She fed tidbits to a tiger crouched below. It was a commercial for laundry detergent. He dozed till a knock woke him and jumped to his feet terrified. He had to ask who it was three times before he felt safe enough to open the door. He'd been dreaming about Tiger-Eye. Marcello stood in the hall holding bags. "A change of clothes, Signor?" Adamson told him he didn't have any money but Marcello bowed. "I selected some items to make your stay and journey more comfortable. We are sorry for the inconvenience." Marcello said he'd arrange for phone calls.

Adamson splashed his face with water and tried on the black T-shirt, black jeans, and purple sweater. Who was that dashing man in the mirror? He pretended to smoke a cigarette using a hotel pen and said out loud, "Stirred, not shaken." In another bag, he found two miniatures of Johnny Walker Black Whiskey, a small bottle of champagne, some snazzy men's underwear, an issue of *Life* magazine, a German photography magazine, a small box of Belgium chocolates that he gobbled instantly, a leather-bound nail scissor set, and a leather-bound writing case with paper, envelopes, and a fountain pen, all embossed with "TWA."

He ordered orange juice from room service and asked for the long-distance operator. The juice, freshly squeezed in a pitcher, arrived before the operator called back. She'd had to search for his parents' number since Adamson didn't know it.

"Darling, what are you doing in Rome?" said Victoria. "George, it's Henry. He's still in Rome!" Everyone wanted to talk and George got angry with Inkblot. He was asked numerous times, "You what?" Victoria cried, but he cheered her up by listing the contents of his complimentary loot and promised he'd send a photo of himself in Italian gear. She wanted him to come right back but all he wanted was to go home to Sal's. George said he'd call Sal's father.

The stewardesses seemed to give him an extra twinkle the next day. It was the clothes. He'd bought film and shot a final mélange of Italian airport scenes while waiting for his passport: aunties kissing nieces; lovers greeting in Arrivals; the young, the lonely, the stranded.

On the plane, he scrutinized every passenger to make sure there were no hijackers. The only troublemakers were the 12th-grade class from Boston Latin. As he rested, he dreamed. A taxi exploded near a fountain. Sima tore his arm open with her fingernails as he chased a pair of Arab gunmen. He shot them with his Nikon and the flash killed one of them. He kicked over the corpse and gazed into Alistair's face.

✳   ✳   ✳

The plane landed safely without incident. When the automatic doors of Customs wheezed open, there holding a white banner with red lettering were Sal and Hannah. The banner read, "Welcome Home, Adamson!" Paulette grinned over their shoulders. He stepped forward into flashing cameras.

"Let's have one of all of you," said a man with a Canon from the *The Globe*.

"Me?" said Adamson. "What did I do?" He was standing now with a girl on each arm.

"You survived, you goose," said Paulette.

"Koch saw your name in the paper," said Lou. "He said that when he told you to shoot airplane interiors, he didn't mean literally."

"Let's go to Atlantis tomorrow," said Sal, throwing his arm around Adamson's shoulder as they walked to the car. Adamson nodded, numb. When would it sink in? When he'd re-read all his letters? Would he ever feel normal again? Maybe he'd carve Alistair's initials under the Onset pier? Maybe Paulette would help him. Maybe he could call Alistair's dad after a decent interval. Maybe… "I've got a new girlfriend," Sal was saying. "She plays the harp! And here's news you can use," Sal lowered his voice, "Paulette dumped Clyde."

There were the familiar streets, the naked trees, the pond frozen in ice, scabs of snow by the roadside. Sal's house, his motorbike. Adamson peered at himself in the mirror on the handlebars. He looked roughed up and worried. The house smelled great. Paulette brought him an OJ and he sat on the sofa. They ate some Mexican rolled-up things and set up a game called Twister. Paulette was good because she was double-jointed. She had to straddle him at one point. He wasn't any good at playing the game but that made it funny. "Almost time," said Lou.

"For what?" asked Adamson. It was New Year's Eve. "Oh, that's what the party's for."

"Did you think it was all for you?" said Lou, with a wink.

"No," said Adamson, but he did. "I'd like to develop my film tomorrow, if that's all right."

"Be my guest. Anything good?"

"Might be," Adamson said.

"All right," said Lou. "Let's immortalize ourselves. Adamson, can you do the honors?" Lou's camera was attached to a tripod. Paulette wore a floppy hat, Hannah was in granny specs, Lou wore a Groucho Marx get-up, and Sal had on a cowboy hat.

"What should I wear?" asked Adamson. Paulette grabbed a lampshade and balanced it on his head.

"Hurry!" said Sal. "Five, four, three…" Adamson focused the shot and rushed to stand between Sal and Lou. "…two, one."

"Cheese!" they yelled and the camera flashed. "Happy New Year! Goodbye, Sixties!"

Acknowledgements

Although this book is fiction, I owe debts to my brother Alan Burton and my husband Jim Landry for the stories of their youthful adventures. Special thanks for insights from my early readers: Allan Carter, Patricia Connelly, Solveig Eggerz, Melanie Jacobs, Reuben Jackson, Mary Jo Lazun, Joann Malone, Paula Mance, Terryl Paiste, Zara Phillips, Grady Smith, Nora Stork, and Grace Topping. None of my books would be possible without the talents and devotion of my editor, Janet Guinn, and my book designer, Debra Naylor.

Historical Events

All the historical events in the book are true and accurate to my knowledge though one was moved from August to December for the author's convenience. I hope that English, history, and social studies teachers of high school and college students will use *Adamson's 1969* as an adjunct text and a gateway to further study of the rich decade of the 1960s.

Discography

New Year's Eve 1968: Hair soundtrack (MacDermot, Ragni, & Rado), "A Whiter Shade of Pale" (Procol Harum)

January 1969: The Monkees

February: "I Love You More Than You'll Ever Know" (Blood, Sweat & Tears), "Dance to the Music" (Sly & the Family Stone), "Delilah" (Tom Jones), Jefferson Airplane, *Piper at the Gates of Dawn* (Pink Floyd), *Sergeant Peppers Lonely Hearts Club Band* (The Beatles), *Truth* (Jeff Beck)

March: Lennon/Ono, *Disraeli Gears* (Cream), "Moon River" (Andy Williams), "I Left My Heart in San Francisco" (Tony Bennett), "Just Like a Woman" (Bob Dylan), "In-A-Gadda-Da-Vida" (Iron Butterfly), "House of the Rising Sun" (The Animals)

April: "We Shall Overcome" (gospel traditional), "Bam Bam" (The Maytals)

May: "A Whiter Shade of Pale" (Procol Harum), "I've Got A Lovely Bunch of Coconuts" (novelty song)

June: "Get Back" (The Beatles with Billy Preston)

July: *Nashville Skyline,* "One More Night" (Bob Dylan), Jefferson Airplane, Jimi Hendrix, Janis Joplin, "Ta-Ra-Ra Boom-De-Ay" (vaudeville song), "Heartbreak Hotel" (Elvis Presley), Blind Willie Johnson, "Dust My Broom" (Elmore James), "San Francisco" (Scott KcKenzie)

August: "Hickory Wind" (Gram Parsons), "Blue Canadian Rockies" (The Byrds), "Knees Up Mother Brown" (Cockney traditional), "I am the Very Model of a Modern Major-General" (Gilbert and Sullivan), "With a Little Help From My Friends" (The Beatles)

September: "Give Peace A Chance" (Lennon/Ono), "1969" (The Stooges), "Purple Haze" (Jimi Hendrix), Jose Feliciano, Janis Ian, "All You Need Is Love" (The Beatles)

October: *Abbey Road*, "She Came In Through The Bathroom Window," *White Album, Revolver* (The Beatles), Janis Joplin, *Electric Ladyland* (Jimi Hendrix Experience)

November: "You Can't Hurry Love" (The Supremes)

December: *Blonde on Blonde* (Bob Dylan), "Isle of Islay" (Donovan), "Repent Walpurgis" (Procol Harem)

Discussion Questions

1. Is it true you can be drafted if you're not a U.S. citizen?

2. How did new forms of birth control like the Pill affect the liberation of women (and men) from sex and pregnancy constraints?

3. What does Adamson's perspective tell us about how the popular culture of the U.S. affected the U.K. and vice versa? How did the countries differ culturally?

4. Why were people drawn to the message of the Reverend Jim Jones and the Peoples Temple? What went wrong?

5. How does the music (and interpretations of the music) of the late 1960s influence us today?

6. Were other art forms—books, theater, film, dance—as creatively explosive as music during this period?

7. How much has American society moved forward with respect to inclusion and integration of peoples of all ethnicities and races?

8. What was "busing?" Did it work?

9. Why was America involved in the Vietnam War? Did any good come of it?

10. How has our experience of the Vietnam War affected our attitude toward the military, patriotism, and government leadership today? If there ever is "a good war," who should fight it?

Bibliography

A few books to help you go deeper on subjects raised in the book.

The Birth of the Pill, Jonathan Eig

Stories from Jonestown, Leigh Fondakowski

Dispatches, Michael Herr

The Story of Jane: The Legendary Underground Feminist Abortion Service, Laura Kaplan

Woodstock: The Oral History, Joel Makower

Blood Chit, Grady Smith

Conspiracy in the Streets: The Extraordinary Trial of the Chicago Eight, Jules Feiffer, Tom Hayden, and Jon Weiner

CPSIA information can be obtained
at www.ICGtesting.com
Printed in the USA
BVHW09s1741210818
524675BV00007B/62/P